The Grotesquerie Games

Jay Palmer

Copyright © 2017 Jay Palmer

All rights reserved.

ISBN-13: 978-0-9911127-9-1

ISBN-10: 0-9911127-9-2

Version 2

All Books by Jay Palmer

The VIKINGS! Trilogy:
- DeathQuest
- The Mourning Trail
- Quest for Valhalla

The EGYPTIANS! Trilogy:
- SoulQuest
- Song of the Sphinx
- Quest for Osiris

The Magic of Play

The Heart of Play

The Grotesquerie Games

The Grotesquerie Gambit

Souls of Steam

The Seneschal

Jeremy Wrecker - Pirate of Land and Sea

Viking Son

Viking Daughter

Dracula - Deathless Desire

Website: **JayPalmerBooks.com**

Cover Artist: **Jay Palmer**

To John Myers

a true monster ...

and friend!

Chapter 1

Rompday / Thursday

Out of this world ...

"Please .....!" Martin Mulberry begged, standing in the doorway to his kitchen.

"Not one more word!" Martin's mother warned. "You're not trying out for any kind of sports. Kids get hurt, and I don't trust those school coaches ..."

"But, Mom ....!" Martin whined.

"One more word and you go to bed right now," Martin's mother said as she bent to slide the last dirty dish into the dishwasher.

"That's not fair!!!" Martin bellowed.

Forty-three seconds later, Martin's left ear, followed by the rest of him, was drug into his bedroom, accompanied by a furiously-barked command to don his pajamas and get into bed. Then his door slammed shut and angry footsteps drummed across the hall and down the stairs.

Martin kicked his bedpost, stubbed his big toe, and hopped twice around his room, cursing his foolishness. Finally he changed into his pajamas for lack of anything else to do. *Why was she being so unreasonable?* His mom hated sports, but all Martin dreamed of was an overtime catch in the end zone, sinking the perfect three-pointer in the last second, or batting a grand-slam game-winning home run right out of the park.

A blinding flash illuminated Martin's bedroom so brightly his pale blue walls reflected white. A loud hum, like a swarm bees had suddenly flown into his ears, blasted his hearing, and then it cut-off suddenly, and something hard and heavy struck Martin's back. Martin toppled, knocked forward into his dresser, then bounced backwards and stumbled over something sprawled on his bedroom floor.

"Aarrgghhh!" a pained cry reverberated. *"My leg ...! I've broken my leg ...!"*

Martin's eyes flew open. He'd tripped and fallen over a ... *nightmare* ... writhing on his floor. It looked like an adult, but it was no bigger than he, had mottled green skin, long, wing-like ears with thick tufts of hair sticking out of them, and a necklace of jade beads around its throat. It was skinny, with bulging, bloodshot eyes over an elongated bread-stick nose, and it was grimacing in pain, gnashing huge teeth, and the twisted angle of its leg looked very unnatural. Martin gasped, and was about to cry out, when his mother's voice echoed up the stairs.

"Any more banging up there and you'll be on restriction all summer! Go to bed!"

Martin stared at the strange creature. Despite its apparent agony, it glanced about his room in surprise.

"Where am I?" the stranger asked through gritted teeth. "Don't tell me that spell didn't work again! *Dratted Dragons!* Old Bastile Wraithbone never could cast a spell right ...!"

His bulbous eyes fell on Martin.

"Will you sub for me?" the creature pleaded. "I'm hurt, but we can't lose the first round; we must win the playoffs!"

Martin stammered a few unintelligible sounds. For the first time, Martin noticed the wiry green man was wearing a bright purple jersey, torn and dirty, with a big number "13" on it. Clutched in his hands was a large ball covered with long, greasy hair. The creature shoved the hairy ball into Martin's chest.

"This spell will wear off any second," the creature said. "Just get the ball into the basket ... or we lose!"

Instinctively Martin clutched the hairy ball as it was hammered into his chest, and then the creature reached out and grabbed his wrist. Its grip felt sweaty; Martin was about to scream ... when the bee's hum and blinding flash returned. Wincing against its brilliance, Martin blinked ... and his bedroom vanished.

A loud roar of cheers and catcalls filled his ears. When Martin opened his eyes, every nightmare he'd ever dreamed of filled his vision. Under a bright full moon and star-twinkling sky, hundreds of monsters surrounded him, most only thirty feet away, and right beside him, a monstrous ogre was wrestling a gigantic minotaur. The ogre snarled agonized-grunts as hard minotaur fists smacked its ribs, while the ogre twisted the minotaur's sharp horns, straining to flip it over. Other creatures were running about, being chased by even worse monstrosities, and the crowd was screaming.

"Go!" shouted the little green man in the purple jersey, and he released Martin's wrist. *"Get the ball into the basket ... atop the silver pole ... or we lose!"*

The long-fingered hand shoved him, and Martin rolled to his feet, the hairy ball still in his hands. Not far away, he saw the tall silver pole, on top of which sat a plain wicker basket.

"Run!" the green man cried. *"Run or die!"*

Martin looked back and saw a colossal troll pounding across a muddy turf, wearing only magenta shorts and spiked iron bracelets, with massive bare feet hammering right towards him. Terrified, Martin ran away, certain those huge feet would trample him. Martin sprinted, but as he neared the silver pole, the wall of monsters just beyond it howled, roared, and trumpeted. Martin froze, afraid to get any closer, despite the heavy-pounding footfalls rapidly approaching behind him.

"Are you daft or dim-witted?" the ball shouted at

him. *"Are you just going to stand here and get us crushed?"*

Startled, Martin rolled the talking ball over. *It wasn't a hairy ball;* in his hands, Martin was holding a rotting, severed head ... greenish, filthy, and covered in stitches ... a zombie head, glaring up at him with blinking, swollen, mismatched eyes.

Martin screamed, and he threw the zombie head high into the air. To his amazement, the rotting, hairy head flew upwards ... flipped over twice ... and fell right into the wicker basket.

Tremendous cheers exploded, and all the monsters ran out onto the field. Martin raised his arms to shield his face, certain he was about to be killed and eaten, when many long-clawed hands grabbed him, lifted him, and held him high over all the monsters' heads. Three loud trumpet blasts resounded over the cheers.

Hundreds of monsters swarmed around him, wildly jumping up and down, parading him around a massive stone stadium.

Suddenly a deafening voice rose above the tumult, a female voice on loudspeakers, sweet, and yet with a wicked chuckle.

"In Round 1 of the three hundred and fourteenth Grotesquerie Games, victory goes to the team of Grand Wizard Bastile Wraithbone, the Shantdareya Skull-crackers!"

Martin stared at the celebrating crowd of monsters, at countless horns, fangs, scales, fur, folded wings, and long, lashing tails. Strangely, almost all of the monsters were wearing some form of jewelry; copper and brass rings, iron medallions, steel necklaces, tin armbands, heavy bracelets, and spiky cornets that looked like barbed wire. Each looked more threatening than the next, but their exuberant jubilation was disarming ... and infectious. Martin began to smile. He had no idea why, where he was, or how he'd gotten there, but somehow, by accident or not, he'd won the game!

Chapter 2

Rompday / Thursday

Into the fire ...

As the monstrous crowd leaped and cheered, Martin didn't know whether to be terrified or elated. Then a huge, calloused hand encircled his entire chest, closed around him, and lifted him high. Martin was turned to face a head like a boulder, with small red eyes, many scars, and a thin iron chain around his neck; the ogre who'd been wrestling the minotaur.

"Bastile Wraithbone wants a word with you," the ogre said.

Wading through the crowd like Martin would wade through waist-deep water, the ogre carried Martin past hundreds of cheering monsters toward the stone stadium, knocking the smaller creatures aside with its huge, bare feet. They passed the silver pole, and Martin spied strands of long, greasy hair still sticking out of the wicker basket. They circled around to a wall behind the stone stands, away from the cheering crowd, entered a wide door, and descended a short stairs. There, the ogre plopped Martin onto a table in a small, lamp-lit room filled with monsters, most wearing purple jerseys. On the table beside Martin was the strange green man who'd fallen into his bedroom, and he was still grimacing and clutching his broken leg. Before all the monsters stood a wizened old man wearing a tall, pointed, purple wizard's hat and robe, examining the injury.

"Hold still!" the old, long-bearded man said to the little green man. "Let me try ...!"

The old man lifted his staff and waved his free hand over the broken leg, wiggling his long, bony fingers at the goblin's bare green knee. A yellow glow emanated from his staff and wiggling fingers, with their many gemmed gold and silver rings. Then light struck the thin, green leg with a flash, and the little man jumped and cried out.

The spellcasting ended instantly, and a silence ensued. The wizened old man examined the leg again.

"That's better," the old man said. "It'll heal properly now, but not quickly ... you're out of the game for at least ... six weeks."

All of the monsters shouted at this, but suddenly a small, beautiful young girl stepped forward, shielding the old wizard with her body.

"It's not his fault!" she rebuked the monsters'

complaints. "Without him, you wouldn't even be a team!"

"We're not a team!" said a small, strange man covered in short brown fur, whose face looked like a rat, with a sparkling gem in one ear and a thick fishhook hanging from the other. "We need three ... and we don't have a spare Small!"

"I'll play ...!" the girl insisted, but everyone shook their heads.

"That's why I invited our new friend," said the wizened old man, and all eyes fell upon Martin. The wizard in purple addressed him personally. "Well met, young man. I'm Grand Wizard Bastile Wraithbone, and for the sake of all of Shantdareya, I want to thank you for helping us today."

"I ... ummm ... you're welcome," Martin stammered.

"This must all seem very strange to you," Grand Wizard Bastile Wraithbone said. "Trust me, you're perfectly safe, and I'll soon return you to the human world, but first, we owe you a debt of gratitude, and, forgive me, I must ask a great favor of you."

Martin glanced at the strange, inhuman faces staring at him, monsters of all types and sizes, each looking nervous and uncertain.

"Shantdareya is suffering from a terrible disaster," Grand Wizard Bastile Wraithbone said. "Our only hope is if we can win the Grotesquerie Games playoffs. The winner earns the ultimate prize, the staff of Master Grand Wizard Borgias Killoff, the most powerful wizard ever. Only with his staff can I undo the disaster and save Shantdareya."

"You join our team," the ogre interrupted in his deep, rumbling voice.

"Yes, we want you to join us, and if we win, then I'll pay you well," Grand Wizard Bastile Wraithbone promised. "Sadly, I've spent all my money outfitting our team for this season. We're broke, and if we don't win, then we'll lose everything, and I'll have nothing to pay anyone."

"You can't ask him yet!" the small green man waved them back. "He can't make a decision like this ... not knowing what he's agreeing to ...!"

"You're quite right, of course," Grand Wizard Bastile Wraithbone sighed. "Very well. Young man, we are the ..."

"Not you ... or any of us," interrupted the green man. "He's never seen monster-folk before; it'll be too much. Let Veils talk to him; at least she looks human."

Grand Wizard Bastile Wraithbone glanced at the other monsters.

"That would seem wise," Bastile Wraithbone said. "We need to speak to Evilla, and attend the closing ceremony, and Veils can explain as well as any of us."

With nods, as if each knew what the others were thinking, Grand Wizard Bastile Wraithbone led the way out. The ogre picked up the wounded green man that had fallen into Martin's bedroom and carried him outside. A giant lizardman, with green-silvery scales, paused to shake Martin's hand.

"No matter what you decide, thanks for what you did today," the lizard man hissed, his forked tongue flicking inside his narrow mouth. Then he followed the others out.

Only the beautiful young girl remained. For her age, she looked muscular, but she was slightly shorter than he, and thinner, wearing a purple-trimmed black robe that fell to the floor, a short half-cape hanging off her shoulders, and a deep frown. She had dark chocolate hair and blue eyes, pale skin, wore a small silver medallion on a chain, and she looked askance at him.

"You don't look like you're twelve," she said.

"I am," Martin said. "I turned twelve last month."

"I'm eleven," she scowled. "I don't turn twelve for two months. Next year I'll be a Small on the Skull-crackers."

"A ... *Small ...?"* Martin asked.

"Each team fields six players, three Bigs ... and three Smalls," she said. "The Bigs fight to control the field. The Smalls score the points ... when the field allows it."

"The field allows it ...?" Martin asked. "How can a field ...?"

"It's basic strategy," Veils said. "The Smalls dodge around their Bigs and try to avoid the Bigs from the other team. Smalls can't touch each other, but their weapons can."

"Weapons ...?" Martin asked.

"Non-lethal," Veils said. "Nets, bolas, bags of

feathers, ...”

“How can a bag of feathers be a weapon?” Martin asked.

“When one hits you in the face, then you’ll see,” Veils said. “Look: we need you. They won’t let anyone under twelve play, and Rude won’t recover in time.”

“Who’s being rude?” Martin asked.

“Rude Stealing, the goblin who broke his leg,” Veils said. “He brought you here, and lucky he did, or we’d have lost. He’s really smart, but brains alone can’t win.”

“But ... my house ... where am I?” Martin asked.

“This is the realm of Heterodox, Home of Monsters,” Veils said.

“Are you a monster?” Martin asked.

Veils hesitated, then lifted her hand and pushed back her long dark hair, revealing small points on her ears.

“I’m a dark elf,” Veils said. “We’re great Smalls ... better than any other monster, but we’re also the most hated. Most dark elves won’t have anything to do with the games ...”

“Why not?” Martin asked.

“The Grand Wizard’s Council won’t return our staff,” Veils snarled. “Our Grand Wizard was killed in a duel, and his staff was taken, so dark elves can’t host a team of our own.”

“How ...?” Martin began.

“Look, we don’t have time for this,” Veils said, leaning toward him. “You’re from the human world; we have no power over you. But we’ll reward you ... with gold and magic ... as soon as we can. We need you ... will you help us ...?"

"But ... my family ...?" Martin stammered.

"You're not the first human to come to Heterodox," Veils said. "My grandfather, Bastile Wraithbone, can set up a spell to bring you here ... and send you back home ... without anyone noticing. We need you to help us win. Will you?"

Veils leaned close, staring into his eyes; *she was very pretty ...!*

"I ... I want to help, bu ..." Martin began.

"Excellent!" Veils cut off the rest of his sentence. "You have a lot to learn, and we'll train you as best we can. The second round starts next week, and we'll need you ready to play by then."

"Ummm, wait ..., I didn't really ...," Martin tried to correct her.

"We can discuss details later," Veils waved off his objections. "By this time next week, you'll be a Small of the Shantdareya Skull-crackers!"

Chapter 3

Smashday / Friday

Martin learns the pitch …

With a few last instructions, and more mumbled thanks from Grand Wizard Bastile Wraithbone, the monsters in purple jerseys faded and vanished, and Martin Mulberry, still wearing his pajamas, dropped onto his soft bed. He glanced about, astounded; his room looked exactly the same, and the glowing digital clock by his bed read 3:47 AM. Martin listened, and amid the silence he heard his father's muffled snores coming from his parents' room. He really was home, and if it wasn't all a dream, then he had to be ready; at the next strike of midnight, if the monsters kept their word, Grand Wizard Bastile Wraithbone would summon him back to Heterodox.

Martin lay fidgeting, staring up at his dark ceiling. *It'd been too real to be a dream!* He sat up, too excited to sleep. He didn't dare move around much or make noise, so he turned on his computer and scanned his media, but nothing on the web equaled the unbelievable experience of meeting real monsters.

Around 5:00 AM, Martin fell asleep. His dreams tormented him ... torn between his favorite fantasy of being a sports celebrity ... and nightmares of being torn apart by monsters. When summoned for breakfast, he staggered downstairs, half-asleep, still in his pajamas.

Martin had three younger brothers, Tom, Terry, and Ron, and an older sister, Vicky. Three bowls overflowing with dry cereal sat waiting before his brothers, while Vicky carried the milk from the refrigerator and began to pour. She reached Martin and stood looking at his empty bowl.

"Not eating ...?" Vicky asked. "Are you sick?"

Martin startled, then grabbed the closest cereal box and filled his bowl, and Vicky poured milk over his sugared flakes. Then he yawned deeply, and Vicky stared at him.

"Bad dreams," Martin excused himself.

"You're lucky it's summer vacation," Vicky said, and she proceeded to fill her own bowl.

After breakfast, Martin headed back to his room. He didn't know what to think; *had it all been a dream?* He paced back and forth, and then spied something he hadn't noticed, something lying on the carpet on the far side of his bed. At night, by only the glow of his clock's dial, he hadn't noticed it, but Martin snatched it up and held it into the bright sunlight beaming in through his window ... his heart hammering ...

In the clear light of day, between his upraised hands, hung a worn purple jersey with a bright white "13" on it, and across its back, it read "Martin".

After ten whole minutes of looking at his reflection in the mirror, Martin pulled off his jersey and hid it under his bed and ran downstairs. His brothers were locked in a loud racing game, motorized roars blasting from overworked speakers, their eyes fixed on colorful cars flashing across the screen, weaving around pedestrians and other cars, and occasionally crashing or running off the road. A fourth controller lay unused, but Martin ignored it. He walked past Vicky, who glanced up from her book to watch him, as he headed toward the back door.

Normally, Martin loved video games, although he preferred shooting aliens to racing cars. Yet Martin had a purpose; if he was going to compete against a bunch of monsters he had to get in shape ... and quickly.

Their fenced backyard wasn't huge, just a thin strip of grass behind their house. There sat an old swing-set in the corner, but the boys preferred video games, so it was seldom used, covered with a light dusting of moss and fallen leaves. Yet it had a ladder, a small lookout fort, two swings, a climbing rope, and a pole to slide down. Martin started with the rope, and pulled himself up with ease, squeezing the huge knots between his sneakers. Yet this was too easy; Martin grabbed the pole, slid back down, and tried to climb the rope using only his arms. This proved difficult, and without his legs, Martin strained to pull himself up the long rope even once. Yet, once he'd done it, he slid back down the pole and started again.

After his arms started aching, Martin began doing wind sprints, back and forth, running the length of his backyard. Unfortunately, his father hadn't recently mowed, and the long grasses pulled at his sneakers. He was starting to sweat when Vicky came out, her book still clutched in her hand.

"You haven't been out here since last summer," Vicky said, leaving her question unasked.

"Mom says I'm too small to try out for sports," Martin explained.

"You're too short for basketball and too light for football," Vicky said. "You'd do best at track and field ... James did long-distance running, and now he pole vaults."

James was Vicky's boyfriend, although Martin had seldom seen him. Martin nodded, considering her suggestion, although he'd have to be in high school before pole vaulting would be an option. Yet he kept training, and Vicky nodded approvingly and went back inside.

The day passed quickly, and Vicky started cooking dinner before their parents came home from work.

Twice Martin exhausted himself, rested, and started exercising again. He didn't feel any different, except that he felt dirty. After dinner, Martin took a quick shower, and when bedtime came, Martin slipped on his purple jersey, and then climbed into bed fully dressed and pulled his covers up to his chin, in case his parents checked on him later. He was determined to watch his clock all night as it scrolled through the numbers toward midnight.

Martin awoke to the unexpected sensation of falling. He started to cry out, and then crashed hard onto slate flagstones. His breath was knocked from him by his abrupt impact, and the back of his head struck painfully; Martin winced, gritting his teeth.

"I told you ...!" Veils sneered. "He thought we were a dream!"

"He's wearing his jersey ... and his shoes ...," Rude said. "Humans don't wear those to bed ..."

"Help him up," Grand Wizard Bastile Wraithbone said, and the ogre's huge hand pulled Martin to his feet. "Thank you, Brain. Now hold still, Martin ..."

Bastile's staff rose, and despite the pain in his head, Martin glimpsed glowing fingers wiggling many rings at him. Then a brief flash of light blinded him, and when the burst faded, so did his headache.

"Better ...?" Grand Wizard Bastile asked.

Martin paused; *his pain was completely gone!*

"Much ...," Martin grinned.

"Good!" Grand Wizard Bastile said. "Are you still

willing to help us?"

Martin glanced around; he was surrounded by the same monsters he'd seen before, and standing among them was Veils and the old wizard. *They were real! He was back!*

"Ummm .... sure," Martin said.

"Wonderful!" Grand Wizard Bastile said. "Now, let's get out there and practice!"

As the monsters started moving toward the door, Martin glanced around; lockers lined one wall, and four closed doors led to places unknown, yet the one opened door, where everyone was heading, Martin recognized; through it he saw the table he'd sat on before; they were inside the stone stadium, under the bleachers. Rude, the small, green goblin whom Martin was replacing, now had a splint binding his leg, and walked clumsily on crutches, but the ogre reached down and picked up the lame goblin, carrying him through the door like a baby cradled in one arm. As they waited in turn, the only woman player caught his eye. She was short for an adult, strongly-built, with ivy skin, smooth like new leaves, and forest green hair ... a dryad ... and then the heavy hand of the troll bounced upon his shoulder.

"New friend!" the troll snarled.

"Be careful, Snitch," the dryad said. "Don't hurt him; he's our last Small." Then she looked at Martin again. "Did Veils introduce us? I'm Murder, Murder Shelling, the best dryad in the league. This is Allfed Snitchlock, the smartest troll I've ever met. Of course, most trolls can't tell their heads from a boulder, so that's not saying much. But don't call him Allfed. Call him Snitch; his full name is too long, so it takes him a while to remember it."

"I'm Stabbing, Stabbing Kingz," the small, smelly rat-creature said, quickly slipping between Snitch's slow-stumping legs. "I'm your fellow Small, human."

"He has a name, Stabbing," Murder said.

"I'll remember his name after he's proven himself," Stabbing sneered to Murder.

"Ignore Stabbing," Murder said. "Ratlings never learn good manners."

Unlike Murder Shelling, who was very pretty, and completely green, with beautiful turquoise eyes, and long, forest-green hair partially covering her bright, golden-yellow topaz earrings, Stabbing Kingz looked like a rat-human hybrid, slightly shorter than either Martin or Murder, and he had a stubby black nose, beady eyes, long buck-teeth, and was covered in short brown hair that looked rather greasy. Both were wearing purple jerseys; Murder had a double-zero on hers, while Stabbing had a seven on his.

They passed through the next room, climbed the stairs, and emerged onto a moonlit walkway around the outside of the stadium. As they walked, Martin heard distant shouts and footfalls. The dirt field was gone; they arrived at a wide lake covered with a low webbing of thick, rough logs, with their bark shaved off, all supported by posts rising out of the lake. Another team, wearing scarlet jerseys, was practicing on the far end of the field, and a third team, wearing green jerseys, was slinking off down a stairs into a different stadium entrance.

"There goes the Barkrover Bullies," Murder said. "They're tough, but they seldom practice, so we were able to beat them last year."

"Grand Wizard Lion Changeling has been working them hard," Stabbing said. "They won't be so easy now."

"The team practicing on the other side is the Wild Wraiths," Murder said. "They're our worst competition. They haven't lost a game all year, and they have a dragling and a shadow."

"A ... *what ...?*" Martin asked.

"A dragling is a Big, not too big, but they're very powerful," Murder said. "They can't fly, but they have tough wings, and can breathe fire."

"Flame-breath is illegal," Stabbing said. "Draglings who use fire once get stunned, and if twice, they get banished for three games. Their wide wings aren't dangerous, but annoying; they spread them to block Smalls."

"Shadows are even worse," Murder said. "Shadows are Smalls, but they're translucent, and can sometimes phase right through solid objects, including other players."

"Perhaps you'd do better familiarizing Martin with his own teammates," Grand Wizard Bastile spoke up. "Veils, take over. The rest of you ... you know what to do."

With nodding heads, his teammates began trudging onto the strange pitch, balancing with practiced ease, walking across the web-work of thick logs suspended over the lake. On his crutches, Rude limped to the edge of the lake to watch. Martin started to follow them, but Veils grabbed his arm and stopped him.

"All right, divide and converge!" Grand Wizard Bastile shouted at them. "Happy, be careful!"

The centaur looked back and scoffed, but he followed the others. On his hooves, he noisily, and cautiously, walked behind the ogre and Murder, both of whom easily strode barefoot atop the wooden web of logs in one direction, while Snitch, the lizardman, and Stabbing went the other way.

"Watch this," Veils said to Martin.

"Smalls, don't combat," Grand Wizard Bastile called out. "Bigs, don't get passed."

As the two sides had split, they both strode farther across the logs, and then turned. Murder, the dryad, and Stabbing, the ratling, darted forward, but the Bigs on each side split, circling to different tree trunks, chasing back the Smalls.

"The Bigs control the pitch," Veils said. "A Big can swat a Small easily, so the Smalls have to wait until they're engaged."

The Bigs seemed reluctant to choose which log they'd advance on, but finally they divided and slowly approached. The ogre and troll walked toward each other, arms raised, ready to grapple. The lizardman advanced upon the centaur; the lizardman was taller and wider, but the centaur had heavily-muscled arms, a thick, solid horse's body, and showed no fear. As they met, the ogre and troll crashed into each other with a meaty *smack!,* but the lizardman and the centaur seized each other's arms, grappling like wrestlers.

"See how they fight differently?" Veils asked. "Centaurs and lizardmen use practiced moves, while trolls and ogres rely upon pure strength. Centaurs have poor footing on this pitch; see how Happy, our centaur, is backing up? That's on purpose. He wants to get to where the logs intersect, so he'll have better traction."

Martin watched, fascinated, as the Bigs struggled. Behind them, Murder and Stabbing seemed to be waiting.

"What're they doing?" Martin asked.

"Watching," Veils said. "On this pitch, there's only three ways around Bigs, unless you're a shadow; you can go between their legs, try to whip around them by using one of their limbs to swing on, or jump over them. You have to move quickly ... and with confidence. Once you start a dodge, either you succeed, or ..."

Suddenly Stabbing ran forward, right at the lizardman's back. With amazing dexterity, Stabbing jumped up onto the leaning lizardman's back, bounced off his head with one foot, and flipped over the centaur. The centaur tried to grab him, but the ratling flew too high. However, just before Stabbing landed, a wide back-hoof kicked out, fumbled his landing, and Stabbing slipped off the log, fell ... and would've landed in the lake ... but he seized the centaur's long, flicking tail, and swung on it like a rope. His weight offset the centaur, and with screeching wail and a deep shout of anger, both fell off the log and splashed into the dark water.

"Wow!" Martin exclaimed as Bastile Wraithbone, the wizard, started shouting at the players.

"They're all right," Veils shook her head. "That was stupid; Stabbing fouled Happy, and if a referee had seen that, then he'd have been stunned. That's dangerous; this isn't a pitch on which one wants to get stunned."

"What's 'stunned'?" Martin asked. "Would Happy stun him?"

"No, Happy Lostcraft is our centaur," Veils said. "Centaurs are proud. Happy can gallop faster than any ogre, troll, or lizardman can run. However, tails aren't legal targets for Smalls, so you can't swing on them. If a referee saw that, then they'd have zapped Stabbing, and a bad zap can stun a player unconscious."

"What do referees zap Smalls with?" Martin asked.

"Lightning bolts," Veils said. "Not very powerful ones, but strong enough to take a Small out of competition for the rest of the game. They stun Bigs, too, and that's just as dangerous to a Small; you don't want to have a zapped Big collapse atop you ... or be trapped in a Big's hand when they're zapped ... or you'll get zapped, too."

Martin swallowed hard; *could he really get killed*

playing this game?

"Murder's starting her charge," Veils said. "Watch ...!"

Before Veils could finish her sentence, Murder bolted forward ... and jumped away from the logs, out over the lake. The ogre and the troll's arms were locked, and both were grunting loudly, each trying to push the other backwards, or fling them off their thick log into the lake. Murder jumped toward the ogre's arm, caught the crook of his elbow with one hand, and swung between the struggling Bigs, right under the chin of the troll. She flipped to her feet onto the troll's far shoulder, and jumped straight up; the troll blindly kicked behind him, but she was still high in the air, and then Murder fell, kicking both of her bare feet against the troll's wide back, bounced far away, and landed cleanly on the thick log.

"That's how you do it!" Veils shouted, and she let out a cheer.

Chapter 4

Smashday / Friday

To avoid the Happy ...

The ogre and the troll stopped wrestling as Murder landed safely, and all turned to watch Happy and Stabbing climb up out of the lake, onto the shore, both soaking wet. Happy was frowning, holding the ratling helplessly in the air, by his neck, and once upon dry land, he tossed Stabbing back into the lake.

"Enough of that!" Grand Wizard Bastile shouted. "All of you: conference!"

"What's a conference?" Martin asked.

"Oh, Bastile will ask each of them to review themselves, what they did wrong, or how they could've done better," Veils said. "While they're doing that, I'm supposed to teach you everyone's names. Now, you know Murder and Stabbing; they're your fellow Smalls, and they're both quick. Stabbing stinks, because he rarely bathes, but he's so greasy he's hard to grab, and can often slide through spaces where others can't. Murder's advantage is her nimbleness; she's graceful, acrobatic, and always balanced. Don't think that saves her; she's taken many a plunge into that lake. Smalls take risks; their job is to get past the Bigs."

Veils paused to catch her breath. Martin heard the others talking to Grand Wizard Bastile, but he tried to focus on what Veils was saying.

"On this pitch, Happy Lostcraft is only our reserve Big, because hooves don't work well on logs," Veils said. "Our ogre is Brain Stroker, and he's about as smart as any Ogre in the league. Ogres aren't as strong as trolls, normally, but Brain Stroker is tough. Snitch is our troll; Allfed Snitchlock is his real name, but he seldom remembers that. Trolls are the strongest Bigs, now that giants are banned from playing, and Snitch can outmuscle most other trolls. Yet he sometimes forgets what he's doing, so when you get close to his ear, it's always good to remind him who his opponents are."

Martin looked at the vacant expression on Snitch, and wondered if he understood what the others were conferencing about.

"Crusto Fernwalker is our lizardman," Veils said. "Lizardmen aren't the strongest, but they have sharp claws, and other Bigs hate them. They're smart, often maim those they wrestle, and one claw can snag an enemy Small and toss it off the pitch. This is Crusto's favorite pitch, as he can swim faster than any other Big or Small, and if he and another knock each other off, then he can be back on the pitch again while they're still splashing toward shore."

Veils smiled.

"Except for me, that's our team, and I won't be old enough to play until next season," Veils said. "Now, since you're a human, we don't expect too much from you. Your job is to avoid trouble ... to look like you're advancing, but stay back, and don't take risks."

"What ...?" Martin gasped. *"Run away ...?"*

"If we lose you, we can't compete in the next round," Veils said.

"No way!" Martin argued. "I want to play ...!"

"It's too dangerous!" Veils insisted.

"Why?" Martin demanded.

"Because you're ... just a human ...!" Veils answered.

Martin stepped back and glared; if she weren't a girl then he'd have hit her. He turned and stomped toward the others.

"Bastile ...!" Martin shouted. *"Send me home! I'm through!"*

The other monsters all turned to look at him ... with shocked expressions.

"Home ...?" Grand Wizard Bastile asked. "But ... you promised ... we need you ...!"

"I promised to play!" Martin said. "I'm not going to hide behind the Bigs until each match is over ...!"

"Hide ...?" Grand Wizard Bastile asked. "Who said anything about hiding ...?"

"She did!" Martin pointed, and they all turned to look at Veils.

"He doesn't know the rules!" Veils argued. "He doesn't know strategy, or have the dexterity, strength, or speed ...!"

The whole team fell silent, and all eyes fell on Martin.

"I play ... or I go!" Martin shouted.

"Get past me," the centaur growled, still dripping water.

"Happy ...!" Grand Wizard Bastile warned.

"Martin wants a chance, let's give him one," Happy said. "Come on, Martin; touch my tail and you'll prove that you can play."

"Not fair!" Murder argued. "Smalls score best when Bigs are entangled."

"It doesn't matter," the lame goblin said. "We let him play ... or we can't play."

"Rude is right," Grand Wizard Bastile said, "but so is Happy. We all need practice ... including our newest member. Happy, train him ... here on the shore. The rest of you, get back onto the pitch."

Happy nodded, and then looked at Martin ... and softly snarled.

Martin hesitated; Happy was huge, a muscular full-grown man from the waist up, and behind his torso, he looked like a racehorse, with thick legs and wide hooves. He wore a shiny, decorative silver armband of nasty-looking spikes over the bulging bicep of his right arm. A wicked grin widened between his thick moustache and his short, curly brown beard. Happy extended his thick arms, ready to catch Martin in his hands.

"Start practicing!" Happy snapped.

Martin stood flatfooted, helpless, and the others stood and stared silently until Grand Wizard Bastile sent them off, but Grand Wizard Bastile, Rude, and Veils remained to watch.

"Murder is correct," Rude said. "Veils, use your foot, and draw a circle around Happy."

"What ...?" Happy demanded.

"Martin has no chance of winning while Happy can run," Rude explained. "If Martin's going to learn, we have to give him a chance."

Grand Wizard Bastile nodded, and gestured for Veils to perform her task. She scowled, but scuffed a circle eight feet in diameter in the sandy dirt around Happy, who scowled even worse than she did.

"Being a Small is all about strategy," Rude said to Martin. "Since Happy can't leave the circle, you control the range. How can you get around him, or get him to turn around, to reach his tail?"

Martin stared at the huge centaur, uncertain. He had no hope of out-muscling him.

"Think it out!" Rude said. "Try ...!"

Martin could think of nothing else; he approached the circle, stopping only inches outside of the centaur's long, muscular reach.

Suddenly Martin dashed to one side, running around the circle. Happy rotated, but Martin abruptly skidded to a stop and reversed his course. He tried this several times, raising small clouds of dust, but each time, Happy easily rotated to face him.

"This is the heart of strategy," Rude said. "The smaller, inside circle needs to turn less than the outside circle to reach the same angle. To defeat him, you need to negate, or reverse, that advantage."

Martin grinned. He may never have played this game before, but he'd watched TV shows all his life; he knew what to do.

Martin repeated his tactic, running around Happy in one direction, then running back the other direction. Then he stopped, froze, and stared at the lake.

"Murder is hurt!" Martin shouted.

At once, all but Rude looked across at their female teammate, including Happy. Martin stepped back, then dove between his front and rear legs, rolling to the other side. Happy realized the deception and turned, but too late; Martin seized his wet, thick tail ... and hung on.

"Well done!" Rude laughed as the others looked back to see what had happened.

Happy flicked his tail out of Martin's grip, spraying droplets across Martin's face, and then he turned to face him again. Martin smiled; it had been a simple, obvious trick, one he'd seen a hundred times on TV, but he doubted if these monsters had ever seen a television.

"Ah, diversion ...!" Grand Wizard Bastile smiled.

"Yes," Rude said. "Control your opponent, control the outcome. How do you think he did, Veils?"

"This is only practice," Veils scowled. "In a real game that wouldn't work."

"This isn't a real game, so that factor doesn't apply," Rude said. "We challenged Martin, and he succeeded, wouldn't you agree?"

Veils sniffed haughtily, but said nothing.

"Happy, keep working with Martin," Grand Wizard Bastile said. "Let him get the feel of riding on your back, jumping over you, and swinging on your arms. Give him every chance ... and see what he can do."

Martin spent several hours working with Happy. He found the centaur was much stronger than he'd expected; Martin could do chin-ups on his thick arms without even straining him, and he found he liked the touch of his soft, hairy back and legs, so much like the dog he'd always wanted to have. Riding on Happy was easy; Martin could jump onto his back, and hold on to his shoulders while he galloped, and lean into the turns, the wind in his face, gripping tightly to protect him from Happy's sudden changes of direction.

"Well, you're not as bad as I'd thought, considering you're only half a centaur," Happy said.

"The better half," Martin said.

"What do you mean by that?" Happy demanded, deepening his voice and glaring darkly.

"The half with the brain is always best," Martin said.

Happy frowned, but then, almost reluctantly, he

nodded. Without another word, Happy trotted away, toward Rude and Grand Wizard Bastile, who were watching the others practice on the pitch.

"For Happy, that was almost friendly," Veils said.

Martin glanced at Veils, and she read his frown.

"Look, I'm not going to apologize ...," Veils said. "These games are tough, and dangerous, and most Smalls spend years studying ...!"

"I'm not to blame because you're too young," Martin said.

"If you get killed, then I'll be sorry you were old enough," Veils said.

Chapter 5

Stompday / Saturday

Dodging your Brain ...

"Martin ...?" his mother asked. "Are you ill?"

Martin awoke to feel his mother's hand pressing against his head.

"Tired ...," Martin grumbled, and he tried to go back to sleep.

"You missed breakfast," his mother said.

"Not hungry," Martin mumbled, unaware if he was really hungry or not; *he needed more sleep.*

"All right, but you can't sleep much longer," his mother said. "We need to visit your uncle today, and then stop at the bank and the grocery store."

Less than an hour later, Martin was tightening his seat belt, still sleepy, and definitely hungry. Half-an-hour later, they arrived at Martin's uncle's house, his mother's brother, who invited them in and signed some legal papers concerning the sale of some land Martin had never heard about. While sipping coffee, he and his mother discussed their other relatives, and Martin and his brothers gladly finished off a plate of store-bought cookies and tall glasses of milk.

While they chatted, Martin ticked off each of his monster teammates in his mind: Grand Wizard Bastile Wraithbone, the elderly, long-bearded wizard whose misfired spell had dropped the goblin, Rude Stealing, the first monster he'd ever seen, into his bedroom. Brain Stroker was the ogre. Allfed Snitchlock was the troll, and Crusto Fernwalker was the lizardman. Martin felt he knew Happy Lostcraft, the centaur, better than the other Bigs, as they'd practiced together for hours. Murder Shelling was the pretty dryad, with green hair and skin, and Stabbing Kingz was the other Small, a ratling, slimy and slippery. He had to remember their names; it would make him a better teammate.

Two sandwiches vanished into Martin when they got home, and he was still hungry, but he returned to the backyard and began to practice, exercising as best he could. His victory over Happy had been lucky, a stupid mistake, one Martin wouldn't have fallen for, and not one with which Bigs on other teams would be likely to be tricked.

Exercising until dinnertime, Martin ate all he could, and the rest of the evening passed in anxious idleness.

His brothers goaded him into playing video games with them, but Martin lost badly; all he cared about was returning to Heterodox, the Home of Monsters.

After the midnight flash, Martin fell ... into the ogrish arms of Brain Stroker.

"Didn't want you hurting yourself," Grand Wizard Bastile said. "You'll be working with Brain tonight. You need to get used to really big Bigs, but we can't let you train with Snitch; a troll might forget you're a teammate and eat you."

Martin hoped Bastile was joking, but then he looked up into the monstrous ogre's face ... and paled. His tumbleweed eyebrows lowered, Brain grinned at Martin ... as if human boys were his favorite food, too.

As Martin approached the lake, he saw the others already practicing on the pitch. Snitch was wrestling both Happy and Crusto, each of whom had a hold onto one of Snitch's thick arms, and yet the troll looked like he was barely straining himself. Veils was among them, and she, Murder, and Stabbing were on the shore, taking turns flinging short ropes at a pole. The short ropes were weighted on both ends, and each wrapped tightly around the pole when they struck.

As they practiced together, Brain Stroker turned out to be nicer than Martin expected an ogre to be. Bouncing upon his thick arms was like jumping from a rock to a tree limb, or climbing a smooth-skinned mountain. Martin stood barely taller than Brain's waist, yet he was much faster than Brain, and obviously smarter.

As they played, Rude came limping up on his crutches. He looked pained, but he was no longer wearing a splint.

"Don't worry about hurting Brain," Rude said. "I've jumped ten feet and landed on his head; he barely noticed. You can hang on the chain he wears and he'll barely notice your weight."

Brain raised both arms, which were as thick as tree trunks. When Martin slipped and fell, Brain caught him with ease and tossed him back up, just a few feet over his head. Sometimes Martin felt like the ogre was a juggler ... and he was being juggled.

"Don't be afraid," Rude said. "Fear is mostly a lack of experience. Once you've done something a few times, you realize it's not that scary."

After a while, Martin stopped being afraid, exactly as Rude had said. Climbing Brain was like playing on a living swing set made of soft tree trunks. Rude gave detailed instructions, and Martin performed all the moves with ease.

"That's fine, and it'll help you for this match," Rude said. "But your goal is to get past enemy Bigs, not climb on them."

Rude had Brain pose in combat positions, and Martin found this exercise even easier. Diving around or between Brain's thick legs was simple, as was running around him, and jumping up, swinging on his still arms.

As quickly as Brain could turn to face him, Martin jumped past him, and ended up behind him.

"Don't get cocky," Rude said. "All right, Brain, now ... don't let him pass so easily."

Brain smiled, a terrible, gruesome grin, and as Martin was deciding how to slip past again, Brain suddenly swatted him, absently, and Martin flew backwards. He landed on the soft sand, stunned, but he felt certain Brain could have swatted him across the whole pitch, had he wished.

"Good strategy takes time to create, and has to be decided beforehand," Rude said. "You can't form good strategy while you're busy defending yourself, and bad strategy usually fails."

Martin picked himself up and wiped his bleeding nose.

"That was your fault," Rude said. "Remember yesterday, your fight against Happy? Brain has no circle to restrain him. This time, you have to control the range ... or you lose. That's the whole point of this log spider web; fast Smalls can't just run around the slower Bigs; you have to pass within their reach."

Brain smiled again, which worried Martin. He tried running to one side, then the other, as he had before, but one of Brain's wide steps covered more distance than three of his, and while slower, Brain successfully blocked his every attempt. Martin tried to dive between his legs, but Brain smashed him to the ground with one finger, then picked him up and gently tossed him backwards, slowly enough that Martin could land on his feet.

"Think strategically," Rude said. "If you try to do a specific move, how will Brain respond?"

Suddenly Martin understood. He stepped forward, just out of reach, then darted to one side, back to the other, and jumped forward to dive between Brain's legs. Again, Brain tried to poke him down with one finger, but Martin had expected it ... and was ready. He jumped aside, grabbed Brain's wrist, swung around his thick arm, and skidded across the sand between his legs.

"Well done!" Rude smiled. "Winners are masters of surprise. Never let your opponent know what you're about to do."

"Good Small!" Brain said, beaming at Martin.

"Very true, Brain," Rude said. "Now, Martin, as long as you're thinking strategically, consider this: you have no experience playing in any Grotesquerie Game, let alone the playoffs. If you get injured, like I did, then we'll have to drop out. I'm not telling you to hold back, and I'm certainly not telling you to only pretend to play. I am telling you that, if you choose to be careful in your first match, where you'll be facing real opponents for the first time, then your chances of surviving to play in the next game will be far better."

"How many games are there?" Martin asked.

"Finals are usually between four and seven games, depending on who wins," Rude said. "As to which game we play, we never know more than one game in advance.

The Grand Wizard's Council announces the game for the next round only after the last round is complete. More than a hundred different games exist, only about three dozen of which are commonly played. This game is called 'Wet-Feather War'."

"Wet-feather War ...?" Martin asked.

"Yes," Rude said. "In play, the opponents can hit each other with bags of feathers."

"But ... feathers are light!" Martin exclaimed.

"True," Rude smiled wickedly, "... until you dip the bag of feathers ... into water ...!"

Martin looked puzzled.

"Each team gets three balls of their color, in our case, purple, and Smalls have to dunk them through a basket in the center of the pitch, which drops them into the lake," Rude said. "Each team's ball that goes through the basket earns one point. The first team to score earns the zombie head, which gets passed to the other team after each score. Getting the zombie head through the basket earns three points. You can't touch any of the other team's balls, but when yours fall into the lake, then you must recover them, and carry our purple balls out at the shore. Regulation gameplay lasts two hours, and then the horns blow, one at the end of regulation, three at the end of the game. In most games, especially if it's a tie, after the next point is scored in post-regulation, then the team with the most points wins."

"What about the feathers?" Martin asked.

"Bigs can whack each other with wet-feather bags,

which deliver quite a wallop," Rude said. "You need to avoid those; one swat by a Big can crush a Small. You'll have your own weapon, but you must be careful about how you use it."

"Me ...?" Martin asked. "A weapon ...?"

"Tomorrow you'll start weapons-training," Rude said. "Tonight, you need to keep practicing with Brain."

Brain smiled again, and Martin tried to not fret; the ogre looked uncomfortably hungry.

Chapter 6

Smiteday / Sunday

You have to throw ...

"Where did you get those bruises?" Martin's mother demanded.

"Ummm....," Martin stammered, still blurry from lack of sleep, and he glanced at his arm, which was spotted with colored bruises in a series of wide round circles ... exactly the size of an ogre's fingerprints.

"Martin's been exercising in the back yard," his sister said.

Martin's mother gave him a piercing stare.

"I said you're not going out for school sports," his mother reminded him.

"I know," Martin answered, and he struggled to keep from smiling.

Rain spattered the windows; after church, Martin couldn't exercise outside, so while his brothers shot digital zombies, enjoying their summer vacation in the virtual world, Martin did push-ups and stretches. He did feel badly bruised, and his shoulders ached from being yanked on by Brain Stroker. Yet, you don't get good at sports without driving yourself physically, so he ignored his pains and pushed on.

At midnight, the tingly sensation Martin was just getting used to flashed over him, the loud buzz returned, and suddenly he fell into the hands of Snitch. The huge troll looked surprised, but then Veils reached out and stopped him from dropping Martin.

"We told you this would happen," Veils said to Snitch. "Remember? We said Martin would appear and land in your hands. Now, you need to set him down; Martin is our new Small, and we need him unhurt."

Snitch looked like he was straining to comprehend her words, but then Grand Wizard Bastile stepped into the room.

"Be gentle with him, Snitch," Grand Wizard Bastile said from the doorway. "This is your new friend, Martin. He helped us win the last game."

Snitch lifted Martin higher and stared at him from small, hungry eyes, as eagerly as Martin might examine a banana split covered in whipped cream and nuts; Martin felt like a snack about to be eaten, but Snitch simply sniffed him with his bulbous nose, and then lowered him to the floor.

"Hi, Snitch," Martin waved up at him, trying to appear friendly.

Snitch only grunted, then held out a stubby finger thicker than Martin's wrist, which was capped by a relatively-short, cracked and broken claw, and poked Martin in the chest, as if testing to see if he were real.

"Thank you, Snitch," Grand Wizard Bastile said. "Welcome back, Martin. Veils, take him out to the pitch while I work with Snitch, will you? You know what he needs."

"This way, newbie," Veils said, and Martin followed as she led the way out of the locker room.

"So ... I get a weapon today?" Martin asked.

"You get weapons-training today," Veils said. "You'd better learn fast; tomorrow night we play."

"What ...?" Martin exclaimed. "You said we only play once a week ...!"

"It's been a week," Veils replied.

"No, a week is seven days!" Martin argued. "Monday, Tuesday, Wednesd...!"

"We don't have those," Veils said. "Our weeks are four days long: Smashday, Stompday, Smiteday, and Rompday. All Grotesquerie Games are played on Rompday."

"But ... I'm not ready ...!" Martin complained.

"You'd better be," Veils said. "This is your last night of training. Tomorrow you play for real."

Murder and Stabbing were again playing with short ropes, weighted on each end. Stabbing was just dipping the ends of his into a barrel of water, while Murder flung hers, throwing a wide spray of droplets ... and wrapping its cord around a pole.

"Think you can do that?" Veils asked.

"It doesn't look too hard," Martin answered.

Overhearing, Murder and Stabbing glanced at each other, and then Stabbing yanked his rope out of the water, spun it once around over his head, and flung it at Martin. Veils jumped aside as the rope struck Martin's ankles and wrapped tightly around both legs, making him topple onto the sandy dirt.

"It's called a bola," Murder said. "It started as a weapon for hunting, and it's pretty dangerous."

"Once the game starts, their Smalls will be hunting you," Stabbing said. "You need to learn how to dodge as well as throw."

Martin pushed up onto his knees, and had to reach back and unwind the bola from around his ankles. Tied to each end of the rope was a small, soft bag of feathers ... soaking wet ... and now layered in wet sand.

"It could be worse," Murder said. "They used to make bolas with steel balls ... some with spikes on them."

"Try it on the post," Veils said. "Do what they did."

Martin stood up and hefted the bola, wanting to throw it back at Stabbing, but obediently he faced the thin post. He grasped the bola by one end, raised it, and spun it over his head. Carefully he aimed ... and then he threw.

The bola sailed right past the post.

"Don't be discouraged," Murder said as Veils and Stabbing laughed. "All weapons require practice to master."

She handed him another wet bola, and showed him how to hold it, and when to release it.

"Try again," Murder said. "As the bola is turning, half of it is rotating forward ... while the other half is rotating backwards. If you aim right at your target, it'll often spin around it as your bola flies forward, and never actually loop your opponent. If you're throwing with your right arm, then aim a foot to the left of your target."

Martin did as instructed, and to his surprise, his bola wrapped neatly around the post.

"Timing your target is just as important as aiming," Stabbing said. "Catching one shin won't trip most Smalls. You have to envelope their legs in mid-stride, while their knees are close together."

They spent the next hour playing on the sand, running back and forth, throwing their bolas. Martin spent a lot of time on his knees, unwrapping their weapons from his ankles. Stabbing was especially good at tripping Martin right before he threw. Murder was more patient, and let Martin trap her ankles with his bola, but she had to stop and wait for him, and she never fell. Throwing the bolas was fun, and Martin enjoyed it. However, Stabbing and Murder could dodge his throws at will, and he often fell, even when he successfully dodged their throws.

They taught him how to test the bolas by squeezing the bags, and if no water dripped, he had to dunk them again. Each rope was no longer than his arm, nose to fingertip, but the wet feathers weren't light; one of the bags splatted him in the face as he tried to dodge, and he thought the wet feathers would knock him out.

Stabbing complained that Martin would never learn how to properly throw in just one night, so Murder suggested he focus on dodging and jumping over the bolas thrown at him. Martin wasn't keen on this, but he had to learn both skills, so he agreed, and they spent the next hour with Stabbing and Murder throwing their bolas at him. It was actually more fun, because Martin already knew how to dodge, and he improved quickly. Soon they found it hard to catch his ankles, for Martin could do handstands on one arm, and lift his feet as the bola passed under him. He also jumped quickly, and could dodge about leaping from one foot to the other.

Finally Murder called for a break, for Martin was breathing in gasps. She gave him some fresh water and made him sit and rest.

"You're doing better," Murder said.

"Thanks," Martin said. "It feels good. I think I can do this."

"I felt the same ... until my first match," Murder said. "I'd seen lots of games, and knew how loud it got, but the roar of the crowd sounds different when you're actually in the game ... and every eye is watching you."

"I've never been in anything like this," Martin said.

"I'm a little nervous."

"Everything is a strategy," Murder said. "How would you advise someone facing their first event, who said that they were nervous?"

Martin had no answer, and didn't know what to say. He liked the concept that he needed a strategy, he just didn't know any strategy that would work. Of course, if Martin knew a strategy that would work, then he wouldn't need to ask ... and he wouldn't be nervous before his first game.

"Look, it's easy," Stabbing said. "First, there are challenges of the body, and that's what we've been trying to teach you to meet. Then there are challenges of the mind, and those you have to teach yourself. Nervousness is a challenge of the mind; only you can overcome it."

"How'd you overcome your nerves?" Martin asked.

"I had no choice," Stabbing said. "In these games, Smalls do what they must ... or we get squished. I've been squished; I didn't like it."

Martin understood that; he'd only seen the final minute of the last game, but he knew what he was facing. Bigs squashed Smalls. Players got hurt. He was only playing because Rude Stealing had broken his leg. Martin was worried; *if he got hurt ... how could he explain it to his mother?*

Murder suggested they let Martin practice against the post for a while, but Stabbing refused.

"Practicing on the shore won't help tomorrow night,"

Stabbing said. "He needs to try it on the pitch."

"Martin, this may be a little late, but ... can you swim?" Murder asked.

"Yes, and I can high-dive," Martin said.

"Good," Stabbing said. "Because you're going to need both."

Martin had his breath back, and they climbed up onto the thick logs. Martin liked running on the logs, and thought he might have an advantage; most monsters didn't wear shoes, and his sneakers offered much better traction than bare feet. Today, Murder wore leather sandals; he wondered how she managed to not slip off, and Stabbing wore no shoes, although his long, hairy toes had small claws that curved downward, and hooked into the log as he ran. Yet, although Murder warned him that she was about to throw, Martin's dodge unbalanced him, and he fell off, splashing into the water. The lake was cold, yet Martin pushed to the surface and swam for the shore, ignoring Stabbing's laughter. Fortunately, land wasn't far away. From the center of the lake, his swim would take much longer.

"Don't be ashamed," Murder said. "You won't be the only one in the water."

"But when you do fall in, there're three things you must remember," Stabbing said. "Stay away from enemy players, because fouls happen, and judges can't see what happens underwater. Also, touching an opponent in the water is a foul, and if a referee zaps you in the water, you could drown."

"What's the third thing?" Martin asked.

"Before you fall in the water," Stabbing said, "look ... to make sure that you don't fall on me."

They spent another hour letting Martin practice dodging on the logs, most of which seemed to be spent swimming toward shore. Stabbing could almost always drop him, but Murder took it easy, giving him a chance. However by the end of the hour, Martin felt he'd improved greatly, and could dodge most throws, if he had time, and if he saw it coming.

Then Murder sent Stabbing to go fetch some balls, and she let Martin rest while he was gone.

"I'm going to be terrible, aren't I?" Martin asked.

"No ...," Murder said, but she bowed her green head. "Yes, but good or bad, we need you. Without you, Shantdareya sinks."

"Sinks ...?" Martin asked.

"Shantdareya ... was a large island," Murder said.

"Was ...?" Martin asked.

"Grand Wizard Maim La Nuormal," Murder hissed, sounding like she was cursing. "She's a Grand Wizard, or Grand Witch, as she prefers. Beluga La Grossie and Lion Changeling told her that Bastile Wraithbone was plotting against her, and had said terrible things about her. She attacked Bastile without warning from her flying palace; Bastile defeated her, and blasted her castle out of the sky, but she revenged herself upon all of Shantdareya. Standing on the top balcony of her sinking palace, Maim La Nuormal cast a terrible spell which sank the whole of Shantdareya Island. Only Topsail Tower remains above water, and all our people are cowering on it; most of Shantdareya lies under many fathoms of ocean."

"That's terrible!" Martin said.

"That's why we must win," Murder said. "Only the staff of Master Grand Wizard Borgias Killoff is powerful enough to lift Shantdareya out of the sea."

"Who is Master Grand Wizard Borgias Killoff?" Martin asked.

"Borgias Killoff was the founder of the Grotesquerie Games," Murder said. "He was the most-powerful wizard to ever rule Heterodox."

"What happened to him?" Martin asked.

"No one knows," Murder said. "Some say he got bored of being king, and others think he was dying. He'd commanded the first Grotesquerie Games ages before, and after centuries, everyone was shocked when he suddenly handed over his staff as the prize for the Grand Wizard whose team won. His last command was to hold a Grotesquerie Games playoff each year, and to surrender his staff to each victor. Then he walked away, into the crowd, and no one ever saw him again."

"His staff ... can raise the island ...?" Martin asked.

"Yes, but we don't have it," Murder said. "Beluga La Grossie won last year, and he wouldn't lend that staff to another wizard even for a moment."

"But ... I'm too new ...!" Martin argued. *"I've never even seen a full game ...!"*

"We know," Murder said. "But, without your help, we can't even play."

Martin bowed his head. *Why hadn't they told him sooner ...?*

Stabbing came back with some large purple balls, like soccer balls, only softer, and they spent the last hour practicing scoring goals, which was just like basketball ... using a broken wicker basket on a pole only five feet above the logs, and you didn't have to dribble. Martin wasn't bad ... but not as good as Murder or Stabbing. Martin frowned; *even if he didn't get himself killed, he was likely to make a fool of himself.*

Chapter 7

Rompday / Monday

The Wet Feather War ...

"How did your shoes get wet?" Martin's mother demanded.

"They got dirty ... in the backyard ... I tried to wash them ... with the hose," Martin said.

His mother gave him a strange look, but shook her head and said nothing else. Martin focused on his breakfast and said nothing; he'd planned this excuse last night, ever since arriving in his bedroom near 5:00 AM, when he'd landed on his bed soaking wet, and then carefully laid his clothes out to let them dry. He'd left his shoes by the window, hoping they'd dry overnight. He should've hidden them under his bed, as he had with the damp bola that was still hidden there.

Fifteen minutes later his mother left for work, and his father left ten minutes after her. As soon as they were gone, Martin fetched a small plastic sand bucket from his toy chest, which he'd once been given when they vacationed at the beach. He filled it with water, dug out his bola, and headed outside.

He threw, and watched the bola wrap around the posts of his swing-set for the twelfth time when his sister came outside.

"What is that?" Vicky demanded.

"Feathers ... on a string," Martin said.

"Let me see it," Vicky said, and Martin surrendered it to her inspection. "Where did you get this?"

"A friend ... before school ended," Martin said.

Vicky examined it carefully, and squeezed some water from the bags.

"You're up to something," Vicky said. "What is this ... a martial arts thing ...?"

"Mom wouldn't let me take martial arts," Martin said.

"I'm not stupid," Vicky said, and she sniffed him. "You smell funny."

She handed back the bola, then returned inside.

Tom, Terry, and Ron came out to see what Martin was playing with, but after a few tries throwing it, they returned to their video games. Martin practiced until he could wrap the bola around any section of the swing-set he aimed at, and then he resumed practicing dodging imaginary bolas.

Martin bathed before his parents came home ... so

that he didn't smell like he'd been swimming in a lake. Eating dinner was difficult; his stomach churned with unspoken worries.

At midnight, wearing damp shoes, Martin fell into Brain's waiting arms, dressed in his bright purple jersey with the number "13" printed in white. Everyone watched in silence as Brain set him on his feet.

"Martin, I can't thank you enough," Grand Wizard Bastile said. "We all thank you. Shantdareya thanks you ..."

"Got it ... thanks," Martin said. "Now ... don't we have a game to win ...?"

Happy and Murder smiled, and they walked together out onto the pitch. Cheers exploded as they approached; a huge, noisy crowd of monsters surrounded the lake, and the stands were standing room only. Martin saw fangs, claws, pale skin, fur, scales, and armored plates all around him, and limbs of all types waving small flags and banners, most over hats and jerseys supporting their favorite team – only a handful wore purple. He even saw some purple t-shirts boldly bearing the name 'Skull-crackers'.

"Here they come!" the loud woman's voice blasted out from huge speakers. "The Shantdareya Skull-crackers, led by Grand Wizard Bastile Wraithbone, and from what I've heard ..." a titter of laughter sounded "... they have a human on their team! You heard me right, folks! Some wizards argued that it violated the rules, but the original scrolls of Borgias Killoff were reviewed, and it doesn't violate any statutes, and trust me, if there's anything yours truly, Evilla, knows well, it's violations. Well, we'll soon see if a human can play against monsters!"

"Who's that?" Martin asked.

"That's Evilla," Veils said. "She announces all the games – be careful what you say around her; she's kind of a hu....!"

Veils faltered, as if she were about to say something that she shouldn't.

"A ... *what ...?"* Martin frowned.

"A ... hu ... hu ... huge pain in the butt!" Veils finished.

Martin knew she meant to say something else, but their path took them into the thick of the crowd, and he let it go. As they reached the edge of the lake, with many hands, paws, and tentacles reaching out to touch them as they slid past, Evilla spoke up, and he saw her centermost in the stands across the pitch. She was tall and thin, with hair like a ripe tomato, and barely wearing a tight, sexy red dress.

"And here comes the Barkrover Bullies, led by their coach, Grand Wizard Lion Changeling. The Barkrover Bullies have had a great season, and we expect to see some magnificent plays from Jackknife Illson, the best cyclops in the league, and Aunt Honey Peekings, the goblin Queen of Trouble. We're in for an exciting game tonight, but sources expect a blow-out ... can the Skull-crackers, only wildcards in this tournament, win with a temporary replacement player - a human - against one of the best teams in the league?"

On a raised post, on each side of the pitch, stood a man in a striped yellow robe and pointed hat, holding a magic wand, and frowning. Martin eyed them warily.

"Yea, those are the referees," Veils warned. "Play clean; as the first human, they'll be watching you."

As the game began, Brain, Snitch, and Crusto lifted up bags of feathers as big as any Small ... and dipped them into a huge water barrel. Afterwards, they shook the heavy bags as if they weighed nothing, deluging gallons, and then they climbed up onto the logs. Martin, Murder, and Stabbing were given new bolas, which they dipped into a smaller water barrel on the shore, and each was handed a soft, purple ball. Stabbing led the way, and stepped up onto a log half-buried in the sand, and then walked up onto the log web-work of the pitch.

Cheering and catcalls deafened them, but then the voice of Evilla blasted above them.

"Here we are, the second contest in Round 2 of the three hundred and fourteenth Grotesquerie Games! The Shantdareya Skull-crackers ... facing the Barkrover Bullies! Let the mayhem begin!"

Nerves consumed Martin. A thousand monsters cheered, and shouts of *"Human ...!"* repeated frequently ... always accompanied by raucous laughter. Eyes of every description, except friendly, stared at him, and someone tossed a crumpled paper cup at his head, which barely missed him, and fell into the lake. Suddenly a horn sounded, and Brain, Snitch, and Crusto unexpectedly charged forward, across the shaking logs, roaring like beasts. Stabbing and Murder chased after them. Finally, amid many laughs, Martin followed.

Neither of the ogres on the Barkrover Bullies looked as big as Brain or Snitch, but their massive cyclops charged forward, spiked armor banded over him with straps of black leather, and an iron grill tied over his face to protect his one eye. Martin had never seen anything so terrifying, but the cyclops charged at Snitch fearlessly, and the huge troll charged straight at him.

The meaty *smack!* of three ogres, a troll, a lizardman, and a cyclops slamming into each other was tremendous, echoing out across the pitch, the crowd, and the stands. As they collided, five figures leaped upon them and bounced high. Bolas flew; a swarthy, black-haired elf on the other side got one bola wrapped around his neck, which flipped him over in midair, and caused his green ball to slip out of his hands; it bounced off the side of the head of the ogre fighting Crusto, and splashed into the lake. Four other balls flew toward the basket, but a purple ball landed inside it: Stabbing had managed to score first, which meant the Skull-crackers got the zombie head first, but Stabbing got a bola wrapped around one ankle and his wrist, and fell right on top of the cyclops' head, bounced off, and toppled into the lake. Murder managed to dodge the bola cast at her, but her bola-throw also missed. However, Murder's purple ball, and the two remaining green balls of the other team, had all fouled each other and bounced away, off the basket's rim.

"What a start!" Evilla shouted, laughing into her microphone. "Jackknife Illson fixed his one eye on Allfed Snitchlock, the strongest troll in the league, and he's holding his own. Stabbing Kingz scored first, but then splashed, and Slid Egg beat him into the lake. Only the human has failed to shoot yet, but look: Aunt Honey Peekings saved her ball from the wet!"

Martin spied an older woman, thin and looking like she was past seventy, but with green skin like Rude, swinging around one ogre in a green jersey toward the other. With an amazing dexterity that denied her apparent age, she bounced off his shoulder toward the broken-bottomed basket, which had dropped Stabbing's purple ball into the lake. Martin couldn't let her score; he whipped up his bola and flung it right at her.

Right before it could strike her, a young goblin man in a green jersey jumped in front of the older woman, a bola swinging in his left hand, and he snatched Martin's bola out of midair with his right hand.

"Aunt Honey Peekings scores, and the game is tied!" Evilla shouted.

Martin gasped; the old woman had scored, but he still had his ball, and he wasn't going to miss ...

"Martin ...!" Murder shouted, and she held up her hands to catch his ball. He wanted to score himself, but he raised it high to pass to her.

The young goblin threw both bolas. One wrapped around Martin's wrists, the other around his ankles. His ball slipped from his hands ... and he tumbled off the log into the lake.

"So falls the first human to ever ...!" Evilla laughed, and then Martin splashed underwater into darkness, and heard only his own frantic thrashings. He tried to pull his hands apart, so he could free his legs, but both were bound tight. He began a spinning motion underwater, circling his hands around the floating bags of feathers; slowly they came free, but it wasted precious time.

Suddenly a huge splash knocked him aside, and as the air burst from his lungs, the pale hand of Brain seized the bola around his legs, pinching one tiny wet-feather bag between his thick fingers, and lifted Martin out of the water. Martin gasped for air, and then Brain twirled him like a marionette, unwinding the bola around his ankles. Brain succeeded, all the while carrying Martin toward the shore, and as Martin became untangled and fell, Brain caught him in his other hand.

"Get up there!" Brain shouted, and to Martin's surprise, Brain threw him toward the shore, skimming him across the water so he skipped like a stone.

The next thing he knew, Brain had slashed his thick arm at the water, splashing toward Martin two floating purple balls. As he fumbled to recover both balls in shallows up to his knees, Martin spied Stabbing just emerging from the water, a purple ball in his grip, and Veils tossed him a freshly-wetted bola. Then Stabbing jumped onto the log in the sand and ran for the center.

Martin slogged through the shallows, gathered both balls, and emerged onto the shore just before Brain splashed out.

"Don't wait, go!" Veils shouted.

His hands full, Veils hooked a new, wet bola around the back of Martin's neck, and then pushed him toward the log. Happy galloped up with a new, large wet bag for Brain, as big as Martin, and Brain followed him up onto the pitch.

Neither Snitch nor the cyclops seemed to like the bags; both had dropped theirs, and they were grappling, but Crusto and the other ogre on the pitch were hammering each other, swinging their bags like baseball bats, and knocking each other backwards with each blow, which landed with a *splosh!,* showering droplets in every direction.

"One side!" Brain shouted, and he stepped right over Martin and ran toward the center, the thick log bouncing under his weight. The other ogre, whom Brain had been fighting, and who had fallen with him, splashed out of the lake and started climbing toward the log spider web. The old woman and dark elf were facing off against Murder and Stabbing, who seemed to be backtracking, trying to find a way to circle close enough to the basket to score without approaching the Bigs, one pair of which was contesting on each side of the basket.

Both Smalls in green were empty-handed, which let them bounce and swing off the limbs of the combatting

Bigs with ease, while Stabbing had a ball and a bola, and Murder carried the zombie head. On the far end, the goblin in green ran up onto the spider web with a bola and two green balls, and dashed forward.

Martin ran, chasing after Brain, carrying both purple balls closer to the basket. Brain reached Crusto and swung his wet sack high, while Crusto swung low; their wet bags struck simultaneously, and their enemy ogre toppled. Then Crusto turned toward the approaching ogre, and Brain ran at the Smalls in green, who scattered before him. Murder ran forward, but the young goblin jumped straight for Brain's face; a stupid move. Brain swung his heavy wet-feather bag, which was bigger than its target, and swatted the young goblin solidly. The goblin flew backwards over several rows of logs, flailing for balance, and almost sticking a landing on the last beam, but slipping off and falling into the shallows of the lake. However, while he was striking the young goblin, the old goblin woman jumped at Brain, swung upon his arm and flipped passed him, landed on the log, and jumped straight at Murder.

"Murder Shelling's in trouble; she passes the zombie head backwards to Stabbing Kingz, who circles back," Evilla shouted. "Martin has two balls, and ... look! Crusto struck Jackknife Illson from behind! Jackknife is down – no, wait! Jackknife has picked up Crusto in both hands, and ... *Hell's Belles!* Allfed Snitchlock has picked up Jackknife Illson, who is still carrying Crusto Fernwalker ... and there they both go!"

Snitch lifted and threw both his teammate and opponent, the cyclops and lizardman, off the logs. As they splashed, a huge deluge gushed up into the air, a veritable column of water rose toward the starry sky ... and then rained down on Snitch as he roared in triumph. Unfortunately, the heavy water struck Murder, and she was knocked off the logs into the lake.

The dark elf threw his bola, not at Stabbing, but to the old woman. She caught it, then faced Stabbing.

His left hand clutching the zombie head, Stabbing dropped the ball he was carrying in his right hand ... and yanked out his bola, spinning it threateningly. They faced each other, one-on-one, ratling and goblin undaunted.

"It's Stabbing Kingz, ready to score big, with only Aunt Honey Peekings blocking his way. Both are armed: who'll win? Rude Stealing was their best Small, but he's sidelined, injured for the rest of the season. Both players are twirling bolas, coming closer ... both throw ... and each caught the other player's ankles! They're falling ...!"

"Martin ...!" Stabbing shouted, and he threw the zombie head. Martin dropped a ball to catch it, and it landed right against his chest just as Stabbing and the old woman both struck the water, wrapped in each other's weapons. No one else was on the pitch except for the dark elf, who held a green ball, but was being chased by Snitch. Martin sprinted to the center; no one stood between him and the basket. *He was going to score ...!*

He was almost there ...!

Suddenly a green ball flew at Martin, struck his leg, and bounced against the log underneath him. The dark elf had hurled it, and Martin tripped over the green ball ... and fell. He managed to stay on the log, but both the ball in his left hand, and the zombie head in his right, fell, loosened by his impact, and they flew out over the water ... and splashed in.

A loud sizzle matched a brilliant flash, and as Martin watched, he saw a lightning bolt arc from each side of the pitch. Both lightning bolts struck the dark elf, who leapt up like a cartoon character, illuminated in yellow light. Then he fell into the water, shaking and twitching.

"Slid Egg gets zapped!" Evilla shouted. "Martin was carrying four points to the basket, but using a ball as a weapon is a foul, and Slid Egg knew it! Maybe he thought it was worth it, but he won't be straightening his hair for a week, at least! Shantdareya owns the pitch, yet all six balls and the head are in the drink! Will Slid Egg survive his risky foul ...?"

One of the ogres in green was wading toward shore, but it turned around and splashed back into deeper water. The zapped dark elf had vanished into the starlit lake ... and not resurfaced.

A streak slashed across the surface of the lake; Crusto the lizardman was swimming for shore, his webbed feet and hands making him fly through the water. Before any of the others reached the shore, Crusto ran back up onto the logs.

A good fifteen minutes passed. Martin hadn't realized how long it took to get out of the lake. He also had no idea how much game time had passed. Crusto arranged them carefully, placing Snitch on one side of the basket, he on the other, with Martin standing between them, right beside the basket, spinning his bola.

"Stand ready," Crusto told Martin, talking over Evilla. "We'll keep them off, and Murder and Stabbing should be able to pass the balls to you."

"Why didn't you grab a ball ... or the head?" Martin asked Crusto. "As fast as you can swim ...?"

"Illegal; I'd get zapped," Crusto said. "Bigs can't carry scoring tools."

"Brain threw me ...!" Martin said.

"That's legal," Crusto said, and he looked past Martin. "Hey, Snitch! You're doing fine! Keep the other Bigs back, but not Brain! Only attack monsters in green!"

Snitch grunted in reply, licking his chops, but his level of comprehension was anyone's guess.

Eventually Brain splashed out and climbed up onto the pitch, a new, wet bag over his shoulder. Murder and Stabbing climbed up onto the logs a few minutes later. Both had new bolas, and Murder held two purple balls. Stabbing held the last purple ball and the zombie head.

The Barkrover Bullies had long been waiting, preparing to play. The stunned young goblin, who'd been batted into the shallows, was standing weakly on the shore, holding the zapped dark elf, who looked partly charred. Another young goblin, a female, and a male satyr had replaced them. The satyr looked uncomfortable; like Happy Lostcraft, he had hooves instead of feet, and much of the log spider web was drenched, making footing precarious. Each of the Barkrover Smalls held a green ball and spun a bola, and looked determined.

As Murder and Stabbing reached the outer ring of the log spider web, the Barkrover Bullies came charging forward, the cyclops in the lead, followed by both ogres, with Aunt Honey Peekings, the young female goblin, and the male satyr behind them. Crusto repeated his reminders to Snitch, who roared at the approaching team, ignoring Crusto entirely. Brain stepped forward and braced, ready to swing his heavy, dripping bag. Evilla was shouting to the crowd, but the roar of cheers drowned out even her loudspeakers.

It was like the game was beginning again, except that Martin and the Skull-cracker Bigs were standing center, guarding the basket, with Murder and Stabbing running toward them from behind, carrying their precious tickets to victory. Yet the Barkrover Bullies were charging from the other side, and they were a lot closer.

The cyclops charged Snitch, then changed course at the last second. He circled around to meet Brain and Crusto on a different log, and both of their ogres attacked Snitch. Martin spun his bola, and waited until the Smalls came within range. He flung his bola at the old goblin woman, who dodged it, as he'd expected. His bola flew past her ... and wrapped around the legs of the young female goblin on the log behind her. She screamed and fell ... and she, her bola, and her green ball landed in the lake.

Two bolas came flying forward. The first knocked Martin back against the post under the basket, and the second wrapped around Martin ... and the post.

While Martin struggled, pinned against the basket-pole, the Bigs met in a *crash!*, shaking the whole pitch, and their soaking-wet weapons struck with a *splash!* Martin struggled against his bonds, but then an aged green face appeared right in front of his; the older goblin woman, laughing at him. Aunt Honey Peekings lifted her green ball and tossed it up with ease ... right into the basket. Seconds later, the satyr tossed his ball to her. Martin managed to pull one arm free, but too late; the old woman scored again.

"Aunt Honey Peekings scores twice!" Evilla shouted. "Barkrover Bullies are winning, three to one!"

Martin yanked free one of the bolas wrapped around him, but the old woman was too close to throw at; Martin swung the rope hard, and the bag struck the old woman like a blackjack.

"Nooooo!" Murder screamed, and then Martin's world became a painful blaze of electric yellow light, searing every fiber of Martin's thrashing body.

Chapter 8

Rompday / Monday

To win the game ...

"Blood-pies! The best!"

"Dragon-burgers! Chocolate skulls!"

"Four-to-one odds! Place your bets here!"

Agonizingly ... Martin groaned.

"I think he's coming around," Grand Wizard Bastile's voice said near his ear.

"Martin ... can you hear me?" Murder asked.

Martin opened his eyes; most of his teammates were leaning over him.

"Did ... did we win?" Martin asked.

"It's halftime," Happy snarled, and then he turned away.

"What ... what happened ...?" Martin asked.

"You fouled Aunt Honey Peekings!" Veils snapped. *"We were outnumbered on the pitch ... and you ...!"*

"Easy!" Grand Wizard Bastile said. "We should've told him all the rules."

"We scored twice, but they got the zombie head," Stabbing snarled. "They threw me in the water and tore it away from Murder, three against one."

"We're losing six to three," Rude said, hobbling up on his crutches. "The odds are against us. Grand Wizard Bastile used his healing spell on you ... he can't use another until after the game."

"That means we can't get hurt," Murder said. "One accident ... and one of us could die."

"Us play ...!" Snitch grumbled deeply.

"Yes, we play," Rude said. "We have no choice ... or Shantdareya washes away."

"They have replacements ... we don't," Veils snapped. "All of them are experienced players ... we have a novice ... a human novice! We're three points down! What chance do we have ...?"

Martin sat up, then turned and looked at each of his teammates, finally staring at Rude.

"We have strategy," Martin said.

"Strategy ...?" Veils started, but Rude cut her off.

"Let him speak," Rude said. "Martin, do you have an idea ...?"

The roar of the crowd was filled with laughter. One creature, a short, long-haired thing with stubby horns and gray tentacles shuffled forward and threw a leather-wrapped bottle at them; Snitch reached down, picked the creature up, and threw the shaggy monster over the heads of the crowd, evoking much laughter. Yet, as the Skull-crackers rose and climbed to the pitch, jeers and insults shouted at them.

"Let the havoc resume!" Evilla shouted.

As the second half started with one trumpet blare, the rush toward the center began again. This time Martin ran with them, only a step behind Stabbing.

The Bigs struck with smacks that sounded painful to Martin, but he kept his cool; *they had a strategy!*

Snitch struck first: he didn't even try to grapple or hit the armored cyclops; he seized him and pulled him off the logs, down into the water.

"Allfed Snitchlock goes down, taking Jackknife Illson with him!" Evilla shouted. "The two strongest players are down!"

Snitch and the cyclops splashed, hurling so much water aloft that a heavy rain fell on all of them. The young female goblin scored first, so the next Barkrover Small to reach the outer log-ring would get the zombie head, worth three points. Seconds later, Stabbing scored.

"Crusto Fernwalker and Brain Stroker are teaming up, attacking two on one," Evilla shouted. "There goes ... Crusto was pulled off, too! One ogre left for each team ... the only Bigs on the pitch ...! Score is seven to four!"

Murder darted forward, flinging her bola, but the old

goblin woman dodged it with ease. Murder jumped up dunked her ball into the basket, then chased the old woman back, preventing her from scoring. Stabbing was blocking the last green Small, the satyr, but the old woman's bola wrapped around him from behind and dropped Stabbing into the water.

Martin ran forward, swinging his bola; the satyr stood his ground. Martin and the satyr threw simultaneously; their bolas caught in midair, and both weapons fell to the water.

With casual ease, Martin plopped his purple ball into the basket, and then stepped back.

"Go ahead ... score," Martin said. "I won't try to stop you."

The satyr looked puzzled, but stepped forward and scored.

"What are they doing?" Evilla shouted. "Is this a game or what? Nine to seven ...!"

Suddenly Brain appeared on the shore. The green Bigs were all still midway in water, slowly slogging through. Brain grabbed a new wet-feather bag and ran up onto the pitch.

"How did he get out so fast?" the satyr asked.

"Strategy," Martin answered.

Martin glanced down and saw something streak through the water. Seconds later, another splash sloshed past. Less than a minute later, Stabbing climbed up onto the pitch, a bola hanging over one shoulder ... and carrying three balls in his hands.

"What …?" the satyr demanded.

"Gotta go," Martin chuckled to the satyr. "Here … play with Brain …!"

The satyr shrieked and ran back as Brain ran forward … and chased after him. Martin ran to help Stabbing, and soon they scored all three balls.

"Nine to eight!" Evilla shouted with their first score. "Tied game!" with their second. "Nine to ten! The Skull-crackers take the lead!"

Aunt Honey Peekings tried to score and failed, but by then, the young female goblin and cyclops had climbed onto the pitch, bringing with them the zombie head. Shortly afterwards, Snitch climbed out onto shore, and, to everyone's amazement, suddenly Martin just … jumped off the log, purposefully splashing into the lake.

The game continued, but the play was chaotic. The three Barkrover Bullies' Smalls outnumbered the two Skull-crackers' Smalls, but Jackknife Illson was no match for Snitch and Brain combined. Barkrover scored with the zombie head, but then they were forced back, and their Smalls couldn't approach the basket, even with the two green balls they'd managed to pull up onto the pitch. Minutes later, Martin was back at the shore … with the zombie head and all three purple balls.

Jeers turned to cheers. The crowd went wild. As fast as they could, the Barkrover Bullies drug all of their teammates out of the lake, with their three recovered balls, and once with the zombie head, and then they charged together. However, each time the Skull-crackers' Bigs could drag the Barkrover Bullies' Bigs into the water, Brain came sloshing out only a few moments later, while it took the cyclops and other ogres ten minutes or more to wade from the center to shore.

It also took Snitch ten minutes to wade out; he was too big for Crusto to carry. Yet the zombie head and balls were returned as fast as Brain, and carried up by Martin, who passed them all to Murder and Stabbing.

Boisterous cheers greeted the horn that sounded the end of regulation, and three horn blasts followed the last ball falling into the basket, which Martin himself scored. Then the whole team, even Happy, lifted Martin up and paraded him around the entire outside of the log ring, much to the riotous celebratory exultations of the crowd.

To Martin's amazement, they exited the pitch upon a log toward the far stands, where before them stood Evilla. Up close, she was exceptionally pretty, her red dress so tight her shapely figure threatened to burst it apart every time she moved. Her dark blue eyeshadow was eclipsed by heavy black eyeliner, which seemed totally weird surrounded by her bright tomato hair and dress.

"Monsters of all kinds ... I give you our winner: the Shantdareya Skull-crackers!" Evilla shouted into her microphone, and a long, loud cheer echoed across the starlit land. When it finally diminished, Evilla smiled brightly and spoke into her microphone. "Final score: twenty-six to seventeen. Grand Wizard Bastile Wraithbone, how did you do it?"

"We have our newest member to thank," Grand Wizard Bastile said, and all eyes fell upon Martin.

"Tell us all, human," Evilla said. "First, what's your name?"

"Martin ... Martin Mulberry ... from Earth."

"So tell us, Martin Mulberry from Ear ... from the human world ... how did you do it?" Evilla asked, and she pointed her microphone at Martin.

"Well, we were losing ... because of me," Martin said. "I'd never even seen a Grotesquerie Game, and here I was ... playing in the playoffs. Well, nothing I could do would give me the years of experience the other players had, but then I realized we had one advantage; Crusto could swim faster than all of us combined. He couldn't carry Snitch, as he was too heavy, and he couldn't carry a ball, because that's a foul. But Crusto could carry me, and I could carry the balls ... and the zombie head. We could all splash in ... and take them with us ... and then we could all be back on the pitch ... with all three purple balls ... and the zombie head ... in half the time it took our opponents to swim back to shore." Martin glanced at Rude. "Because of me, we couldn't out-play them, but, because of Crusto, we could out-score them."

"It was all Martin's idea," Happy said, truly smiling. "Martin won this round."

"Well, congratulations to the Shantdareya Skull-crackers!" Evilla said. "You're entering Round 3 – two wins and no losses – and your victory gave the Barkrover Bullies their first loss, which puts them one loss away from being out before the finals! This is your amorous announcer, Evilla, saying, before we start the next game, once more, a brilliant strategy, and congratulations to all of the Shantdareya Skull-crackers, to Grand Wizard Bastile Wraithbone, and to our newest player, the first human ever to play in any Grotesquerie Game, Martin the Magnificent!"

A thunderous cheer arose, and monsters of every type jumped and applauded. Finally, as the adulations lessened, Brain lifted Martin, and they headed back to the stands.

"So, the Shantdareya Skull-crackers join the Narwhaila Rowdy Reavers and the Barkrover Bullies in Round 3, and the Cruel Creepers are out of the tournament. Next, the Wild Wraiths and the Greasy Golems meet. The Greasy Golems have one loss, and need a win to move on to Round 3 ...!"

Brain carried Martin through the crowd, which pushed up against them despite them all being soaking wet. Martin held out both hands as he was carried, and got high-fived by giant hands, clawed paws, sharp talons, leathery wings, slimy tentacles, and some kind of scratchy insectoid limbs he couldn't even begin to identify. Quickly, the whole team headed toward their locker rooms under the stands, all with broad grins.

They set Martin on the table, and every expression showed joy no words could express. Yet the sweetest thing of all was Veils, stepping forward and smiling at him.

"I was wrong about you, Martin," Veils said. "I'm sorry – you were great!"

"Thanks," Martin replied.

"We owe you everything," Bastile said. "Before we send you home, is there anything we can do for you?"

"Well ...," Martin said, "you don't have any magic that could ... dry my shoes and clothes, do you ...?"

Chapter 9

Smashday / Tuesday

Learning strategy helps ...

Martin awoke early ... smiling. He'd won – *they'd won!* The Wet-Feather War was finished, and they were entering the third round undefeated. He guessed many details they hadn't told him, how each team was kicked out of the playoffs after their second loss, and possibly two teams were already gone, including Grand Wizard Beluga La Grossie's team, the Cruel Creepers, from Camelsnot, who were certainly out of the game. And ... Beluga La Grossie had won last year, so he'd won and carried the staff of Master Grand Wizard Borgias Killoff all year, which he'd have to hand off to the winner of this year's Grotesquerie Games. With that ultimate prize, Bastile could raise the sunken island of Shantdareya out of the sea and restore their homeland.

But, to do that, they had to keep winning.

Martin was first to the breakfast table, which surprised his mother, who'd slept in past her alarm. She asked Vicky to pour cereal for her bothers, then grabbed her computer and hurried out the door. She and Martin's father left at the same time. The TV came on moments after the door closed; Martin's brothers, Tom, Terry, and Ron, were already starting their daily video battle, this time working as a team ... invading a dungeon of zombies, ghosts, and demons.

"So, what's up for today?" Vicky asked Martin. "More exercising?"

"Got to stay in shape," Martin shrugged.

"I will find out what you're up to," Vicky said.

"Game on," Martin smiled at her.

At midnight, Martin fell into Happy's arms.

"Welcome back," Happy said.

"Yes, welcome indeed," Rude said.

"How did it go after I left?" Martin asked, and Happy scowled and looked angry.

"Grand Wizard Peevish Lore, ruler of Barsdoom, lost to Grand Wizard Veinlet Prize, ruler of Lilliesput," Rude said. "That puts the Killer Hooves, the centaur team, out of the finals, and moves Veinlet Prize's Grave Gutters undefeated to Round 3."

"Grand Wizard Crass Gopherly, of DeSpire, badly beat Grand Wizard Maim La Nuormal, Queen of

Wanderlost," Happy said. "So the Greasy Golems and the Wild Wraiths both enter Round 3, each with one loss."

"We face the Greasy Golems next week, and they're a tough team," Rude said. "There's no water in this game, so your winning strategy from last night's game won't work."

"What are we playing this week?" Martin asked.

"Tilted-Tramp Race," Happy scowled again.

"Happy, they need you on the pitch," Rude said. "Send Veils in, would you?"

"Sure," Happy snarled, and he walked away grumbling, toward the stairs. Martin and Rude watched him depart in silence ... except for each *clack!* of his hooves upon the stone floor.

"What's his problem?" Martin asked.

"Centaurs are proud," Rude said. "Justly so, in many ways. They've never before been out of the playoffs before Round 3, so they're deeply ashamed. However, I'm glad we have a moment alone ... I wanted to tell you how impressed I was with your victory."

"Our victory ...," Martin said.

"We all won the game," Rude said. "Your victory was devising the strategy that let us succeed. Many monsters didn't think humans could endure our games, let alone triumph. That's the victory you won.

"In practice, you trust your strengths, and work to lessen your weaknesses," Rude said. "In play, you drive your strengths, and defend your weaknesses. You utilized a great strategy. Everyone was impressed ... even Evilla."

"What is Evilla?" Martin asked. "She looks human ..."

"No one knows," Rude said. "Evilla came from the Forests of Ambler, and as far as we know, she's the only resident to ever leave it."

"What's Ambler like?" Martin asked.

"Only Evilla knows," Rude said. "Many have entered the Forests of Ambler, hoping to discover its secrets, but none have ever returned."

"What about the grand wizards?" Martin asked. "Where did they come from?"

"Again, no one knows," Rude said. "Heterodox wasn't always peaceful; monsters once fought and killed each other just to survive, battling to the death over our few feeding grounds, preying upon each other to eat. The wizards ended that; they came out of nowhere, and with their magic staves, they provided food for everyone. Once everyone was fed, our need to kill each other vanished, and so Heterodox was civilized almost overnight. However, some wizards argued and magically contested against each other. Many monsters died in their duels, and so the most powerful wizard, Borgias Killoff, devised the Grotesquerie Games, to keep their arguments from becoming lethal."

"Borgias Killoff ... he owned the staff that the winner gets," Martin said. "What happened to him?"

"You have a gift for spotting what one knows," Rude

said. "He had a fight with Maim La Nuormal, some people said ... and he handed over his staff ... walked off into the crowd, and vanished forever."

"This is a strange land," Martin said.

"Monsters are naturally curious," Rude said. "Many have investigated these mysteries ... none have lived to solve them."

"Perhaps they need a better strategy," Martin said.

Rude smiled, and then Veils arrived.

"You're supposed to go work with Snitch," Veils said to Rude. "He's still tilting the tramps."

Rude sighed and shook his head. "I'd better get out there."

"We can go, too," Veils said to Martin. "I'm supposed to teach you how to play Tilted-Tramp Race ... so you don't commit any more fouls. That'll be easier if you can see the new pitch."

The three of them left the meeting room and approached the lake ... only there wasn't a lake anymore. Martin stared; where the log spider web had been, now stood a huge structure, a framework of two levels. The brightly-lit lower level had a polished wooden floor, and consisted of a circle the same size that the lake had been, with posts along the outside holding up the next level, and had many small poles hanging down from the ceiling.

The second level was the strangest Martin had ever seen. It had no roof, and the only floor between the lower and upper level were dozens of round, transparent trampolines, all linked together, with gaps between them. The outer ring of trampolines was all tilted inwards, and most of the others were horizontal, but as Martin watched, Brain grabbed a hanging pole on the lower level and moved it, and the trampoline above him tilted.

Even crazier, Murder and Stabbing were bouncing on the second level, arcing up from one trampoline to bounce upon another, and then flying toward a third. As Stabbing came down onto the trampoline Brain had tilted, he bounced off at a sharp angle, in a totally different direction.

"Tilted-Tramp Race," Veils said. "They're not dressed, but you get the general idea."

"Dressed ...?" Martin asked.

"They wear Ram-armor," Veils said. "See those nine flagpoles ... with the purple flags? Smalls grab flags of their color, bounce to the center post, and drop them into the basket. It's not hard ... once you get the hang of it, and learn not to bounce into flagpoles ..."

"Sound like fun," Martin said.

"Not really," Veils said. "Now, it's a foul to punch, grab, hold, or pull an opposing player. You can't kick them, shoulder them, or head-butt ... unless you want to get zapped by the referees. You can ram into opponents using your chest or back Ram-armor ... and they can bounce into you. It's possible to collide very painfully, if you're off-balance. The worst is missing a trampoline ... if you fall between them, you land on the hard lower level, where the Bigs play."

"Play ...?" Martin asked.

"They wear Ram-armor, too, much thicker, but they aren't limited by the same rules," Veils said. "If Brain, Crusto, or Happy get to you first, they'll throw you back up, so you return to the second level."

"What about Snitch?" Martin asked.

"Snitch isn't too particular ... and he's usually hungry," Veils said. "Asking him to recognize teammates in the midst of a fast game is kinda ... asking too much. In this game, we tell Snitch to eat the Smalls, and the other Smalls run away, terrified of him."

"Has he ever actually eaten a Small?" Martin asked.

"Not that we know of, but he's bitten a few really deeply," Veils said. "He got zapped for it, of course, but pain doesn't teach Snitch. If you end up falling between the tramps, just run to Brain, Crusto, or Happy." Veils lowered her voice and glanced around to make sure no one else was listening. "If Snitch comes near, roll on the ground rather than run away; we told him that only bad-tasting food rolls."

Martin didn't know whether to laugh or be worried.

"The rules are simple," Veils said. "You line up outside the pitch, and when the game begins, each Big throws a Small up onto the second level. The Smalls jump from tramp to tramp. Your goal is to snatch purple flags from the flagpoles and put them in the basket, which is atop the post in the center. When a team gets ten flags in the basket, a bell automatically rings, and the zombie head appears at a random spot around the outside. The team that rang the bell has one minute to get the zombie head and put it in the basket. You can never pass the zombie head; the Small who gets to it has to score within a minute ... or throw the zombie head away."

"Or what ...?" Martin asked.

"Zap-city," Veils said. "If you get the zombie head into the basket within one minute, then our team earns one point, and all flag-counts revert to zero. If you get rid of it in time, by throwing it down to the lower level or outside the pitch, then gameplay continues uninterrupted. If you're still holding the zombie head after one minute ... or take it from someone else ... well, the referees are not your friends."

"How do you know if it's been a minute ...?" Martin asked.

"Oh, the zombie head will tell you," Veils said. "He doesn't like getting zapped, either."

"So, that's it?" Martin asked. "The team that baskets the zombie head the most wins?"

"Yes, but it's harder than it looks, and more painful," Veils said. "Six Smalls all bouncing toward the same basket; there's a lot of collisions."

"What do the Bigs do?" Martin asked.

"The Bigs control the pitch," Veils said. "They grapple, push, pull, and run into each other, and try to knock each other down. When they can, they look up; that's why the tramps are transparent. When they see a teammate bounce above them, they can tilt the trampoline to help them bounce better, and when they see an opponent, they tilt the tramp backwards, to send the opponent off in the wrong direction."

"Can they grab, pull, or punch ... a Small?" Martin asked.

"No, but they can trample or fall on a Small ... and you don't want to get crushed," Veils said. "Accidents happen ... and in Tilted-Tramp Race, accidents happen with amazing frequency."

"Can I try bouncing?" Martin asked.

"Not tonight," Veils said. "One bad bounce and you could hurt yourself. Bastile wants you to watch and ask questions; tomorrow you start bounce-training."

"There're no weapons in Tilted-Tramp Race, are there?" Martin asked.

"Yes; in Tilted-Tramp Race, the Smalls are the weapons," Veils grinned. "But don't worry; you're also the targets."

Martin watched Murder and Stabbing bounce, and he didn't feel comforted.

Chapter 10

Stompday / Wednesday

Understandings come hard ...

Martin's mom awoke early, and served hot oatmeal with butter and brown sugar for breakfast. Martin was delighted - oatmeal was much healthier than cereal - and he was still eating when she and his dad left. Vicky ate with her nose stuck in her newest book, and Martin slipped quietly outside and began practicing, jumping all over everything in the backyard. He even pulled the trashcans into the middle, and practiced jumping over them.

Brain caught Martin when he arrived, and they walked out to the pitch together.

"No, Snitch!" Rude was shouting. "Leave the poles

alone! Focus on Crusto and Happy. See how they're wearing burgundy jerseys? That color is burgundy. Attack only the burgundy jerseys ...!"

Veils, Murder, and Stabbing were bouncing on the tramps, and wearing the strangest outfits. As they approached, Grand Wizard Bastile stood there watching, another strange outfit hanging from atop his tall wizard's staff.

"Martin, welcome back," Grand Wizard Bastile said, and he leaned his staff toward him. Brain lifted the bulky purple outfit off the staff and held it out; it looked like a stiff, thick, padded poncho, with a smooth, hard outer shell, a hole for Martin's head, and long strings to tie around the front and back halves.

"It's Ram-armor," Grand Wizard Bastile said. "Put it on; you'll need it for practice."

Martin stuck his head through the hole, and tied the back strings around his chest while Bastile tied the front strings behind his back. The armor was heavy, and Martin felt like a fat turtle.

"Your fellow Smalls will teach you all you need to know," Bastile said. "Brain, give him a lift ... gently."

Brain uttered a soft growl, but grinned, lifted, and carried Martin to the pitch, under the transparent trampolines, which looked like a stretchy, rubbery, clear plastic. Brain lifted him up and set him on one. Martin sank into it, feeling its surface flex under his weight like any normal trampoline.

"Martin ...!" Veils called, and she bounced toward

him.

"Martin the Magnificent, beloved by Evilla," Stabbing chuckled, and he also bounced toward him.

"Don't tease him," Murder said, and she joined them on the same tramp, which made it crowded. Each tramp was about eight feet in diameter, a padded, nearly one-foot rim around an almost seven-foot translucent, elastic skin.

"He's only got hours to master bouncing," Veils said.

"Ever bounce on a trampoline before?" Stabbing asked.

"A few times ...," Martin said, although it was only twice.

"I'll start him, and the rest of you, stay out of his way," Murder said.

"He's got to know how to hit ... and be hit!" Stabbing said.

"Later," Murder said. "Let's get him bouncing first."

Veils and Stabbing took a break, and Murder took Martin by his wrists, making him bounce in tandem.

"The trick is to target every landing," Murder said, her thick forest green hair flopping every time she landed and bounced again. "Aim for the centers, for now; you need to avoid the gaps."

Murder let go, bounced high, and landed dead center on the trampoline behind her. Then she bounced back toward him, landing with such perfect timing she didn't upset Martin, and she grabbed his wrists again.

"Now, hold tight," Murder said. "We're going to

jump together ... exactly as I did."

They jumped together, and repeated the exercise three times before Murder proclaimed that Martin should jump solo. She told him to follow her, and set off on an easy route around the pitch. Martin matched her jumps, although nervously glancing at the deadly gaps that could drop him into the lower level, which had a wooden floor that looked uncomfortably hard. His Ram-armor made him heavier, so he had to kick his legs harder than he would've without the extra weight.

Then Murder showed Martin how she bounced against the outer ring, where the trampolines were all set at a 45 degree angle. She bounced low, catching it at a steep angle, so the tramp bounced her right back. Martin tried it, and found it was more fun than bouncing only on flat trampolines. Murder had him try this several times.

"You need to master this," Murder said. "In play, few of these tramps will remain level for long, and that opens bigger gaps to fall through."

Murder called down to Happy, who was on the lower level, and he tilted a tramp so it faced the outer ring, and Martin found it much harder, bouncing back and forth, tilted-tramp to tilted-tramp. Bouncing low flung you faster, and Martin had to push off more carefully or he'd end up bouncing off the edge, rather than from the center of the tramp. Once he got used to it, Murder bounced between him and his target landing spots, risking collisions each time. Yet Murder was an expert;

she could fly past Martin by inches and never touch him.

After a few more exercises, doing both long jumps and short bounces, Murder had him stop and rest.

"This is ... fun ... but harder ... than it looks," Martin said, pausing for gasps.

"Yes, but you'll get used to bouncing," Murder said. "The danger is in the haphazard chaos of the game, when we're all playing together. You never know when you'll be hit, or from what angle. Good players will try to knock you into falling between the gaps ... and sometimes outside the outer ring – that gets dangerous."

"What can I do?" Martin asked.

"Focus on bouncing cleanly," Murder said. "Your strategy should be to stay away from opposing players, and that means always stay aware of where they are. They may try to target you, as they know you're new, so it doesn't hurt to stay near Stabbing or I."

"Are you asking me not to play?" Martin asked.

"No, I want you to focus on flag-gathering," Murder said, pointing up at the flagpoles. "We always need that. But ... what do you need?"

"Me ...?" Martin asked.

"Yes," Murder stared at him intently. "I know why we're doing this ... we grew up with the Grotesquerie Games. Every monster child dreams of playing in the finals. I know why Brain and Stabbing are here. Why are you here?"

"Why ... I just ...," Martin stammered a reply. "Well, how many chances like this does someone get ...?"

"I was afraid you'd say that," Murder said.

"Afraid ...?" Martin asked.

"It shows a lack of commitment," Murder said. "I'm a dryad; do you know what dryads are?"

Martin shook his head.

"Dryads are tree-spirits," Murder said. "Most trees live longer than humans ... and far longer than most monsters ... so we tend to think deeply."

"Humans think deeply," Martin said.

"Humans can think deeply, but seldom do," Murder said. "Strategically, as Rude would say, ability only blooms with constant practice. Humans seldom think deeply about eating their meals, tying their shoes, or getting ...!"

"I tie my shoes!" Martin argued.

"Long ago you learned how to tie your shoes, and have you thought deeply about them since then?" Murder asked. "Professional athletes think very deeply about tying their shoes. Barefoot, feet are most comfortable and have the best circulation, but if you have to walk far, or over rough terrain, then shoes protect your feet from getting sore. Loose, floppy shoes may work while indoors, and still be comfortable, but you couldn't run in them. Snug shoes work fine for running straight, but don't give the best traction for turns. Tight shoes give the best traction, but constrict circulation. Too tight shoes can help you twist and turn quickly, but choke your circulation, and can permanently damage your feet. Professional athletes are studious about foot-care; they need the highest performance, but can't risk damaging their feet."

Martin listened carefully; he understood all of this ... mostly ... even if he'd never once talked about it.

"Right now, playing our games may be fun ... because it's new, but novelty wears off," Murder said. "Choosing to be an athlete is a life-long dedication, not to be taken lightly. It always seems fun ... at first ... but even for those with natural talent, our skills are hard-won. Many monsters spend years, their whole lives, fighting for every improvement, drilling, training, and practicing until total exhaustion claims them ... and then they do it again. They ignore pain. They push their bodies to the limits of endurance, no matter the effort required.

"Playing against the Barkrover Bullies, you impressed me, but you also got zapped, and I know what that feels like. You will feel that again; accidents happen, and even the best make mistakes, and sometimes referees make bad judgements or zap the wrong player ... lightning bolts are hard to control. I need to know ... today ... what your long-term goal is. Competition will get tougher the farther we go. Are you going to quit when you get hurt ... or it's no longer fun?"

Martin looked up into her dark eyes, so deep that their turquoise looked almost black. Murder was very pretty, and sturdy, built like an oak tree ... when not wearing her Ram-armor; obviously she was an adult, even though she was barely three inches taller than he.

"I want to be an athlete, but my mom won't let me

play in ... the human-world," Martin said. "I'm determined ... and willing to do whatever it takes."

Murder smiled sweetly.

"Being an athlete gives you a steady purpose in life," Murder said. "Nothing contributes so much to tranquilize the mind as a steady purpose. If you have any questions, feel free to ask me. You've a lot to learn, and very little time ..."

"What can I do right now ...?" Martin asked.

"Train ... and practice thinking deeply," Murder said.

Murder stood up and pulled Martin to his feet, then pointed up at a flagpole.

"See that purple flag?" Murder asked. "If I asked you to get it, would you jump straight toward it?"

"Sure," Martin said.

"Wrong answer," Murder said. "If you jump straight at a flagpole, you'll smack into it, and slide down to the Big's level. You need to pick a target trampoline on the far side of it, and jump for that tramp ... in an arc that lets you pass by the flag close enough to reach it. Not every flag can be grabbed from every tramp; sometimes the angles don't align. Let's play 'follow my tail' again; match my jumps, but don't grab the flags ... you might fall. For now, just try to touch them as you pass by."

Murder led the way, starting slowly, bouncing from tramp to tramp, and then she kicked off hard, flew high, and brushed her hand against the flag on a flagpole. Martin managed to equal her jump, but after touching the flag, he fumbled his landing and bounced off at an angle, and had to bounce twice more before he got behind her again.

Murder pushed hard, leading a difficult course, and Martin struggled to follow her. Yet soon she had him pull off the flags, which were held on only by gentle spring-loaded clips, and Martin quickly got the hang of snatching flags.

Then Stabbing and Veils returned, walking outside the pitch.

"It's time," Stabbing said. "He needs to know ... the real game ...!"

Murder nodded, and Stabbing called to Brain, who tossed him and Veils up to the tramps. They each bounced apart several times, and then they bounced right toward each other ... and collided in mid-jump.

Martin winced, both from the loud *clack!* and the jolt of their impact; every hair covering Stabbing flew forward, and Veil's long, dark hair, slender arms, and legs flailed like she'd just been punched by Snitch. Yet both bounced backwards and landed with practiced ease.

"Stiffen your neck so you don't bang foreheads," Murder said, and she nudged him. "Veils, go light on Martin."

Worries filled Martin as he bounced; Veils was younger, smaller, and a girl. He didn't want to hurt her. Yet, as he bounced toward her, he saw her fly at him, a mischievous grin on her lips and a wicked gleam in her eye.

Clack!

Martin flew backwards, and landed on his back, off-center, whacking his arm on the padded rim, which wasn't nearly as padded as he'd have liked. He bounced off at an odd angle, and landed feet-first on another padded rim, waving his arm to keep from falling to the level below. Then Stabbing's furry, clawed hand seized his arm, and pulled him safely back onto the tramp.

"Better get used to it," Stabbing said. "Day after tomorrow we face the Greasy Golems, and they won't hit so nicely."

Chapter 11

S[illegible]y / Thursday

Ram-armored bouncing ...

"What happened to your arm ...?" Martin's mother exclaimed.

"What happened to your arm ...?" Martin's mother exclaimed.

"Wha ...?" Martin glanced at his arm, which had a wide bruise reaching above and below his elbow, light brown, with a wide outline of dirty yellow. "Oh, I ... bumped something."

"Bumped ...?" his mother's voice rose.

"Show me," his father said, and he turned it to see the underside, where the bruise was darkest. "How did you do this?"

"Playing ... on the swing-set," Martin said.

"You got this swinging ...?" His father frowned.

"Exercising ...," Martin said.

"Why ...?" his father asked. "Your mother said no sports ..."

"I ... don't want to be little," Martin answered.

Martin's parents exchanged a knowing glance, and Martin wondered what conversations about him they'd had in private.

"If you're hurting yourself that much, then you need to take it easier," his father said.

Martin nodded but said nothing.

After his parents left, Vicky found Martin still sitting at the table.

"Not exercising today ...?" Vicky asked, and she set her book on the table to pour some orange juice.

Martin glanced at the book's cover; a picture of a starship passing a planet like Saturn, only with a wide, maroon ring, and what looked like a black hole in the background.

"Do I bug you about reading?" Martin asked.

"I'm not bugging you," Vicky said. "I should exercise more ... and you should read more."

"I'm thinking," Martin said.

"Impressive," Vicky said. "Thinking is always best."

Dressed in his purple Ram-armor, Martin walked beside Happy out to the pitch, and to Martin's surprise, he saw Aunt Honey Peeking in green Ram-armor, bouncing on the Small's level with the dark elf who'd fouled him, Slid Egg, his hair still frizzled and sticking out, and the other Smalls of the Barkrover Bullies. In the distance, he saw the backs of several ogres and the armored cyclops, Jackknife Illson, walking away. Beside them walked an old man wearing a green wizard's hat and carrying a tall staff: Grand Wizard Lion Changeling.

"Teams have scheduled practice sessions," Happy said. "Their turn is just ending."

Aunt Honey Peekings spied Martin, paused to glare at him, and then gestured to the far stands, and her fellow Smalls departed. Aunt Honey Peekings bounced to the nearest flagpole, and slid down it to the lower level. With obvious contempt, she stood awaiting their approach.

"Good evening, Aunt Honey Peekings," Happy said.

"Good evening, Happy Lostcraft," Aunt Honey Peekings said. "Congratulations, human ..."

"His name is Martin," Happy said.

"Yes; Martin the Magnificent," Aunt Honey Peekings said. "We out-played you. If not for your ... strategy, we'd have beaten you."

"Yes, 'mam," Martin said, unsure what else to say, and not wanting to anger her.

"We have a bye in the next round," Aunt Honey Peekings said. "If you lose to the Greasy Golems, then we'll face you again in the quarter-finals."

"We'll be ready, if that should happen," Happy said firmly.

Aunt Honey Peekings gave both of them a

contemptuous glare, and then turned and walked back toward her stands.

"Not just sour grapes," Rude said, hobbling on only one crutch, out from a shadow as Aunt Honey Peekings stepped too far away to hear. "Apparently Aunt Honey Peekings knows strategy, too. Martin, what strategy was she employing?"

Martin shrugged.

"Intimidation," Rude said. "Instilling fear in your enemies makes them either reckless or inhibited ... either of which gains an advantage. Do you know how to fight intimidation?"

Martin shook his head.

"When someone reminds you of your weaknesses, also remember your strengths," Rude said. "When you fear your enemy's strengths, also remember their weaknesses. Know your enemy ... and know yourself; in a thousand games, you will always win."

"Good advice, but Martin needs practice," Happy said.

"Let him bounce alone," Rude said. "Murder and the others will be right back. Snitch spied a bunch of drunken gremlins ... and thought that they were snacks."

"Want a lift?" Happy asked.

"In a minute," Martin said. "What's a bye?"

"An odd number of wizards made it into the playoffs," Happy said. "When it's uneven, teams pair off, and the odd team gets automatically promoted to the next round."

"The Greasy Golems got a bye in the first round, and then lost in Round 2," Rude said. "Now they face us, and if they lose again, then they're out, so we must play hard; they'll be holding nothing back, and we must equal their determination."

Alone, Martin bounced freely, and focused on snatching flags, which he quickly mastered. After he'd snatched all the purple flags, he went after the burgundy flags, and soon he had all of them, too. Then he decided to try putting the flags in the basket, so he took a purple flag and bounced toward the basket.

As Martin neared the basket, he reached to drop one flag ... and startled; laying inside the basket was the zombie head!

Surprised by the zombie head, Martin fumbled his landing, and had to bounce twice more to regain his balance. He stared at the basket, then bounced past it again. After several more passes, Martin plucked the head from the basket as he flew by it, and carried the zombie head down to a tramp.

"Oh, thank you!" the zombie head said. "The Wild Wraiths were practicing before the Barkrover Bullies, and they left me ... I thought I'd be stuck up there all night."

Martin just stared at the head; it was pale, and sickly green, with long stitches closing rips in its skin, and it had mismatched, blood-shot eyes and thick, greasy hair.

"Hey, you're that human," the zombie head laughed. "You scored me in Round 1. Man, I laughed about that."

"Why ...?" Martin asked.

"Just the look on your face," the zombie head chuckled. "Never seen a zombie before, eh?"

"No, I hadn't," Martin admitted. "How do you ..., I mean, where's ...?"

"Where's my body ...?" the zombie head grinned. "Probably in a hole somewhere, rotting without me. If I knew where ..., well, there's not much that I could do about it."

"How do you live without a body?" Martin asked.

"Live ...?" the zombie head exclaimed. "Ha! I've been dead for almost a century!"

"How did you end up being a ball?" Martin asked.

"I certainly didn't ask for this job," the zombie head said. "Somehow I got decapitated ... by a mummy with a sword ... and he tossed me to a bunch of child mummies to play with ... and I ended up here."

"Does it hurt ... to be a ball ...?" Martin asked.

"Only when I get zapped," the zombie head said. "Hey, that's a very thoughtful question! You're a nice guy ... for a human!"

Martin shrugged.

"Don't dismiss being nice," the zombie head said. "Some monsters can't feel anything but their own wants and needs. They can't look at things through the eyes of others, or imagine how others feel. Being nice is an amazing skill, and it has equally amazing rewards."

"Like what ...?" Martin asked.

"The nicer you are, the sooner you'll find out," the zombie head said. "I have a comfortable little cabinet under the stands, in the referee's office; could you put me there ... after your practice?"

"Sure, if I can," Martin replied.

"Until then, you can leave me anywhere," the zombie head said. "Just ... please, don't leave me face-down."

"Okay," Martin said. "I need to keep practicing, anyway."

Martin set the head on a tramp near the tilted outer ring, facing inwards, so that the head could watch. Then he returned to practicing, and managed to drop all of the flags, one at a time, into the basket, with little difficulty.

Dragging Snitch, which took all of their strengths combined, Martin's teammates returned. Snitch looked very unhappy, but Grand Wizard Bastile waved his staff and created a small pen filled with live turkeys, and Snitch tossed the big, squawking birds into his mouth like candy.

Brain tossed Veils, Murder, and Stabbing up to join Martin, and he welcomed them.

Stabbing smiled, and rapped the hard outer shell of his Ram-armor with his thick, stubby claws.

"Ready, Martin ...?" he grinned.

"We've got a big game tomorrow," Martin said. "You need to make me ready for it ... if you can."

Stabbing leapt strongly, bounced twice, and then bounced right over Martin's head, onto the tramp behind him, and his next bounce slammed into Martin from behind. Martin flew forward, but Murder and Veils caught him before he slammed forward onto the barely-padded rims.

"Tormenting isn't training!" Murder scolded Stabbing.

"Compared to what the Greasy Golems will do, that's nothing," Stabbing said.

"Leave him ... to me!" Martin said, and he pushed to his feet ... and started bouncing.

For several minutes, Martin chased Stabbing, bouncing all around the upper pitch. Stabbing led a merry chase, using the slanted outer tramps to test Martin's skill, and purposefully bounced off-center on the tramps, so his leaps bounded him away at strange angles. Finally Stabbing managed to leave Martin behind, bounced four tramps away, and then turned back to face him. Martin and Stabbing bounced straight at each other, determination steeling each face. They met in midair ...

Clack!

Martin and Stabbing both fell back, slightly apart, and landed just inside the rims of two adjoining tramps. Their on-center striking angles had made them bounce far apart.

"Yaaaa-hoo!" the zombie head cheered.

"Excellent!" Murder shouted. "Now come here ... let's talk."

Both Martin and Stabbing checked their bounces ... and approached, slowing to land without bouncing again.

"That was a good hit," Veils said. "Clean, hard, and no fouls, ..."

"Yes, but notice where you landed," Murder said to Martin. "You hit right over a tramp's edge, and you struck head-on, at the tops of your bounces, so you both bounced backwards about five feet ... and landed safely. Other Smalls will try to hit you off-center above their tramp, and not from the same circle of tramps, to try and drop you between the rims to the Bigs. Striking another player off-center means you bounce apart in different directions, and colliding when you're not at equal points in your bounce can send you off in almost any angle, and worse; it could tilt you, so you land on your face ... or your back ... or your head."

"Understood," Martin said.

"Understanding isn't enough," Murder said to Martin. "You need experience, so get bouncing; all three of us are going to aim for you."

After two more hours of bouncing, Martin called for a halt. He was gasping, drenched in sweat, he had a headache, was exhausted, and even the thought of another *clack!* hitting him from an unexpected direction sent shivers up his spine.

"I ... need ... rest ...," Martin gasped.

"And water," Murder said, and as she raised her hand, a flash of light erupted, and a full glass of water appeared in her hand, and she handed it to him. Martin looked down as he drank; through the transparent tramp, he saw Grand Wizard Bastile, who was still wiggling his fingers and shaking his staff, which had created his glass of water. Grand Wizard Bastile was standing beside Happy, Brain, Crusto, and Snitch.

"Drink slowly," Veils said. "We have one more lesson we have to show you."

"I can't ... do much ... more," Martin said.

"We can't let you go until you know this," Murder said.

"It's easy," Veils said. "No hitting. Just follow me."

Martin drank all he could, then forced himself to bounce. As Veils jumped away, he followed. They bounced three tramps away, and then three tramps back. Martin had almost landed on the last tramp when he saw, through the transparent tramp, Brain below him, his ogre-hand on the short pole. At the last second, Brain moved the pole ... and the trampoline Martin was about to land on tilted from horizontal to a 45 degree angle.

Martin cried out, hit the tramp, and sprang away wildly, completely out of control. Martin bounced hard over several tramp-tarps and their rims, and ended up hanging in the undersection, his fingers above him dug into the thin padding of a rim.

"Welcome downstairs," Happy grinned at him. "It gets even worse down here."

Chapter 12

Rompday / Friday

The Tilted-Tramp Race ...

Rain poured; no playing outside today.

"Don't worry," Vicky told Martin after their parents had left for work. "Your body needs to recover sometimes. Do some stretching, but let your body heal today."

Martin and his brothers killed a thousand zombies that day, and Martin hoped the zombie head in Heterodox never found out about it.

Martin fell into Snitch's hands ready to play. The whole team was there.

"Now, listen," Grand Wizard Bastile said. "I have some bad news: Maxivoom Snydho was supposed to be injured and out for the season, but they're letting him come back."

All the monsters groaned, and Martin glanced between them.

"Who ...?" Martin began.

"Maxivoom Snydho is terrible!" Rude said. "He's a were-boar, a human-boar, and he's a legendary bouncer."

"It doesn't matter," Veils said. "We have to win."

"How is Martin supposed to survive against Maxivoom Snydho...?" Happy demanded. "He's committed the most fouls of any player since Liverea Squiggly, who killed fourteen Smalls and one Big."

Martin's eyes blazed at this revelation.

"Martin, this comes down to you," Bastile said. "The Greasy Golems have been plagued with injuries; they were down to two Smalls, both novices, third-stringers; that's why they brought Maxivoom Snydho back. He's the biggest Small in the league, thick and strong, and an expert bouncer."

"I'm not afraid," Martin said.

"It's not about fear," Murder said. "If we lose you, we lose the finals. You need to stay away from Maxivoom Snydho ... he could do worse than hurt you."

"I understand," Martin said.

"We'd better go," Stabbing said, holding out to Martin a purple suit of Ram-armor. "We don't want the late-penalty."

They trudged out together, toward the pitch.

Monsters cheered as they appeared, and Brain and Snitch led the way, knocking aside any monsters blocking their path. Martin noticed that more fans were wearing purple now, and waving purple flags and pennants. Yet he was facing a player who could vastly out-skill him; *how could strategy defeat a better opponent?*

"And here they come, the Shantdareya Skull-crackers!" Evilla's voice blasted over the crowd. "Fresh after their stunning come-from-behind win last week, with two amazing players: Allfed Snitchlock, the strongest troll in the league, and Martin the Magnificent, whose strategic brilliance led to the downfall of Aunt Honey Peekings and the Barkrover Bullies. But the fantastic swimming speed of Crusto Fernwalker can't help today. Will Martin the Magnificent be able to repeat his victorious insights today ... against the Greasy Golems?"

The crowd roared loudly, an inarticulate drone that made speech impossible.

"And here comes the Greasy Golems, and look who's leading them!" Evilla shouted. "You heard it here first: Maxivoom Snydho is coming off injured reserves and back into play! Today, Maxivoom Snydho returns to defend his fellow players in their last chance after losing to Wild Wraiths in a dramatic upset in Round 2. Yes, the player that Monster Today nicknamed 'the dirtiest player to never bathe' is back to entertain us with more injuries ... and maybe a death! Will we be that lucky?

We'll see: Round 3 of the Grotesquerie Games, the Shantdareya Skull-crackers against the DeSpire Greasy Golems, is about to begin! Place your bets now! Grand Wizard Bastile Wraithbone, against the legendary Grand Wizard Crass Gopherly, meeting today in a war neither can afford to lose!"

Across the pitch, a small crowd of players came out of the far bleachers wearing burgundy. They had no ogres, but four trolls, and one Big that looked like a statue, made of stone; he barely came up to the troll's shoulders, but monsters jumped to get out of his way.

"What's that?" Martin shouted to Murder, pointing.

"That's Ton Eat-oddly, a golem," Murder shouted. "Golems are statues brought to life, and they're slow, but very tough."

As they neared the pitch, Martin saw their Smalls. Maxivoom Snydho stood foremost, a short, squat man with the head of a pig, but with thick, sharp tusks curving up from his sneering mouth. Just over the collar of his burgundy Ram-armor, he wore a steel chain hanging numerous brass coins. Behind him stood a female ratling and a male goblin, both of whom looked rather small and thin, and who looked strange for their absence of jewelry. Behind them were three other Smalls, one on crutches, one in a wheelchair, and the third with both arms in casts. Martin paled; *if he got really hurt, how could he explain it to his parents?*

"Take your positions!" Evilla shouted, and Happy picked up Martin, Brain picked up Murder, and Snitch, under Rude's direction, picked up Stabbing, and then the horn sounded. "Let the mayhem begin!"

Happy gently tossed Martin upward, onto the Small's level. Martin landed bouncing, Murder on one side, Stabbing on the other. The female ratling and the male goblin landed opposite them. Maxivoom Snydho was thrown high, and flew longer, and bounced with incredible force. Maxivoom bounced halfway across the pitch, slammed into a tilted tramp on the outer ring, and fired himself at Stabbing.

"Maxivoom Snydho starts the show!" Evilla shouted as the crowd burst into cheers. "Stabbing Kingz dodges, bouncing high ... and Maxivoom Snydho challenges the human!"

The boar-faced beast in burgundy sailed at Martin with amazing speed, and Martin jumped to the side, bouncing lightly. Maxivoom Snydho shot past him, his coin-necklace jingling loudly, and he bounced off a tramp, headed back to the outer ring. Murder cut him off, bouncing straight at him, a grazing shot, a mild *clack!* that only slowed him down.

"Get the flags!" Murder shouted at Martin.

Martin glanced over, saw the female ratling and the male goblin going after burgundy flags, and Stabbing chasing the goblin, a purple flag in his hand. Martin bounced hard, gained speed and height, and jumped for the nearest purple flag, got it, and went for another. Soon he had three, and he turned and bounced for the basket.

Clack!

Murder blocked Maxivoom Snydho right behind him, bounced off badly, and had to bounce twice more to regain her balance. Maxivoom Snydho was blocked, but only barely; he was at least twenty pounds heavier than Murder, who was heavier than Martin. Maxivoom Snydho was deflected, but passed by Martin close enough that Martin flinched away from him, and Martin's next bounce flew past the basket. Martin shoved his three purple flags into the basket ... they landed atop several burgundy flags.

The female ratling flew at him; Martin steeled himself ... *clack!* They struck in midair, and she bounced back toward the tramp, and Martin was falling beside the basket-pole ... right toward a gap between the tramps. Martin kicked the pole, propelled himself away, and landed on all fours on the innermost ring of tramps. Yet, as he landed, through the transparent tarps, he saw the chaos below; Snitch was on his back, Brain and Crusto ramming a troll in burgundy, hammering it from both sides, with the stone golem charging both of them.

"Murder Shelling dodges Maxivoom Snydho, and Stabbing stuffs the basket," Evilla shouted. "The bell rings; that's ten! Where's the zombie head ... there it is! Stabbing is heading for it! All of the Greasy Golems are aiming toward him!"

Martin looked up, too late to join in. Murder was bouncing high, and she slammed into the goblin at an angle, and ricocheted off him into the female ratling, blocking both, but Stabbing had to jump to the side to avoid Maxivoom Snydho. The half-boar flew fast, bounced hard, and Stabbing darted around him. Murder bounced straight at Maxivoom Snydho, and managed to barely *clack!* off him, only slightly deflecting either's trajectory. However, as Martin bounced toward Stabbing, he saw the goblin and ratling aiming at him, cutting him off from reaching the basket. Martin leaned in, bounced hard, and flew forward. The goblin and ratling were both poised to block Stabbing, but Martin bounced right at them ... and suddenly they bounced apart, and Martin flew right between them. Yet he'd opened a hole; Stabbing followed Martin, bouncing for the basket, holding the zombie head high ...!

Clack!

Maxivoom Snydho slammed into Stabbing so hard both tumbled off-balance, out of control. Both managed to land on a tramp, but the zombie head tumbled down through a gap to the Big's level.

"The Skull-crackers fail to score!" Evilla shouted over the screaming crowd. "Ton Eat-oddly is dominating below, where the fighting is fierce; Allfed Snitchlock is down again, and the Greasy Golems are knocking back Brain Stroker!"

The bell rang again, and Martin saw the ratling streak away from the basket; she'd stuffed it, and the burgundy flags totaled ten. The zombie head came floating up on the outside and over the outer ring.

Martin was closest, he bounced toward it, ready to

block, as all the Smalls converged. He saw Stabbing and Murder, and the goblin and ratling ... but where was Maxivoom ...?

"Martin ...!" Stabbing shouted.

... Jingle ...

Clack!

Martin flew toward the edge, unbalanced and flailing, and struck the outer tramp. He bounded backwards, twisting to try and see where he was headed, and saw Maxivoom Snydho headed for the zombie head. Martin flung himself head-over-heels, targeted his landing, and braced himself for the impact ...

A shadow moved beneath the tramp ... and the tramp tilted away from him! Martin scrambled to avoid the hard rim, caught the thin padding with his right sneaker ... and tumbled over it. He fell onto the tramp beyond it, bounced to the rim ... and almost off. Martin grabbed the padded rim to keep from falling over ... and clung for his life. He looked up; Murder had dodged the burgundy ratling and bounced to block Maxivoom Snydho, while Stabbing blocked the goblin so hard that he slammed into a flagpole and slid down to the Big's level.

Clack!

Maxivoom Snydho and Murder met again, and both bounced in opposite directions, but landed off-center and leaning, and both bounced straight for the basket. Stabbing flew past it seconds too early; Murder and Maxivoom *clacked!* again, and the zombie head flew up as they hit and bounced apart, and when it fell, the head dropped right into the basket.

"Maxivoom Snydho scores!" Evilla shouted. "One point to the Greasy Golems!"

The crowd went wild. Cheers escalated; Evilla was shouting but her words were lost. Martin frowned, then climbed to his feet and jumped to start bouncing.

Beneath his feet, the tramp he was on suddenly tilted, and Martin fell. He landed hard on the wooden floor below, but staggered to his feet. The pitch underneath was bigger than he'd expected, as big as a basketball court, only round. He saw a troll pick up the fallen goblin and toss it back upstairs. Then he saw a giant stone statue running toward him, and he jumped up and ran.

"Help!" Martin shouted, and suddenly Happy came galloping around and past the stone golem. Martin held out his hands; Happy snatched him up and galloped away. Martin caught one glimpse of the golem's angry expression, and saw the word "LOVE" written on its forehead. He paused to wonder what it meant, and then Happy tossed him up between the tramps, and he was back among the Smalls.

"Get flags!" Murder shouted at him.

Martin started bouncing, then collected two more flags, and got both in the basket, before he got hit again. The goblin smacked him head-on, but he'd seen it coming and gave as good as he got. Murder was keeping Maxivoom busy, and Martin noticed a dark green bruise on her cheek. Stabbing had a fistful of flags and bounced toward the basket. The other ratling was chasing him with a fistful of burgundy flags, but Stabbing slammed into the center-pole, dropped his purple flags into the basket, and bounced backwards, slamming with his back-plate into the oncoming female ratling. She fell backwards, head over heels, and many burgundy flags dropped from her fingers and fluttered down in all directions.

"No!" the goblin shouted, and he went bouncing after her.

Martin took advantage of the situation, and bounced past flagpoles, grabbing four more purple flags. Determined, he turned, and unopposed he bounced for the basket. He stuffed his flags in and heard the bell ring.

The other Smalls were on the far side, and the zombie head again appeared near him. Martin bounced toward it, grabbed it, and headed back for the basket.

Every Small was bouncing toward him. Maxivoom Snydho purposefully aimed at him, poised to block him hard, but then the tramp he was going to bounce on tilted, and Maxivoom shot off in the wrong direction, shouting a curse. Martin spied Brain's ogre hand on the pole beneath the tilted tramp and smiled. Martin jumped toward the basket ... bounced past Murder, who was shielding him, and he slammed the zombie head into the basket.

"Martin the Magnificent scores!" Evilla screamed, and

cheers roared across the land.

Martin almost fell on his landing; the tramp he'd hoped to land upon was already tilted, and as Martin bounced to another, he noticed how many tramps were tilted – almost half. The pitch up here kept changing, and the longer this lasted, the more bizarre this level would become. Targeting a landing spot became harder ... and riskier.

Gameplay became harder, too. Angry, Maxivoom Snydho bounced hard, and his greater bulk struck brutally. Martin almost got knocked over the outer ring, then had to fall flat to avoid a collision he was sure would've killed him. Maxivoom Snydho was targeting him, but Murder stayed close on his tail, leaving the were-boar little opportunity.

Yet Martin couldn't keep pace with the burgundy goblin and ratling. Stabbing was better than either, but he couldn't match both, and several times Martin almost fell just bouncing around the pitch. Suddenly the tilted tramp before him flattened out; he saw Happy gallop underneath, and one after another tramp before him turned horizontal. Martin bounced better on flat tramps, and started gathering flags; every time a flag of one color was pulled free, the rope on that flagpole lowered, and then rose back up with a flag of a different color. Martin plucked three purple flags, then heard the bell ring. The zombie head rose on the far side of the pitch, and the Smalls converged, including Martin, but once again Maxivoom Snydho grabbed the head and scored.

"Maxivoom Snydho does it again!" Evilla shouted. "The Greasy Golems are back in the lead!"

The game got harder as the players got winded, and exhaustion came quickly. This was a fast game, with no hope of rest, and all breaths became gasps. Still they played, but they couldn't gain an advantage. Martin ended up on the Big's level twice more, and several times Maxivoom Snydho plowed him down, usually hitting him from behind.

Both sides scored several more times, and the female ratling was charging him down when the horn blew. She reached out and caught his shoulders rather than slam into him. They dropped to a tramp together and bounced to a stop.

"What ...?" Martin gasped.

"Half ... time," she gasped, pressing a hand against her burgundy Ram-armor. Up close, she was as rat-like as Stabbing, but she wasn't ugly, as he'd expected. When Martin looked confused, she pointed at his teammates, who were gathering on the far side of the pitch. Struggling to catch her breath, she started walking across the tramps in the other direction.

Martin headed as she'd directed, walking rather than bouncing, and having to veer around the tilted tramps. Stabbing and Murder were headed in the same direction, and he followed.

Brain lifted them down, one at a time, using only his left hand; he was holding his right arm at a weird angle, as if it pained him. Glasses and buckets of water were passed around, and they all gulped greedily.

Martin couldn't believe how beaten the Bigs looked. Snitch looked like he was ready to fall down, and Happy wasn't limping, but he was favoring three of his legs. Brain looked hurt, and Crusto was helping, holding a thick, wet bandage against his bleeding ogre-knee. Murder and Stabbing were obviously bruised and exhausted, and Martin felt little better; bruised, scraped, and with one finger bleeding badly. How they were going to survive another half Martin had no idea.

Chapter 13

Rompday / Friday

Give to your foe write ...

"This is a tough match," Grand Wizard Bastile said. "We're barely holding up. Happy, you shouldn't have tried to hurt that horrible golem ... he's too tough. Snitch and Brain hurt both of their trolls from the first half, but their reserve trolls will be playing in the second half, and they're fresh. Their goblin Small was also injured, and they don't have a Small reserve, so he may have to play in the second half, even if he's hurt."

"We can't hurt Ton," Happy grumbled.

"Golem can't be hurt," Brain snarled.

"Rock hurt," Snitch growled.

"If we can't get Snydho down to you, we're not going to last up top ...," Murder sighed.

"Even if we could knock out the others, he's killing us," Stabbing agreed.

"Don't lose heart," Rude said. "Martin, how do you feel?"

Martin looked up at Rude ... and winced; the movement of lifting his head hurt.

"There has to be a way," Crusto said. "I could relieve one of you ..."

"You're a speed-Big, not a power Big," Rude said. "That's not a plan."

"Martin, you figured out our strategy last week," Grand Wizard Bastile said. "Any ideas ...?"

Martin shook his head.

"We need to try ... something new," Martin wheezed. "What we're doing ... is not working ... so we need to ... do something different."

"Halftime is only 20 minutes," Rude said. "Martin, if ever we needed a plan ...!"

Martin focused, but it seemed impossible. They had to try something ... unexpected, something everyone knew could never work ...

"Does Maxivoom have any weaknesses?" Martin asked.

"We wish ...!" Murder said.

"What about Ton?" Martin asked.

"Rocks don't have weaknesses," Happy said.

"Why does he have 'LOVE' written on him?" Martin asked.

"That's the word that brought him to life," Grand

Wizard Bastile said. "Making a golem is tricky magic. Once done, only that emotion, written in blood across his forehead, makes him live."

"Can we scrub it off?" Martin asked.

"No, the blood soaks into the stone ... and becomes permanent," Bastile said.

The others sighed and shook their heads. Martin kept thinking, but nothing came to mind. Then his eyes widened.

"Yes ...?" Rude asked.

"Logically, we can't win," Martin said. "Like in chess, when you're over-powered: checkmate, you lose."

"That's reassuring ...," Stabbing sneered.

"We need to do something ... crazy," Martin said. "We need to ... change the dynamics of the game ..."

"How ...?" Crusto asked. "If there's anything we can do ...?"

"I need to do it," Martin said ... and he glanced at Murder. "You need to leave ... Maxivoom ... to me."

"He'll kill you!" Murder snapped.

"No, he won't," Martin said. "I'll ... chase him. Look, we need to score points. You and Stabbing can jump rings around the other Smalls; Maxivoom is our only threat. I'm the worst at scoring, so let me run interference ..."

"We can afford one defeat," Grand Wizard Bastile said. "We can't afford to lose you."

"You won't," Martin said. "Maxivoom can't focus on me while both of you are scoring."

"That's crazy!" Happy said.

"I know ... but ...," Martin left his sentence unfinished.

"But crazy is all we have," Rude finished for him.

"What about downstairs?" Brain asked.

"I don't know," Martin said. "I'll try to think of something ... but how do you stop a rock ...?"

The crowd was still cheering, less than before, and Evilla's commentary was running non-stop.

"The Neverlive Nasties' victory keeps them in the finals, and the Grave Gutters now have one loss," Evilla said. "We're all looking forward to the next match, pitting the undefeated Wild Wraiths against the Rowdy Reavers, who have one loss. Lucky you; I'll be there, your sexy madam of the microphone, bringing you every thrill! But first, we're all looking forward to the end of this game, and we're about to start the second half ...!"

"Better get ready," Rude said. "We can't miss the horn ..."

The team rose, dispirited, and took their places.

"... about to begin!" Evilla babbled. "Hold on for an exciting ... me ... and an almost as exciting second half! I'm being told the players are ready ... are you? Very well! Let the mayhem begin again!"

The horn blew. As before, each Small was tossed up to their level by a Big. Martin bounced hard, then straight at his enemy. He heard, this time more aware, the initial *crash!* of the Bigs colliding below, before he made his fourth bounce.

"Ton Eat-oddly takes the lead below!" Evilla shouted. "Above, Maxivoom Snydho is foremost, headed toward Murder Shelling! But wait ...! Martin the Magnificent is bouncing forward!"

Maxivoom turned his focus to Martin, but then Martin bounced away from him at the last second, and dodged a possibly deadly head-on collision.

Martin turned at once, bouncing hard, and chased after Maxivoom Snydho. The were-boar seemed surprised, and bounced away from him, then reversed and charged ... but again, Martin dodged him.

"Martin and Maxivoom ... dancing around, but no real hits!" Evilla shouted. "What are they up to? Greasy Golems lead 6 to 5! The Skull-crackers can't afford to play nice!"

Apparently Martin had angered Maxivoom Snydho, for he snorted and cursed in some grunting pig-language. Their next pass was too close to dodge ... *clack!* Martin managed to deflect it slightly, but the impact still shook him to his teeth, and both bounced awkwardly, landing with their momentum spent, only one empty tramp between them.

"I'm gonna kill you, human!" Maxivoom Snydho shouted over the roar of the crowd.

"Bacon is my breakfast!" Martin shouted back.

Martin bounced away; *angering a were-boar was probably a bad idea!* Yet he had to keep him distracted ...!

Just then, the bell rang.

"Zombie head to the Shantdareya Skull-crackers!" Evilla shouted.

Maxivoom Snydho paused his chase, and Martin looked back at him; he could almost see realization dawn on the tusked boar-face. Snarls rose, and the glare he shot at Martin carried deadly threats, but then the zombie head rose up close to him.

Martin reversed his course; Maxivoom Snydho couldn't touch the zombie head, but he could prevent the others from scoring. Martin charged the were-boar, but he seemed to have realized Martin's tactic, and bounced straight toward Stabbing, while both his companions were blocking Murder.

They only had one minute. Martin bounced to the zombie head and grabbed it; *now he alone could score!* Maxivoom Snydho slammed into Stabbing, colliding hard, and both looked staggered.

"Martin, score ...!" he heard Veils shout from just outside the pitch.

Martin bounced for the basket, but Maxivoom Snydho cut him off. He dodged, veering sharply, and all the Smalls converged on him. Murder blocked Maxivoom, but the goblin and the female ratling both slammed into him ... and Martin dropped the zombie head.

"Get it!" Stabbing shouted to Martin, bouncing back into the fray, going after the other ratling.

Martin dropped down; the zombie head had fallen onto a tramp, and bounced almost to the padded rim, but as he approached it, the goblin bounced center on that tramp, and the greasy head bounced to an adjacent tramp. Martin raced to pick it up ... *but how much time had elapsed?*

Martin snatched up the head, and jumped to start bouncing, but all the Smalls were bouncing toward him.

"Run across the rims!" the zombie head shouted.

Martin obeyed, balancing between the rims and the drop to the lower level, and dodged aside as all five of the other players group-collided behind him. Stabbing and the goblin both fell below, but Maxivoom Snydho bounced after him.

"10 ... 9 ... 8 ... Listen to me!" the zombie head shouted. "No time! Give me to Maxivoom!"

"What ...?" Martin shouted.

"Now!!!"

As Maxivoom Snydho bounced straight at him, Martin tossed the zombie head straight at his hated enemy. As Martin had first done when Rude had shoved the zombie head into his hands in his bedroom, the hands of Maxivoom instinctively closed upon the greasy hair.

"Zero ...!" the zombie head grinned.

Crackling energies flew from the referees, two bolts of lightning searing across the pitch, powerful enough to stun even the strongest Big. Holding the zombie head, Maxivoom Snydho took both blasts as thunderclaps deafened all ears.

"Maxivoom Snydho is down!" Evilla shouted. "The

'Boar that Gives More' has been zapped, and he falls ... right through a gap! Maxivoom Snydho is unconscious on the floor of the lower level!"

Martin saw the zombie head fall onto an adjacent tramp ... and jumped toward it. Yet he didn't touch it, *he didn't want to get zapped.*

"Are you all right ...?" Martin asked, his voice full of concern.

The head looked partially cooked, its greasy hairs still steaming, and it smelled even worse.

"Yea ...," it muttered weakly, "and ... thanks for ... putting me away ... last night."

"Anytime ...!" Martin smiled.

The next few minutes seemed a paradise. Martin and Stabbing kept the goblin and ratling busy, while Murder stuffed flags and scored twice more.

"Murder scores again!" Evilla shouted. "The Skull-crackers now lead 7 to 6! And look: Maxivoom is safe! The Greasy Golem Bigs drug him out! Yet he doesn't look good ... he came off of injured reserves early, his health was questionable. It looks like he's out for the rest of the season."

Martin grinned but the female ratling sneered.

"You've put us out," she snarled, "but you can't play another round either ... with only one Big ...!"

Martin paused, bounced away from her, and glanced down. Snitch and Brain were struggling to hold down the golem, while Happy was galloping around, leveling all the tilted tramps. However, they all looked terrible, as if they'd been beaten to a pulp. The two trolls had carried Maxivoom Snydho off the pitch, and swapped places; their replacements, the trolls from the first round were running back onto the pitch, in burgundy Ram-armor, fresh and ready to fight again.

Martin didn't hesitate; he jumped into a gap and caught the edge of the rim, then dropped himself to the wooden floor.

"Martin ...!" Happy shouted, galloping up. "What ...?"

"Distract them!" Martin shouted, pointing at the burgundy trolls.

Quickly Martin ran to Snitch and Brain, while Happy galloped away. Martin ran up behind Brain, who was kneeling to hold the golem down, and bounced off the back of his calf ... up onto the golem's chest.

"Martin ...?" Brain gasped.

"Hold him!" Martin shouted, and he climbed up the statue's stone body to kneel by his stone chin.

"What you doing ...?" Brain asked.

"Remember what Bastile said?" Martin replied. "*Only that emotion, written in blood across his forehead, makes him live.*"

"But ... can't scrub it off!" Brain argued.

"I'm not going to scrub it," Martin grinned. "I'm going to add to it!"

Martin's finger was bleeding, and he bent down and drew the letter 'G' onto the golem's forehead ... right in front of the word 'LOVE'.

The golem opened its mouth and gnashed its stone teeth at Martin ... and then, with a loud grinding sound, it stopped moving, its whole body solidifying. Brain and Snitch looked equally confused; the golem's body had turned rigid, like any other statue.

"GLOVE," Martin said. "Written in blood; that's not an emotion ... and it can't give life!"

"Small good ...!" Snitch grinned wickedly.

"Can you two handle those trolls?" Martin asked, pointing at the trolls chasing Happy.

"Yes," Brain said, and he looked at Snitch. "Let's help Happy."

"Wait!" Martin said. "Toss me back up!"

Brain grabbed Martin and started to throw him.

"Wait ...!" Martin said. "Over there ... ready ... now!"

Both Smalls of the Greasy Golems were closing on Stabbing. Thrown by Brain, Martin came hurling up, between the tramps, and slammed into the goblin.

Clack!

Martin and the goblin collided so hard both were rattled. Martin fell backwards, bouncing upon his back, and the goblin flew over the tilted outer tramps and outside the pitch.

"No!" screamed the female ratling.

Bouncing, she watched her last Small teammate leave the game; he flew into the cheering crowd and landed atop an abominable snowman; the crowd loved it. Below, she heard her troll Bigs cry out. In frustration, the female ratling stopped bouncing and crossed her arms, standing perfectly still.

The remainder of the game was a rout. Murder, Stabbing, and Martin scored at will, laughing all the while. The attractive ratling didn't bother to stop them; she just stood and watched, unwilling to subject herself to fighting against odds she couldn't defeat. Finally, the warning horn blew, and Martin took the zombie head and leisurely headed toward the basket.

"Thanks again!" Martin said to the head in his hands.

"My pleasure!" the zombie head grinned.

Martin bounced high and gently set the head in the basket, scoring the final goal.

As the three horn-blasts blared, the crowd was cheering, laughing, and celebrating.

Snitch stood on the edge of the pitch, and lifted the purple Smalls down. The fanatic joviality of the crowd didn't infect the players; all were bruised and sore. Yet Snitch petted Martin, knocking him off his feet; Crusto stopped Snitch before he accidentally killed Martin.

"That was brilliant!" Grand Wizard Bastile shouted excitedly, walking up beside Rude and Veils.

"Indeed," Rude said. "Two successful strategies!"

Veils seemed to be unable to speak, and lacking words, she leaned forward and kissed Martin on the cheek; he startled, not knowing what to say.

"We have to visit Evilla," Crusto said.

"I ... I don't want to talk to her," Martin said.

"Rude, you're our best speaker," Bastile said. "You talk to her."

Rude nodded, and they slowly pushed through the crowd. Hands reached out to pat their shoulders, but the players were so covered with bruises they couldn't enjoy it. Finally they squeezed through. Before them stood Evilla, now with flaming orange hair and a sun-yellow dress, seemingly sewed on, as tight as ever.

"Martin ...!" Evilla cried, but Rude stepped forward.

"I've been asked to speak ...," Rude said.

"Your fans want to hear from ...!" Evilla began.

"The Skull-crackers are weary from the game," Rude said. "If you don't wish to speak ...!"

"Very well, Rude Stealing," Evilla said. "Tell us what happened!"

She shoved her microphone toward Rude, but he merely grinned.

"Submitted for your approval ...," Rude said into her microphone with infinite calmness. "The Shantdareya Skull-crackers entered these playoffs with the odds-makers against us, and after Round 3, we stand undefeated, with the Wild Wraiths the only other undefeated team. Our turn of fortunes coincide with the joining of our newest member, who has turned out to be a blessed gift. Martin Mulberry, whom you have named Martin the Magnificent, has shown us all that humans can play, and with each game he gets better."

Evilla drew back her microphone.

"We all laughed when Martin handed the zombie head to Maxivoom Snydho, making him foul," Evilla said. "What happened to Ton Eat-oddly?"

"Gee ... I must confess that ... Ton had a bad spelling issue, which led to his ... statuesque ending," Rude said. "He'll be out for a ... spell, assuming that Grand Wizard Crass Gopherly can restore him ... for next season."

"Yes, the DeSpire Greasy Golems have two losses now and are out of the playoffs," Evilla said. "Grand Wizard Crass Gopherly won't be happy about that! Is Grand Wizard Bastile Wraithbone worried about possible retribution ...?"

Evilla shoved her microphone at Grand Wizard Bastile. Rude reached for it but Grand Wizard Bastile waved him away.

"I would not disgrace the Council of Grand Wizards with unfounded accusations," Grand Wizard Bastile said, deepening his voice and staring coldly into Evilla's scarlet-painted eyes. "Grand wizards are justly proud, and we're too dangerously powerful to be goaded into pointless rivalries by a sports reporter ... appointed to her position by the Council of Grand Wizards."

"Thank you, most honorable and respected Grand Wizard Bastile Wraithbone!" Evilla answered quickly, worry crossing her features. "Congratulations also ... and best wishes ... to the Shantdareya Skull-crackers ... for this dramatic victory in Round 3 of the three hundred and fourteenth Grotesquerie Games playoffs! Now, let's see if we can get a word from tonight's most-unhappy player, Maxivoom Snydho, assuming he's regained consciousness ...!"

Chapter 14

Smashday / Saturday

In a fine restaurant ...

Martin awoke to the sounds of his brothers arguing ... and felt like he'd been punched by Snitch. He hurt everywhere, and even moving his arm to push back his blankets stabbed.

His clock read 9:14 AM; it had to be Saturday. Martin crawled out of bed, saw bruises covering most of his skin, and put on a long-sleeved shirt and jeans to hide the colorful, swollen lumps from his parents.

Martin shook his head, and then regretted doing so; his head felt like he was in a long tunnel filled with echoes. Staying up all night wasn't working; he wasn't getting enough sleep. Bodies need sleep to recover, and he had to recover more.

Staggering into the kitchen, Martin found three different cereal boxes on the table, which meant his brothers were awake, and the soft sounds of gunfire from the TV speakers told him they were attempting, however poorly, not to awaken their parents.

Martin sat and poured his bowl full of dry cereal. He needed to walk to the refrigerator to get milk, decided he was too tired, and dropped his head onto his elbow, trying to fall back asleep.

"Martin ...?" Vicky asked.

Startled, Martin tried to sit up ... without getting dizzy.

"What happened to you this time?" Vicky demanded. "Didn't sleep ...?"

"Ummmm .... bad dreams," Martin lied.

"Well, finish eating," Vicky said. "Mom's getting dressed; you're going with her."

"Me ...?" Martin asked.

"I babysit all week ...!" Vicky said.

"I don't need a ...!" Martin began.

"Actually, I don't think you do, not any more ...," Vicky agreed, looking at him, "but your brothers do."

Martin frowned; *he couldn't disagree with that.*

"Vicky ... could I ... borrow a book?" Martin asked.

Vicky paused, looking surprised.

"Why ...?" Vicky asked.

"Well, ... never mind," Martin said.

"No ... I mean, yes. Wait here."

Vicky went back into her room, and then returned with a worn paperback.

"I wouldn't lend this to you if I thought I'd get it back torn or with the page corners folded down ...," Vicky warned.

"I'll be nice to it," Martin promised, taking the book from her hand.

Vicky stared at him, and then went back into her room. Martin put his head back down on the table and tried to sleep.

When he heard his parents approaching the kitchen, Martin opened the book to the first page and pretended to be reading.

"We need groceries ...," his mother began, and then she stopped and looked at him. "Is that one of your sister's books?"

"She lent it to me," Martin said.

"Well, you can bring it with us," she said.

"Can't I stay here?" Martin asked. "I really want to read this book ...!"

"Bring it with us," she repeated. "We leave in ten minutes."

His father went out to the garage to get the lawn mower; their grass was growing like weeds. Martin reluctantly followed his mother out to the car, but he brought Vicky's book. He only glanced at its cover: a pretty girl with pointed ears was shooting a laser pistol – exactly the kind of story Vicky would like.

The pharmacy, the dry cleaners, gas for the car, and finally, the grocery store; Martin wasted half of the day running errands with his mother. After carrying all their bags into the kitchen, Martin insisted on going to his room to read. His mother made him wait, and quickly made lunch for the whole family except Vicky, who was spending the day with her friends. When Martin finally got to his bedroom, he set the book on his nightstand, beside his clock, fell onto his bed, and passed out.

Vicky still hadn't returned by dinnertime, when they woke Martin. He felt refreshed, but not fully, and he gobbled down his meatloaf, silently reliving his victory in the Tilted-Tramp Race while his brothers argued over whose online character had the best virtual gear.

Martin startled awake when he fell ... and Brain caught him. The whole team was gathered around him, but they weren't in their locker room; Martin glanced around at the dark, noisy, crowded, unfamiliar setting, assaulted by a dull roar of strange music and many voices.

"Where are we ...?" Martin asked.

"Manticore Tavern," Happy answered. "Here, have a drink."

Happy handed Martin a wooden mug filled with a frothy, yellow-white liquid. Martin sniffed it, then drank ... it was ice-cold, and tasted like a spicy butterscotch; *delicious!*

They were in a rustic restaurant. Martin looked around and saw most of his teammates seated at a tall table, and an empty chair was saved for him between Murder and Veils. These chairs were also tall, which allowed Snitch, Crusto, and Brain to sit in low chairs big enough for them. Happy stood on the far end, rather than sit; no chairs for a centaur. However, Happy wasn't bare-chested, as Martin usually saw him during practice. Happy was wearing a plaid shirt of bright colors. Brain wore a clean, purple Skull-crackers t-shirt, as Martin had seen some fans wear, and Snitch was wearing a brown leather vest. Murder and Veils were both wearing dresses, and Stabbing looked almost unrecognizable in a fancy dark blue sports coat and a crisp white shirt. Grand Wizard Bastile sat at the head of their table wearing golden robes instead of his customary purple, and he wore a tall gold crown on his head.

"We got the bye ...!" Stabbing practically cheered, and everyone smiled.

"What ...?" Martin asked, feeling confused and very underdressed.

"We're automatically promoted to the semi-finals!" Murder explained. "There are only five teams left, and in the quarter-finals, the Wild Wraiths play the Neverlive Nasties, and the Grave Gutters face the Barkrover Bullies. All of the other teams are out."

"You should've seen the Wild Wraiths take out the Rowdy Reavers!" Veils said. "They were pitiless! Their Bigs broke the pitch, and tramps and Smalls rained on their heads!"

"I'm glad that we didn't have to face the Rowdy Reavers," Bastile said, and he raised his crystal goblet, which was filled with a light green goop that seemed to splash around of its own accord. "They have three sasquatch Bigs, and those beasts have bad tempers. Let's drink; to the defeat of the Rowdy Reavers!"

Everyone raised their tankard, mug, or glass, and drank. Martin noticed that Veils' drink looked just like his, but all of the others' looked different. The pink concoction in Murder's tall glass bubbled and churned, and tiny flashes of light swirled in it.

"What's that ...?" Martin asked her, nodding toward the drink in her hand.

"Angel's Spittle," she chuckled, waving it before him. "The finest ... but you've got a few years before you can try it."

Veils scowled and set down her drink disgustedly. Martin looked at her.

"Oh, pixie-slushes are tasty, but I'd like to try something stronger," Veils said.

"You will ... when you're older," Happy said to her. "Don't feel bad; we've all drunk pixie-slushes."

"More ...!" Snitch rumbled, and Grand Wizard Bastile gestured to a passing waitress, who had green snakes for hair.

"More Amber Dragon-ale for Snitch, please," Grand Wizard Bastile said.

She nodded to him and hurried off.

Martin looked around; Manticore Tavern wasn't exactly elegant, but it looked clean, well-built, and it was packed with monsters. The noisy, boisterous establishment seemed to be built of thick beams of polished wood, stained dark, and lit candles glowed in sconces along the walls, although what looked like electric lamps shined down from the ceiling onto each table.

"What happened to Maxivoom Snydho?" Martin asked.

"Boar will recover," Brain snarled.

"He really shouldn't have been playing." Murder said. "He suffered three cracked ribs near the end of regulation, and healing spells only work so much."

"Ton Eat-oddly is the 'Big' question," Stabbing said, and several groaned at his pun. "That was some idea, changing his life-word. Crass Gopherly's not sure if he can be fixed."

"Grand Wizard Crass Gopherly has filed a complaint with the Council," Grand Wizard Bastile said. "He thinks changing a life-word should be a foul. Yet, Grand Wizards Veinlet Prize and Clod Pains argued that golems are too invulnerable, and that any team would gladly foul them just to have golems removed from the game. No decision will be made this year, but we could have a new ruling by next season."

"Giants could break a golem, so no one used them until giants were banned," Murder explained.

"Humans are also a topic of conversation," Crusto said. "Evilla said that Lion Changeling isn't happy, and Pester Crushings, Peevish Lore, and Maim La Nuormal all think the Grotesquerie Games should be monsters-only."

"Ghost's blood!" Grand Wizard Bastile exclaimed, which sounded like swearing to Martin. "No complaints have been filed. Evilla's just stirring up trouble again."

A loud squeal arose, and from behind Martin came the familiar voice of Evilla.

"Did I hear my name?" Evilla pushed through the crowd and pressed against the back of Veils' chair, and Evilla looked down at her. "Was that you, Veilscreech Hobbleswoon? I hear I'll be doing commentary on your rookie year next season."

"It's Veils!" Veils glared up at Evilla, who was wearing a low-cut dress of pure silver glitter, although she still had flaming orange hair.

"And here's our season's best strategist!" Evilla laughed, and she reached over and tousled Martin's hair. "I really missed not speaking to you after the game; Rude Stealing is far too proper. Speaking of Rude, where's he hiding?"

"Rude is attending a personal engagement ...," Grand Wizard Bastile began.

"With a lady ...?" Evilla interrupted.

"... a personal engagement which is nobody's business but his own," Grand Wizard Bastile completed his sentence, but at which Evilla gave him a sly, penetrating stare. "And now, if you would be so kind, Evilla, I was about to have a private word with my team ..."

"Oh, I'll be quiet as a mouse, as always," Evilla said with a wicked smile. "You know me: Lady Discretion!"

She stood smiling, and showed no desire to depart.

Grand Wizard Bastile was about to object, but Stabbing waved him off.

"Evilla, my lovely, would you honor me with a private walk ... somewhere secluded ...?" Stabbing asked.

"Why, Stabbing Kingz, what are you suggesting ...?" Evilla asked, fanning herself dramatically with a slender hand bearing many gaudy rings.

"Oh, nothing indecent," Stabbing said. "We'll take Snitch along as a chaperone; he's hungry ... and maybe we'll find a bite for him ... somewhere ...!"

At the word *'bite'*, Snitch grinned broadly.

"As flattered as I am, I think I might be needed elsewhere," Evilla said suddenly. "You know me; there's a center of attention somewhere, and I think hear it calling!"

With a bright smile and a wiggling wave at everyone, Evilla vanished back into the crowd.

"Martin, never let Evilla, or people like her, steal your joy for your accomplishments here," Grand Wizard Bastile said. "Never regret anything you've done with sincere affection; nothing is lost that is born of the heart."

"I won't," Martin promised, although he remained torn - he liked Evilla and thought she was funny ... when she wasn't shoving a microphone in his face.

The waitress with green snakes for hair wheeled out a narrow, sturdy cart, on which rested a tankard that looked like a small barrel with a handle. Brain assisted her to swap it for Snitch's huge empty mug, and she coyly drummed her fingers on Brain's broad shoulder and gave him a sweet, flirtatious smile as thanks.

"Dinner will be out shortly," she said to Grand Wizard Bastile. "It took a while to talk your foul-mouthed bass into the oven."

She wheeled her cart back, calling for the crowd to make room for her.

Conversation began again, and broke into small groups, as it was so loud. Those sitting next to each other leaned close to be heard, and Martin found himself quietly left alone. He glanced to one side, hoping to join in the conversation, and noticed the classy, pale green silk dress Murder was wearing, which flashed in the light yet made her dryad skin stand out. It had bare shoulders and showed off her full, adult figure more than Martin had ever noticed before, so he turned back the other way to talk to Veils.

Veils, he noticed, was wearing a sapphire blue dress, and if he hadn't known she was nearly his age, he would've guessed she was much older. She looked surprisingly pretty, and Martin swallowed hard, uncertain what he should say to her.

Food arrived just then, and Martin was spared from any attempts at conversation. The snaky waitress darted around them with casual ease, yet moving amazingly quickly, and soon plates were set before each of them.

"Ahhh, dragon-steaks!" Brain exclaimed.

Martin also got a dragon-steak, while Grand Wizard Bastile got his foul-mouthed bass, and Murder received a plate of steaming vegetables over rice, covered in a rich, red sauce. Snitch got a huge roasted leg of something that looked like lamb, heavily sprinkled with spices, and with a big bone sticking out of it.

"Martin, you must be excited," Crusto said between mouthfuls. "This week you get to watch your first Grotesquerie Game, rather than play in it."

"What are they playing?" Martin asked.

"Net-Door Maze," Crusto said. "I almost wish we didn't have the bye ... I always play in Net-Door Maze."

"What's it like?" Martin asked.

"You'll see," Crusto said. "I don't want to spoil the surprise, but we'll need you at practice tomorrow and Smiteday ... just because we're not playing on Rompday doesn't mean we take every night off."

"Yes, this is our celebration," Grand Wizard Bastile said. "Tomorrow, it's back to work. We've got a lot to do."

"I just want to see the Shantdareya Skull-crackers in the finals," Stabbing said. "If the Wild Wraiths win, then the Neverlive Nasties are out, and if the Grave Gutters win, then the Barkrover Bullies are out."

"I'll be rooting for the Grave Gutters," Crusto said. "Rumor has it that Aunt Honey Peekings is still angry we beat her."

"I just hope the Neverlive Nasties win," Veils said. "Then we'll be entering the semi-finals as the only team with no losses."

"No losses!" Brain grinned, and he raised his glass

and drank.

"Losses are unimportant in the last game ... when only two teams are left," Crusto said. "The winner of the finals wins the season ... and the staff."

"No team has ever won the Grotesquerie Games undefeated," Stabbing reminded everyone.

"Then let's be the first!" Grand Wizard Bastile said, and they all raised their glasses and cheered.

Chapter 15

Stompday / Sunday

Exercise your friendships ...

Sunday breakfast was hot scrambled eggs with bacon, blueberry muffins, and steaming grits with gravy ... all of Martin's favorites, yet he could barely eat a bite. He was still full of dragon-steak, but he couldn't tell them that.

"Are you sick?" his mother asked him.

"No," Martin said. "Just ... not hungry."

After church, Sunday was a lazy day, and Martin relaxed and napped. His brothers made him play video games, but after an hour, Martin grew bored. *How exciting could a virtual game be compared to throwing wet-feather bolas or bouncing across tramps holding a talking zombie head?*

Reality was the difference. Every game, and every

practice, Martin got better – improved himself – in reality. Each day was an accomplishment; he could look back and be proud of what he'd done. The cheers, adulation, and excitement of the crowd were music to his ears, proofs of his accomplishments. Video games were fun, but only momentarily … and were forgotten the next day. Martin liked having fun, and video games helped pass the time, but reality delivered the most fun, and Martin craved all the fun reality held.

Martin fell into Snitch's arms, dressed in his jersey and eager to start practicing.

"Hello, Snitch," Martin said.

Snitch looked surprised to see Martin suddenly appear in his hands, but this time he seemed to recognize him.

"Friend Small …!" Snitch growled.

"That's right," Martin said. "You … you can put me down now."

Snitch looked confused.

"Put him down, Snitch," came Rude's voice. "Put Martin down."

Slowly comprehension dawned, and Snitch lowered his hands, and Martin slid to his feet.

"Thanks!" Martin said to Snitch, and then he looked at Rude. To his surprise, Rude was using a sleek, black cane instead of a crutch.

"Hey, good news!" Martin said.

"Yes, I'm feeling better, but not fully," Rude said.

"Was that why you weren't at Manticore Tavern?" Martin asked.

"No, I had a ... date," Rude tried to grin, obviously shying away from the subject. "I heard that you had a good time."

"It was delicious," Martin said. "Dragon-steaks ... and pixie-slushes!"

"Now you pay for frivolity," Rude said. "Let's get out onto the pitch ... they're waiting for you."

"What about Snitch ...?" Martin asked.

"Oh, Snitch doesn't need exercise," Rude laughed. "Snitch needs educating. We take turns explaining the rules over and over ... eventually he remembers it ... for a few days."

Martin startled as they approached; the pitch was a huge building, and the stands had risen thirty feet taller.

"Net-Door Maze," Rude said. "There's no ceiling, so the stands look right down into it."

"What is it?" Martin asked.

"It's a maze ... except that the walls move," Rude said. "Bigs control the pitch, the Smalls score; it's a thinking game as much as a muscle game."

"What's the best strategy?" Martin asked.

"To get the bye ... so you win without playing," Rude grinned.

"No, really ...," Martin said.

"I'm serious," Rude said. "Every time you play, you risk losing. The goal is to win, which means not losing. Zero risk is the best; either you win a little ... or you win a lot."

"But every game needs playing ...!" Martin argued.

"Yes, but games constantly change ... only winning remains," Rude said. "Everything is a competition, and the victor is usually the one who controls which game you play. In Wet-Feather Wars, the odds on the logs were even, but you focused us on using our best strength, Crusto's swimming speed. You changed the focus of the game to the water, so we won. In Tilted-Tramp Race, we were outmatched, so you focused on removing their strengths, Ton and Maxivoom. You changed the game above and below, and we set a scoring record for that game in any playoff."

"That was the ball," Martin said. "I was nice to the zombie head ... and he told me how to take out Maxivoom ..."

"Friendship is the best strategy," Rude said. "You make friends once, by being nice, and friends always help you."

"Martin ...!" Murder called, waving one hand. "Let's get started ...!"

Practice started out the hard way: pushups. Martin, Murder, and Stabbing dropped at Rude's command, and started working out. Martin managed twenty-seven pushups before he had to stop and catch his breath, but Murder and Stabbing kept going.

"Humans ... can't keep up ... when it ... gets hard," Stabbing gasped between pushups.

"We've been ... training for years," Murder said.

"Martin ... has only had ... weeks."

"Is this gossip time, arguing time, or complaining time?" Rude asked. "You never heard me wasting breath while exercising."

"No ...," Stabbing said. "That's because ... you talk too much ... when you're not ... exercising."

"Martin, ignore Stabbing," Rude said. "Catch your breath and start again. Training your body to a new routine is hard, and conditioning your body to a new sport takes six months, not six days. Athletes who push too hard hurt themselves."

"But you ... don't want to ... baby yourself ... either," Murder gasped between pushups.

"Double-workout ...!" Rude ordered. "While doing pushups, exercise the muscles that hold your mouths closed!"

After pushups came deep drinks of water, then long-distance runs around the pitch. As they passed each end of the new building, through the wide doors on each side, Martin saw another team practicing inside the building that covered the pitch. One player was a vampire, who didn't look like a Big or a Small, and another who looked like a Frankenstien's monster, as big as Crusto, but stitched and bolted together. Both were pushing against a wall, and the wall was slowly sliding backwards. Yet Martin, Murder, and Stabbing ran by too fast to see more. No one was visible inside the door on the other side, and when they circled the building, the vampire and Frankenstien's monster were gone, but an iron door that hadn't been visible before stood wide open.

Martin was better at running than pushups, but he was gasping before Murder or Stabbing started breathing hard. Again, Martin had to quit early, and Rude brought him more water while he rested.

After several other common exercises, Brain appeared carrying all sorts of weapons, including wet-feather bolas, javelins, nets made of thick cord, five-foot staves, and sticks with padded balls on each end.

"These weapons are commonly used," Rude said. "We should practice with all of them, so Martin gets used to them."

Stabbing and Murder demonstrated the weapons, and Martin watched in awe. Both could hurl a javelin 160 feet, with good accuracy, which Rude said was only half of what Happy could throw. Yet, at only thirty feet, both could hit the exact center of a target, and Martin secretly prayed that no one would be throwing javelins at him. At twenty feet, Martin usually missed the target.

Net fighting proved to be more difficult than Martin expected, and Stabbing excelled at it. Anyone could throw a net at another player, but to fully-entwine them proved difficult. As they had a net, too, they could swing their net to block yours, or dodge your throw, and then entangle you while you were pulling back your net from its failed toss. Stabbing was especially good at stepping on an opponent's net, preventing them from recovering it, and he often released it just when Murder pulled her hardest, making her fall backwards off-balance.

Martin found playing with the nets awkward, and twice managed to entangle himself, which earned titters from Murder and howls of laughter from Stabbing, but Rude only smiled. Murder let him entangle her just so she could show him how to escape, but Martin's fingers got caught in the net every time, and he struggled to extricate himself.

Murder excelled at the staves, which were used just like in every Robin Hood movie, so Martin had seen this kind of fighting before, and thought that he could hold his own. Murder proved him wrong three times, and then walked off twirling her staff. Bruised and embarrassed, he and Stabbing worked at half-speed, under Rude's direction, until Martin felt he had the basics, and then they played for real ... just with lighter blows. Martin even won a few.

As with the rims on the trampolines, the sticks with thick, padded ends weren't as padded as they looked. Murder and Stabbing preferred different styles; Murder held hers with one hand near each pad, and Stabbing held his like a baseball bat. Both styles worked, and each won half of their matches. Martin, of course, lost every match against both of them, and one hit to his stomach dropped him to his knees.

"This is what we talked about," Murder said. "This is where athletes must look inside them for the strength to continue ... even when it gets unpleasant."

Martin gasped, then slowly climbed back to his feet

and lifted his weapon against her.

"Again ...!" Martin snarled.

As they practiced with weapons, Happy charged past them at a full gallop. In his dust, Brain, Snitch, and Crusto came running. All the Bigs glanced at the Smalls, but they didn't wave or smile; even Snitch looked like he was sweating.

A short while later, Veils and Grand Wizard Bastile arrived.

"How'd it go?" Rude asked.

"Veils did very well," Grand Wizard Bastile said, glancing at Veils, who blushed slightly. "She worked the Bigs until they were ready to drop. How's Martin?"

"A novice ... but with real potential," Rude said, glancing at him.

"Well, we need to get him home now," Grand Wizard Bastile said. "We don't want him being missed."

"Drink more water when you get home," Rude instructed.

"I will," Martin promised. "Could you ... check on the zombie head ...?"

"I will," Rude promised.

"Prepare yourself for the trip home," Grand Wizard Bastile said, and he raised his staff ... which began to glow.

Chapter 16

Smiteday / Monday

To learn your history ...

Vicky was fixated on her book and Martin felt too tired to think. He tried exercising in the backyard, but he hadn't had enough sleep, and he didn't want to hurt himself, so he soon quit.

Inside, his brothers called for him to join them, and Martin picked up a controller, sat beside them, and created a wizard character. Clicking, he joined their game, and started throwing level one fireballs at a monster that looked like a fur-covered troll with tusks like Maxivoom Snydho, only larger. He played for almost an hour, and then he asked his brothers the question needling his brain.

"Wouldn't you rather be doing this for real?" Martin

asked. "I mean, where would you rather be; sitting here, playing this game ... or in a real dungeon, fighting real monsters, risking life and limb ...?"

His brothers looked at him like he was crazy.

Monday, or Smiteday, was the same. After two solid hours of exercise, Martin fell exhausted, gasping for breath so hard he couldn't even drink water. They all ceased practicing to make sure Martin was all right, and half-carried him to the front steps of the stands, where they all sat and rested.

"You're doing fine, Martin," Rude said.

"I'm ... curious," Martin finally gasped. "How ... do they choose ... games ...?"

"Choose the games in the playoffs?" Murder asked. "That's easy. You know that there are lots of games to choose from; each member of the Council of Grand Wizards gets to write the name of one game on a scroll, and they throw them all into an urn. One of the Grand Wizards, who doesn't have a team in play, randomly draws a new scroll after the end of each round, and the announcements are made at the closing ceremonies, just before dawn."

"You know, after Round 1, Bastile Wraithbone did a lot of finagling to get the midnight spot for all our games," Stabbing said. "Before so many teams got kicked out, there was an early game at 9:30 PM. Now, the second game starts after the midnight game ends, around 2:30 AM. If you wanted to stay and watch ..."

"He has to be back in bed when his parents awaken," Rude said.

"Ahh, the human world must be terrible!" Stabbing said.

"The human world is no worse than we were before the wizards came," Rude said. "Monsters preyed on each other for food, shelter, and property. We were little more than animals ..."

"Since the pantries, Heterodox changed ... and we did, too," Murder said.

"Pantries ...?" Martin asked.

"The Grand Wizards created pantries, magical sheds filled with food, that never empty," Murder said. "Once we didn't need to kill each other, we became peaceful, and the wizards began teaching us, and we found friendships that never could've existed before."

"We became intellectuals ... jewelers and artists," Rude said.

"And sportsmen ...," Stabbing added.

"Three hundred years of peace," Murder sighed, her voice softening. "I remember the bad years, the killing, the brutality ..."

"I've only studied about those days, but every record is horrific," Rude said. "It's hard to believe different types of monsters hated each other ...!"

"Earth ... the human world ... suffers a lot of that," Martin said. "But we have cars and malls and television ...!"

"What are those ...?" Stabbing asked.

This question was too much to answer fully, but Martin gave it a good try, and explained how advanced science gave humans many benefits. Stabbing didn't believe in computers or microscopes, but Rude seemed fascinated.

"I wish we had those things," Rude said.

"I wouldn't mind, but I wouldn't trade our peace and friendships for technological toys," Murder said.

"You have some ... electric lights and loudspeakers," Martin said.

"The grand wizards gave us those," Rude said.

"Maybe we could go get some more ... quietly?" Stabbing asked.

"I wouldn't say that to Bastile Wraithbone," Rude said. "Monsters aren't allowed to visit the human world. The few that have made it over there were all killed ... or had to flee back here. Then they were imprisoned for defying our laws ... or expelled from civilized lands."

"The Garden of Eden ...," Martin said.

"What's that?" Murder asked.

"It's the oldest story in the human world," Martin said. "The first humans lived in a wondrous garden, but they defied God, who made the single law that they had to live by ... and so they were cast out."

"The laws of the grand wizards exist to protect our lands," Murder said. "If humans ever find a way to cross over, to come to Heterodox, with their advanced weapons, our paradise would fail."

"I'm afraid that's true," Martin said.

"Can't your ... human technology ... produce enough food for everyone?" Stabbing asked.

"It already does," Martin admitted.

Murder, Stabbing, and Rude stared at Martin in disbelief.

"Humans ... choose the violence they suffer ...?" Murder asked.

"Our grand wizards aren't nice people," Martin confessed.

Rude broke the long, uncomfortable silence that followed by suggesting they resume practice.

"Martin, have you ever used a boomerang?" Rude asked.

Until they'd handed him one, Martin had never held a boomerang ... and didn't really believe they'd return until Rude tossed one ... and it came back so gently he caught it.

"Hold the boomerang with its flat bottom against your palm," Rude said. "Place your thumb over the top, and throw smoothly; a good spin is more critical than a forceful throw."

"Angle your throwing arm halfway between horizontal and vertical, but hold the boomerang almost level," Stabbing said. "In a strong wind, raise your throwing arm higher."

"Release the boomerang with the outer edge slightly higher," Murder said. "Aim high, as if at the tops of trees on the horizon. Throw too low and it will end up climbing too high."

"Throw 40 to 60 degrees off the wind," Rude added.

Martin tried ... and it dropped to the ground about sixty feet away.

"Let the boomerang gently fly out of your hand," Murder said. "It will turn itself."

Five boomerangs fell in the distance, but the sixth came back and landed only twenty feet away.

"Very nice!" Murder said.

"Before you try to catch a boomerang in your hand, you need to know how," Rude said. "Stabbing ...?"

Stabbing picked up a boomerang and hurled it like a pro, and only had to step two paces away to catch it.

"Decide carefully before you catch a boomerang," Rude said. "Too fast and it can take off fingers. A well-thrown boomerang hovers softly towards you."

"Throw too hard, it won't return," Stabbing said. "Too soft, it won't make it back."

Martin practiced for quite a while and got used to it. He even caught two of his own throws.

Then Stabbing set out a target, and Murder fetched several bows and quivers of arrows. They strapped a leather guard over the inside of his left arm, and then tested his pull-strength with several bows.

"You want a bow as tight as you can hold drawn for a good minute, but not much more," Rude said. "Stand with your feet shoulder-width apart, ninety degrees from your target."

"Hold the bow so its grip squeezes the meaty part of your hand just below your thumb," Happy said, coming up behind them. "Point your thumb at your target."

"Ah, Happy ...!" Rude said. "Listen to him, Martin; Happy taught us everything we know about archery."

Martin nodded and did as instructed.

"Place the arrow on the arrow rest, and rotate it so the odd fletching is farthest from your bow-arm," Happy said. "Wrap the tips of three fingers around your bowstring, and gently pinch the nock of the arrow. Draw the bowstring back toward the side of your face, your bowstring-hand slightly above the level of your nose. Lift your back elbow to point directly away from your target. Line up the bowstring with the center of the bow, then raise or lower your point to match, and slowly release."

Martin had never shot an arrow before, but by following the instructions, he hit the target on his first try. Happy was a strict instructor, which took all the fun out of learning, but Martin soon put two arrows into the bullseye.

"Thanks," Martin said to Happy.

"What other weapons will Martin need?" Murder asked Happy.

"That's hard to say," Happy said. "All of the grand wizards have specific likes. Veinlet Prize probably picked Wet-Feather War, and Clod Pains undoubtedly picked Tilted-Tramp Race. Either Crass Gopherly or Pester Crushings picked Net-Door Maze, while Peevish Lore likes Cracked Ice-Whip. Lion Changeling chose Trip-Hook Roller last year, so I doubt if he'd do that again ... since he lost. Maim La Nuormal always chooses

Wire Web-Walk. Yet grand wizards who don't have teams can also add a game, and no one knows which, or in which order, the games will be picked."

"We can't train Martin with everything," Murder said.

"You don't need to train him with everything," Happy said. "Learning weapons is secondary. More important is learning the will to fight, to defend, and to survive, which must be instinctive, or it will never succeed. Timing, controlled movement, and constant, undivided awareness of your surroundings improves every fighter, no matter the weapon."

"Very true," Rude said. "It is the warrior, not the weapon, that wins the battle."

"Besides ... he doesn't have to fight tomorrow night," Stabbing said. "This is just general training. We'll have all next week."

"After the drawing, we'll only have three days to train him with a specific weapon," Murder said.

"Martin learns quickly," Rude grinned. "After all ... what other choice does he have?"

Chapter 17

Rompday / Tuesday

To sit and enjoy ...

"Martin won't play with us!" Ron screeched at the top of his lungs.

Half of the family winced from his pitch and volume, and stared at the youngest child. The boys sat at the breakfast table, while Vicky poured juice, and both parents were hurrying to leave for work.

"Martin, play with your brothers today," his father said. "We'll figure this out tonight ... when we're not so rushed."

Martin tried to object but no one listened. His parents picked up their briefcases and hurried out the door. Martin fumed; *his parents had left, and they hadn't even listened to him ...!*

Two hours later, all of Martin's brothers were screaming. Martin was ruthless, snipering from cover, shooting point-blank, and tossing concussion grenades right at their heads. He recovered all the health, and collected all the ammo, or blew up the supplies when he couldn't carry more, and then he ran past them while they were still recovering ... and killed them again.

It was easy; they were younger, and Martin could usually beat them, but now, with his new understandings of tactics, Martin recognized their simple strategies and countered them with ease. He experimented with tactics that had never occurred to him before, and most worked. Virtual weapons weren't as responsive as real weapons, but the concepts were the same. Martin repeatedly murdered his brothers without giving them any chance to recover.

Sadly, Martin didn't enjoy it. If anything, he felt angry. He'd played this game a hundred times and always enjoyed it before, but somehow, being ordered to play, rather than choosing to play, took all the fun away. He wasn't playing to enjoy himself; Martin was playing to insure that his brothers didn't enjoy themselves ... especially Ron.

Screaming overtop all of them, Vicky charged in and threatened to unplug the game, and was assaulted by an endless barrage of shrieking complaints. Three minutes later, with the boys still voicing grievances even though no one was listening, and Vicky grabbed Martin and pulled him out into the back yard.

"Was that really necessary?" Vicky demanded.

"I was just playing ...!" Martin argued.

"No, you were infuriating ... on purpose," Vicky said. "You know your brothers can't keep up with you ... any more than they could do your homework ... just like you couldn't do my calculus!"

Martin glowered but said nothing.

"You're angry with mom and dad and you're taking it out on your brothers," Vicky said. "You want to be treated like an adult ... and you act like a child!"

"That's how the game is played ...!" Martin argued.

"People are judged equal to those they compete against," Vicky said. "You're lowering yourself to their level!"

Astounded, Martin suddenly froze, and stared at Vicky.

"That ... *that's strategy ...!"* Martin exclaimed.

"It's maturity," Vicky said. "If you want to be considered mature, maybe you should think about what maturity means ...!"

Martin screamed in terror as he plummeted ... until Brain caught him. They weren't in the locker room or Manticore Tavern; the whole Shantdareya team sat in the raised stands, in the front row, looking down at the tall, roofless building Martin and the other Smalls had jogged around and around. From this angle, he could see the shapes of the inner walls, the placements of the doors; the whole pitch of the game. Yet his heart was still pounding; rather than fall from the ceiling, Martin had appeared in midair, at least forty feet above the ground, and fallen ten feet before smacking into Brain's huge hands.

The cheers of the crowd seemed louder ... now that he was part of them, and the game hadn't even begun yet. He and his teammates all wore purple, but on one side of them stretched a line of emerald shirts, the Cruel Creepers from Camelsnot, with their emerald-robed Grand Wizard Beluga La Grossie, whose team was out of the tournament. On the other side of them, in turquoise, sat Grand Wizard Pester Crushings, from Narwhaila, with his team, the Rowdy Reavers. Beyond them was a section with no seats, filled by a dozen bare-chested centaurs wearing deep azure bandanas and sashes, and one who wore elaborate robes that even covered his equestrian half, who had to be Grand Wizard Peevish Lore, leader of Barsdoom, and his centaur team, the Killer Hooves. Only one purple shirt stood among them: Happy Lostcraft, and he was in deep conversation with other centaurs.

Brain sat down on a seat so low his knees rose; his seemed to be just a cushion on the floor. He sat Martin down next to him, on a seat equally low, but at the push of a button, Martin's seat rose higher, until their heads were at the same level, and both see down into the pitch.

"Gonna be good game!" Brain said excitedly.

"Veils, explain it to Martin," Rude said, and Martin noticed Veils was seated on the other side of him.

"Look," Veils pointed at the pitch. "See the tops of those walls? They're color coded, so the players on the pitch can't see them, but we can. Over the two main doors, that yellow mark; that's where both teams enter ... and score, if they can get the zombie head out of their opponent's door. The outer walls are black, solid and unmovable, with no doors except the main yellow ones. The purple inner walls can't be moved. The blue inner walls can be moved, but blues can't be pushed past a door. The green walls are the key; green walls can be pushed past a door ... or used to permanently block one; a closed door with a green wall against one side can't be opened."

Martin looked down and saw what looked like a large office building with dozens of rooms, all marked across the top.

"I thought ... Net-Door Maze ... would be a ... maze," Martin said.

"Ah, it will be!" Veils smiled wickedly. "That's the goal! See the colors above the doors? Maroon doors are the worst; every time a player goes through a maroon door, it automatically closes behind them ... and stays closed for ten minutes. See that little room in the corner? It only has one door; a maroon door. If someone runs in there, the door will close behind them, and then they'll be trapped."

"Trapped for how long ...?" Martin asked.

"Ten minutes, but that's a lot of game time," Veils said. "It's possible to get locked in a room for the rest of the half ... if a green wall gets pushed across the only door of a room you're in."

"What are the others doors?" Martin asked.

"Pink doors are just normal; no locks," Veils said. "Red doors look like normal doors; once you open them, you can leave them open, but if you close them, then they lock for ten minutes ... and no one else can get through ..."

"Monsters, welcome!" came a deep, growling voice over the microphone. "The games are about to begin! And here, for your ultimate pleasure, is that Lady of Laughter, that Mistress of Mirth, the sweetest, sexiest Courtesan of Cuteness, that Paramour of Perfection: Evilla ...!"

With a fanfare of trumpets, Evilla jumped up through a trapdoor onto the platform about ten feet away.

"Kisses and kills!" Evilla shouted into her microphone, raising both arms, wiggling, and beaming her brightest smile. "It's game-night, and as you all know, there's nothing I like more than a night that's a little game ...!"

The crowd cheered and laughed, and Evilla posed and waved at them, blowing kisses.

"Tonight ... the excitement rises!" Evilla said. "Thrills are in store ... and that's a store where I like to shop! The Grave Gutters ... in the quarter-finals! Grand Wizard Veinlet Prize, that mysterious loner from Lilliesput, is back today, straight from his loss to the Neverlive Nasties, facing the formidable Barkrover

Bullies, refreshed after last week's bye, and led by the ever-awesome Grand Wizard Lion Changeling, who suffered their loss in Round 2 to the Shantdareya Skull-crackers! Each is playing for their life, and determined to make it to the semi-finals at all costs! One will make it, and one will go home! Which team are you betting on? Let's hear it: cheer for your team!"

Explosions of shouts deafened everyone in the stands, and Evilla jumped up and down, challenging every thread in her dress. She was wearing sea green today ... with hair as pink as bubblegum, with streaks of purple shot through it.

Vendors came by, handing out food from a large box full of treats.

"Basilisk beans!" Veils shouted, and he threw a box at her.

"Chimera Chocolates, Wight Wraps, Griffon Gnocchi, and Unicorn Ugali!" the vendor shouted.

"Got any Wyvern Wings?" Brain asked, raising his voice over the crowd.

"BBQ or Arsenic Spice?" the vendor asked.

"Arsenic!" Brain shouted.

A greasy bag came flying at Brain, who caught it with a wide grin.

"Could I get some ... BBQ?" Martin asked Brain.

"Sure," Brain said. "Hey, need a BBQ over here ...!"

Another bag came sailing, and Brain elbowed it toward Martin. He caught it and glanced inside; it looked like three freshly-cooked chicken wings ... if the chickens were as big as vultures.

"Here come the Barkrover Bullies!" Evilla shouted into her microphone, regaining the attention of the crowd. "Here's Jackknife Illson, who's got the best eye for trouble ... and Aunt Honey Peekings, proof that age doesn't slow the wicked!"

Evilla continued naming the rest of their team, but having played the Barkrover Bullies, Martin was intimately aware of each of them. He glanced back at the cheering monsters in the crowd, wearing t-shirts, headbands, and holding waving pennants of their team's favorite color. They could be fans at any sports stadium, except for the antennas, horns, wings, fangs, claws, tentacles, fur, armor, beaded skin, and scales of both fish and snake.

"And here come the Grave Gutters!" Evilla cried. "Led by the always-impressive Slug Gormet-Wreather, the only sphinx in the league, with everyone's favorite brownie Jangelly Kurtails riding on her back. Behind her comes Slug's fellow Bigs; bigfoot Pansthorny Chopkins and yeti Bruise Clambell. Barbaric Steal is a naiad of eight years, one of the most experienced players still alive, and the legendary Damhell Hairy, the Blistering Banshee, who seems to most enjoy fouling her enemies!"

Martin looked down at the monsters approaching the pitch with tremulous anxiety; their sphinx was bigger than Snitch, and the bigfoot and yeti were thick, hairy, and looked daunting. The brownie and naiad were his size, but the banshee looked ... bloodcurdling. Martin didn't relish meeting them on the pitch. On the other hand, facing the Barkrover Bullies again worried him; he'd made serious enemies there.

Each team approached their yellow doors on opposite sides of the pitch. In the stands, the fans were wildly cheering, howling, roaring, and hissing.

"Now, hold on to your fangs!" Evilla said. "The quarter-final round of the three hundred and fourteenth Grotesquerie Games playoffs are about to begin! Are both teams ready? I'm getting the signal from the referees - the horn is about to be blown! Here we go: let the mayhem begin!"

The crowd exploded, jumping to their feet as both teams ran through the big, yellow doors. The Smalls glanced inside unknown inner doors, then stepped through them, glanced back to see if the door automatically closed, and then drew a small mark on the wall beside the door, and tried another door.

"Each team has a different mark ... to identify what the doors are," Veils shouted to Martin over the roars of the crowd. "They mark each door so they know what it is, and map the closest rooms."

The Bigs each ran to a different wall, pushing hard against it, testing to see if the wall was movable. Most moved, and as they widened the first room, the rooms on the other sides of those walls shrank.

"The Smalls are exploring the doors, the Bigs exploring the walls," Evilla said. "Aunt Honey Peekings has already reached the mid-corridor, and she's going beyond ... Aunt Honey Peekings and Barbaric Steal have seen each other! Nets are swinging ... and they run toward each other! Aunt Honey swings, Barbaric blocks ... look at them flail! Aged goblin against young naiad, both are maneuvering ... Barbaric Steal is stronger and more aggressive ... driving Aunt Honey Peekings backwards. Nets are thrown, no one entangled yet ... both are dodging ... Barbaric forces Honey back past two doors ... Honey throws ... Barbaric is entangled! Honey shoves her through a door to an empty room ... and closes it behind her! Barbaric is trapped! Aunt Honey Peekings runs on ... but she's lost her net!"

Martin watched amazed; Net-Door Maze was a savage, physical game. From above, he could see the explorations, and wondered what it would be like wandering blindly through unknown trap doors. The brownie, Jangelly Kurtails, seemed to be drawing a map on her inside forearm, of each room and door, and then she approached another door, which Martin could see was a maroon door. Sure enough, as she ran through it, it closed, and it caught one corner of her net as is slid shut. There was an open doorway, a pink door, to her right, but the room beyond that was a dead end.

"Jangelly Kurtails is trapped!" Evilla laughed. "Ten minutes penalty for her! But look; Damhell Hairy has seen Slid Egg! She's chasing him, banshee against dark elf ... he throws ... Damhell dodges ... her net traps Slid Egg! Damhell Hairy has Slid Egg trapped ... and she's pulling him back, dragging him across the floor! Slid Egg fights to extract himself, but Damhell snatched up his net, too, and Slid Egg is caught in a second net!"

Brain bellowed, shaking his ogre fists in the air, cheering the battle below. Veils was on her feet, cheering, and Martin jumped up, joining in the excitement. Watching the game was different than being in it ... safer ... and Martin was glad he wasn't playing Net-Door Maze.

"Damhell pulls one net free ... and shoves Slid through a red door!" Evilla shouted. "She closes it; Damhell Hairy traps Slid Egg in a dead-end room, trapped in his own net!"

The remaining Smalls carefully raced through other rooms, but their routes kept them apart.

"Barbaric Steal is free!" Evilla shouted. "Is she exploring ... no, she's heading back! Take a breath, folks; time for comparing notes! But no one has found the zombie head!"

The zeal of the crowd suddenly lessened, and Martin looked puzzled, and he caught Veils' eye.

"After they explore as much as they can, they run back and compare notes," Veils explained. "Now it's time for the Bigs to take over."

Jangelly Kurtails, and then Slid Egg, were finally released, and both headed back to join their team. The Smalls knelt, and their Bigs leaned over them.

"They're drawing maps on the floor," Veils said. "They're making plans, and then the Bigs will follow those plans."

The Bigs control the pitch: never was this truer than in Net-Door Maze. Suddenly, the Bigs ran to walls and began pushing. The crowd cheered, although not as loudly as during the net-fights. The Smalls ranged out again, but not far; they seemed to be doing reconnaissance, watching for enemies. As Martin watched, the movements of the walls seemed random, but slowly he realized it; they were converting the collection of small rooms into a maze of narrow, long corridors.

"See that section?" Veils asked. "The Grave Gutters are setting a trap! They're sealing off those rooms, making those three maroon doors into traps that go nowhere. Look at the Barkrover Bullies! They've arranged a single passage along the far wall; that's the only way to get through! That's dangerous, but it will give them a good first half!"

Slowly the pitch changed, and soon Martin was looking down at a complex maze on both ends, the middle section still mostly small rooms. Martin scanned the mazes on each side; *how would anyone navigate through their enemies' territory to score ...?*

Chapter 18

Rompday / Tuesday

The Net-Door Maze …

"Aunt Honey Peekings found the zombie head!" Evilla cried.

The reaction of the Grave Gutters to this announcement was instantaneous; *no secrets in Net-Door Maze!* Holding the zombie head aloft, displaying it to the crowd, Aunt Honey Peekings ran back to Jackknife Illson, her massive, armored cyclops. The two groups kept rearranging the walls, building their separate mazes … and approaching each other. The crowd shouted encouragements.

Slid Egg spotted Damhell Hairy, and she chased after him, her net swinging. Suddenly Jackknife Illson burst through the door, swinging his bigger net. Smalls carried nets of rope, but Bigs carried nets of hard, heavy chain, and even the roar of the crowd couldn't drown the hammering of his chain net as it slammed into the floor. Damhell Hairy barely dodged it, and then ran back. Jackknife Illson charged after her, and suddenly a green wall slammed into him. Slug Gormet-Wreather, the massive sphinx, pushed the wall from the other side, and trapped him between a green wall and an immovable purple wall. Both Barkrover Bullies' ogres ran to help, but the Grave Gutters' yeti and bigfoot met them swinging nets of chain.

"The battle is met!" Evilla shouted. "Four Bigs chain-dueling, and Jackknife Illson trapped by Slug Gormet-Wreather! The 'Psychotic Cyclops' is no match for the pure lion muscle of the sphinx! He's trapped! But has he enough strength to save himself, or will the 'Jinx Sphinx' crush him to death?"

"They Bigs are engaged!" Veils shouted. "Look! There go the Smalls!"

"Damhell Hairy, Jangelly Kurtails, and Barbaric Steal make their move!" Evilla shouted as the crowd was screaming. "Jumped up onto Slug Gormet-Wreather's back, bounced off the heads of Pansthorny Chopkins and Bruise Clambell, and the Grave Gutter Smalls are in Barkrover territory! All throw nets ... and Damhell Hairy leaped over the nets! She landed on Aunt Honey Peekings! Both have hands on the zombie head, goblin and banshee! The other green Smalls are entangled ... and Barbaric Steal tears the zombie head from Damhell and Honey! She tosses it to Jangelly Kurtails! Jangelly Kurtails is running to score, Barbaric Steal following!"

As one, the crowd leapt to its feet, screaming riotously.

"Bigs distracted, Grave Gutter Smalls run to score! Jangelly Kurtails passes backwards to Barbaric Steal, but keeps the lead! She's running interference, but will that be enough?"

Jangelly Kurtails reached a fork, and stared down both ways, as Barbaric Steal caught up to her. Half of the crowd was directing her one way, and the other half the other way, all trying to influence the game. Jangelly Kurtails tore off to the left, then ran through a door; it automatically slammed shut behind her, and Jangelly Kurtails screamed.

Holding the zombie head, Barbaric Steal heard her screech, and instantly took the right fork.

"Aunt Honey Peekings is chasing Barbaric Steal!" Evilla screamed into her microphone to be heard over the tumult. "Barbaric Steal has the zombie head! Will she find the right path?"

Martin leaned over so far he felt he might fall out of the stands. Her path was pretty clear ... unless she went through the wrong door. Yet both were experts; they ran for the yellow door. One hallway ... one last turn ... into the big room ... across the big room toward the yellow door, Aunt Honey Peekings only a step behind ...!

"Barbaric Steal scores!" Evilla screamed, and both stands erupted.

Aunt Honey Peekings looked furious, but Barbaric Steal tossed the zombie head aside, then took off running around the outside of the building. Aunt Honey Peekings turned and ran back the way that she'd come. Moments later, Damhell ran right past her; neither had a net.

"When a team scores, their Smalls have to run out the opponent's yellow door and around the outside to their own," Veils said when the cheers died down. "It balances the game. Once the last of the scoring Smalls exit, the zombie head will reappear hidden in some corner of the other team's zone. See? The Grave Gutter Bigs are moving back to rejoin them, and it all starts again."

"Pansthorny Chopkins and Bruise Clambell are forcing Slug Gormet-Wreather to release Jackknife Illson," Evilla shouted. "She looks unhappy, but she lets him go! The wall's not moving, but both ogres are running to help. There's Jackknife Illson, squashed between the walls! Jackknife is staggering; he looks dazed; his teammates are helping him walk ..."

Jackknife looked crushed, with several spikes of his armor bent. Martin didn't know which bothered him most; his fear that he might be facing Jackknife Illson and Aunt Honey Peekings again ... or his fear of meeting a team even worse.

"Jackknife is out, taking a breather," Evilla said. "Looks like Jerk Goldboom, rookie minotaur, is coming in to replace him. But can the Barkrover Bullies recover?"

The crowd sat back down while the players took positions. Jangelly Kurtails was finally freed, and she ran out the yellow door past the Barkrover Bullies' Bigs. Jerk Goldboom started toward her, but the referees raised their wands threateningly, and both ogres grabbed and held him back.

Jangelly Kurtails shouted something insulting, and then ran off.

The game began again, but now the maze was set.

"Slid Egg finds the zombie head!" Evilla shouted. "Now, can the Barkrover Bullies even the score?"

Utter brutality reigned. Once the maze was set, the battle became vicious. Nets of iron chain crashed like thunder, and the Smalls waited until the Bigs were engaged, then leapt over them only to contest against the other Smalls with nets of rope. Aunt Honey Peekings and Slid Egg got entangled, and the younger goblin girl had the zombie head stolen from her. Barbaric Steal got slammed against a wall by one corner of an iron net, and Bruise Clambell had to defend her, while Slug Gormet-Wreather and Pansthorny Chopkins held their own against the Barkrover Bigs without Jackknife Illson. The Grave Gutters scored again, and shortly afterwards, the horn blew for halftime.

The crowd loved it – the more violence the louder they cheered. Brain was especially delighted.

"In halftime, they make quick plans," Veils said. "Each opponent knows the route to score ... now they'll change it slightly."

Another vendor came by, and Martin got a bag of Sugared Ent-nuts, which didn't taste nearly as good as his BBQ Wyvern Wings.

At the end of halftime, Jackknife Illson was back, and he looked angrier than Martin had ever seen.

"The second half is going to be a true grudge match!" Evilla shouted, and the crowd cheered. "The Barkrover Bullies are down by two, and facing expulsion from the playoffs. They have only one chance: utter domination of the second half! The horn is about to sound ... wait for it ... Let chaos reign!"

Both teams charged inside their yellow door. The Bigs began running through halls and doors, rearranging the shape of the pitch, while the Smalls searched for the zombie head. Yet one Big charged into the center.

"What's he doing?" Evilla shouted. "Jackknife Illson is crossing into Gutters' territory! He sees Jangelly Kurtails; he's chasing her! He's got her boxed in! This could be deadly ...!"

The crowd rose to its feet. Jangelly Kurtails had been searching a dead-end ... and now was trapped. The huge cyclops converged on her, both holding nets; chain against rope. Jangelly Kurtails backed up as far as she could go ... and Jackknife swung. Jangelly Kurtails tried to dodge, but the brownie was slammed to the floor ... and after the cyclops pulled back his clanking net, she looked unconscious.

"What ...?" Evilla gasped. "Jackknife has raised his

net again, but Jangelly looks out of play ... he's looking at the referees, who both have their wands pointed at him ... looks like he doesn't want to get zapped today!"

Jackknife turned away, leaving Jangelly wounded and helpless. Many booed him, but Evilla's speech had been heard by all the players. Her beautiful face twisted with rage, Slug Gormet-Wreather dashed up the corridors, slamming her huge lion's shape into the walls on sharp turns, dragging her net of chain.

"Slug Gormet-Wreather charges to avenge Jangelly Kurtails, and Jackknife Illson raises his net to meet her; a battle of titans! She raises her net, they're about to strike ...! Nets clash! Again! A battle royal! What ...? Jackknife Illson fouled both their nets ... he's grabbed her arm! Wrestling! Referees aiming ...!"

ZZZzzzaaaaapppppp!!!!

Electric bolts arced over the pitch from both ends ... and Jackknife Illson dropped low. He slid underneath Slug Gormet-Wreather's golden-furred four legs ... and both bolts struck her!

"The referees missed!" Evilla screamed. "Jackknife Illson slides underneath her, and Slug Gormet-Wreather takes the foul! She screams ... and collapses on top of him! Slug Gormet-Wreather is down!"

Jackknife Illson pushed her off, climbed to his feet, and waved to the stands on both sides. Exuberant cheers met his cheating; the crowd loved it. Only the referees looked furious.

Suddenly Damhell Hairy charged Jackknife Illson,

her rope-net swinging. Everyone gasped.

"A Small attacks a Big!" Evilla cried. "Rope against chain? Is she ...? Damhell Hairy throws ... her net wraps around Jackknife Illson's head! But that can't stop a cyclops ... Damhell Hairy has jumped on his head! She's punching his eye-grill with her fist ...!"

ZZZzzzaaaaapppppp!!!!

"Referees shoot again!" Evilla screamed. "Damhell Hairy ... and Jackknife Illson! She's wrapped around him! They both got zapped!"

Jackknife toppled, and to Martin's amazement, Damhell Hairy jumped and landed on her feet. However, she only staggered two steps before she fell.

"Jackknife Illson is down!" Evilla screamed. "Damhell Hairy is stunned, but she's moving, trying to climb to her feet! Banshees are tough ... or maybe she's just been zapped so often she's getting used to it. She's on her feet ... and she's limping toward Slug Gormet-Wreather. She's trying to awaken her!"

Eventually she succeeded, but before she did, the strong Barkrover trolls met the Gutter's yeti and bigfoot, and Aunt Honey Peekings scored. Damhell Hairy helped Slug Gormet-Wreather to her feet, and then went after Jangelly Kurtails, whom she had to carry back. Afterwards, it was no contest; Jangelly Kurtails was too hurt to return, but three against two Bigs overwhelmed the advantage of three against two Smalls, even though Damhell Hairy played as if she were in a fog. Jackknife Illson never recovered, and after the three horns finally blew, his troll teammates carried him from the pitch.

"Final score: four to two!" Evilla shouted. "That's it for the Barkrover Bullies, their second loss ... out in the quarter finals! Grand Wizard Lion Changeling is out of play! Grand Wizard Veinlet Prize has won, and they'll be celebrating in Lilliesput today! The Grave Gutters move to the semi-finals, and Jangelly Kurtails may not be joining them ... will they field enough Smalls without her? We'll see next week! Until then, this is Evilla, your sexy bestie ... saying I can't wait to see how they'll fare!

"Now, we have our next game coming up, the undefeated Wild Wraiths once again against the Neverlive Nasties, whom they defeated in Round 1. Can they do it again? Or will the Nasties from Neverlive avenge themselves? Better sharpen your claws now! Tonight's excitement ... is standing before you ... and a new game is about to start!"

Amid the cheers, Grand Wizard Bastile Wraithbone leaned forward, around Crusto, and called to Martin.

"Did you enjoy your first game as a spectator?" Grand Wizard Bastile asked.

"Oh, yea!" Martin beamed. "It's a lot less painful than watching from the pitch."

"Well, I wish you could stay for the next match, but you know ..."

"Perhaps ...?" Martin began.

"We can't risk you not playing next week," Grand Wizard Bastile said. "Humans don't sleep during the day, and every player needs rest. We won't get a bye again, so we need you rested and ready to practice tomorrow night. Say good-day, Martin ... time to go."

Martin frowned ... but nodded.

Chapter 19

Smashday / Wednesday

The mystery of the Wizards ...

Sunshine allowed Martin to return to the backyard, and on the short, freshly-mowed grass he pushed himself hard, sprinting, rope-climbing, and jumping trash cans. He also did many pushups, which weren't his favorite, but he heard Murder's voice every time he felt like quitting ... and forced another push.

That afternoon Martin joined his brothers, managing resources and sending out troops. Within an hour, he was winning again, but then he divided his troops, sending out small armies his brothers could easily destroy. He felt bad about demolishing their fun, and considered teaching them how ineffective their strategies were, but he feared they were too young ... *perhaps in a few years ...*

Vicky came in and watched their game long enough to realize what Martin was doing, and then she smiled and nodded approvingly.

"Have you started my book yet?" Vicky asked Martin.

"I will," Martin said. "Lately, I've been ..."

"Busy," Vicky finished. "I hope you read it ... but what you're doing now is important, too."

Crusto caught Martin, who winced at the sharp points of his claws.

"How are you doing?" Crusto asked as he set him down.

"I wish I could've watched the second game," Martin said.

"It was ferocious," Crusto said. "The Neverlive Nasties avenged their Round 1 defeat. They're both moving into the semi-finals with one loss ... and we will be facing the Wild Wraiths."

"What's the game?" Martin asked.

"Trip-Hook Roller," Crusto shook his head.

"What's that?" Martin asked.

"An easy game ... to get hurt in," Crusto said. "There's a large, heavy ball, six feet in diameter, that Bigs have to push into their goal-pit. Smalls need to be careful; if that ball rolls over you, you could get crushed."

Martin understood that these games were dangerous, but Crusto seemed to want to say more, so he tried to be patient.

"Water monsters ... usually aren't friends with others," Crusto said. "I ... don't express myself often, but I ... wanted to thank you. My people lived in the shoals of Shantdareya, and I've been a Skull-cracker for four years. I was one of the first to attempt life among the land monsters."

"Why did you fear them?" Martin asked.

"We didn't fear them," Crusto said. "The land monsters were savages. They wandered, killing and feeding off each other. Rumors say some even found ways to enter your world, only back then, they called it 'The Food World'. My people fled to the depths, but our feeding grounds were in the shallows. We had to swim there, and the land monsters saw us ... and they were hungry ..."

Crusto sat on the desk and bowed his head.

"Lizardmen didn't need grand wizards," Crusto continued. "We could've lived peacefully on our own ... if the land monsters would've left us alone. Even after the wizards arrived, the land monsters didn't stop fighting instantly ... some refused to be civilized."

Crusto fell silent for a long time, and finally Martin spoke up.

"What happened ...?" Martin asked.

"The land monsters suddenly had plenty of food, but a few savages still wanted to hunt," Crusto said. "The other monsters slaughtered those savages ... and the grand wizards helped. Lizardfolk were always peaceful;

the sea provided all we needed. We only fought to protect ourselves. Among ourselves, our currency is songs; we sing to each other to exchange goods. Once we realized we were no longer being preyed upon, some of us risked poking our heads above the surface for the first time in a century. What we found, except for the elves and centaurs, were primitives, barely capable of speech. When we realized what was happening, we helped civilized them ... and they're still a work in progress."

"Thank you ... for telling me," Martin said.

"You need to know," Crusto said. "At first, I didn't realize how civilized humans were; our knowledge of you is limited. With the aid of the grand wizards, we've appropriated certain technical devices from your world, such as lights and Evilla's loudspeakers ..."

"Someone knew our ways enough to take exactly what they wanted," Martin said.

"Yes," Crusto said. "Many of my people fear that the grand wizards came from your world."

Martin fell silent, contemplating this possibility.

"Why are you here ...?" Crusto asked. "I know how you got here ... I'm wondering why they let you come back ..."

"I don't know," Martin said. "Because you needed a new Small ...?"

"Other teams have been forced to drop out of the games when they couldn't field enough players," Crusto said. "They could've easily done that ... ruled that no humans could play ..."

"So ... why am I here?" Martin asked.

"My people don't know," Crusto said. "But you ... you learn quickly, have a strong imagination, and think on multiple levels ... which most monsters can't. We lizardfolk wanted you to be aware of what's going on, as you've demonstrated the ability to understand deep thoughts. The land monsters will get wilder as the final game approaches. One civilized being to another, you need to be warned; the Grotesquerie Games may not be ... the only game being played ... involving you."

In silence, they walked out onto the pitch, each lost in their own thoughts.

"You can't be the best athlete with divided loyalties," Crusto said. "For both our sakes, best that you forget what we talked about and focus on exercising. Trip-Hook Roller is not like any game you've ever played."

"Martin ...!" Stabbing called, and Crusto patted his shoulder.

"Exercise well," Crusto said. "Say nothing of what we discussed."

Crusto walked away, leaving Martin walking toward Stabbing. To his surprise, Stabbing was holding a crooked staff ... taller than he was, and hooked, like a shepherd's crook.

"Don't look too closely," Stabbing said. "You might not like it."

"Why not?" Martin asked.

Stabbing swung his hooked staff towards Martin's

ankles, pulled, ... and Martin fell onto the grass.

"Trip-Hook Roller," Stabbing said. "You'll get one of these, too. The Bigs get the roller, but we Smalls get trip-hooks."

"What ... we just trip each other?" Martin asked.

"We have to," Stabbing said. "A tripped opponent makes it easier to steal the zombie head."

"How do we score?" Martin asked.

"That's the rub," Stabbing said. "Smalls don't score. In this game, the Smalls control the pitch, and the Bigs score the points."

"How can we ...?" Martin asked.

"The zombie head is the key," Stabbing said. "The pitch is covered with divots and barriers. The Bigs roll this huge ball around and try to get it into their own score-pit. The problem is the lightning bolts ..."

"Lightning bolts ...?" Martin asked.

"Not as powerful as the ones the referees cast, but seriously uncomfortable," Stabbing said. "They rain down in random patterns all over the pitch ... except near the zombie head."

"The zombie head protects us ...?" Martin asked.

"The zombie head protects everyone within its ten foot circle, with it at the center," Stabbing said. "Our goal is to get the zombie head and use it to protect our Bigs, so that they can score. Our problem is ... the other team will be trying to do the same."

"But ...!" Martin started.

"Again, grappling is a foul," Stabbing said. "Hitting

someone with your hook-staff is also a foul, and in this game, lightning bolts from the referees are exceptionally potent. Yet our biggest danger is that we have to stay near the Bigs; they can't purposefully hurt us, but ... accidents happen."

"Get over here, you two!" Murder shouted. "We need to start practice!"

Murder, Veils, and Rude were standing by the pitch, which again looked completely revised. The building was gone, but in its place was a ... he didn't know. The closest comparison that Martin could think of was a giant Chinese checkers board littered with large wooden blocks. The floor was smooth and flat, but had divots, almost three feet in diameter and a foot deep, arranged in a geometric pattern ... and randomly covered by squared wooden blocks of all sizes, many stacked so they looked like a crude stairs. Also, on each end of the pitch yawned one deep hole, six feet in diameter, into which even Bigs could topple.

When Stabbing and Martin arrived, Veils dropped to one knee on one side of him, Murder to another, and each strapped onto a different leg a stiff, hard purple legging.

"They're greaves," Murder said, and Martin noticed both girls were wearing the same. "These greaves are waxed leather, and you'll need them to play Trip-Hook Roller."

The greaves covered his calves from the knee down, with little flaps overhanging his sneakers, covering his ankles. Then Veils lifted a weapon, such as Stabbing carried, and handed to Martin a long, hooked-staff.

"You can't hit an opponent, on purpose or by accident," Murder warned. "We'll be playing in close quarters with our opponents, Bigs and Smalls, and you can't hit anyone."

"Especially don't hit us!" Stabbing added, and Veils chuckled.

"Veils, you start him," Murder said.

She and Stabbing stepped back, leaving Martin alone with Veils. As he looked at her, she slashed her hooked-staff down to slap the dirt behind him, yanked hard, and dropped Martin onto his butt.

Stabbing laughed.

"Do the same to her ... but don't hit her," Murder said.

Martin tried, but Veils blocked his hooked-staff with hers. He backed off, then inched forward and tried again; she jumped up high and let his attempt scrape the empty ground beneath her, and a second later, Martin was falling again.

An hour later, Martin was holding his own. Experience was all that taught this game, and a painful butt was a powerful teacher. Individual strategies varied with each body type. Veils was nothing compared to Murder and Stabbing; Murder used her hooked-staff to block anything Martin shoved at her, and Stabbing could leap almost anything. Then Martin figured out that, if he could get them to jump, then he could suddenly shove the crook of his staff under their feet, and make them struggle to land anywhere but upon it ... without entangling their feet. If either failed, Martin pulled hard ... and smiled as they toppled to the ground. Yet all were better than he, and Martin soon felt he needed armor-plating for his aching backside as well as his calves.

Rude offered several suggestions, including how to quickly extend his grip or choke-up on the pole. He showed Martin ways to flip his hook-staff quicker, so he could switch targets, taking out a different Small than he was first attacking. Then Rude fetched the zombie head, and moved them onto the smooth-floored pitch. They stayed out of the divots and off the blocks, and Rude tossed the zombie head into the air. Murder whipped up her hook-staff, and caught it in the crook, and spun the pole so the zombie head rotated without falling, and then she tossed it to Stabbing. He caught it in his hook-staff, slashed it low, and sent it skittering across the pitch toward Veils.

Angry, Martin dropped his hook-staff, jumped in front of Veils, blocking her with his body, and reached down and caught the zombie head with his hands. To the disbelief of his companions, he turned the zombie face toward his.

"Are you all right?" Martin asked.

The zombie head rolled his eyes.

"I've learned to accept it," the zombie head said. "It's better than getting zapped."

Martin frowned, but Stabbing stared dumbfounded.

"What are you ...?" Stabbing started.

"Leave him alone!" boomed a deep, hissing voice.

Rude, Veils, and all three Smalls turned and looked as Crusto stepped out from behind a stack of blocks.

"Martin, it doesn't hurt the zombie head, but it's nice of you to ask," Crusto said. "Your compassion is very ... civilized."

Martin stared, uncertain, but Crusto nodded approvingly to him, and then walked away, leaving all the Smalls dumbfounded.

Chapter 20

Stompday / Thursday

Secrets are revealed ...

"Martin, you're in charge today," his mother said as she lifted her briefcase from the table.

"What ...?" Martin asked, half-asleep, sore, and exhausted from practicing too long.

"Vicky has to go with Maria Myers," his mother said, "Her mother is taking them to a class at the university on how to apply for college. She'll be doing that next year, and we've already paid."

Martin looked across at Vicky, whose smile was beaming.

"Just feed your brothers and keep an eye on them," his father said. "No fighting. Vicky, what time ...?"

"Mrs. Myers will be here at 10:00," Vicky said.

"Behave yourself," their mother said, and then she turned to Martin. "All of you."

Before they left, their father gave Vicky some cash for lunch, and then the kids were alone. Martin looked up at Vicky and found her looking at him.

"There's bread, mustard, and baloney for sandwiches," Vicky said. "If you play outside, they'll trash the house."

"Video games ...," Martin sighed.

"You always wanted to be in charge," Vicky said, staring at him. "Or ... is there something else going on ... something you're not telling me ...?"

Martin clenched his jaw and said nothing.

Martin startled as he fell into Happy's hands. Happy noticed his reaction and looked offended.

"Sorry!" Martin said quickly. "I ... was expecting Crusto."

"Why?" Happy demanded.

Happy set Martin down, but kept his eyes locked upon him. Martin looked around, but they were alone. He racked his brains for something to say ...

"Why ...?" Happy repeated more forcefully.

"We ... Crusto and I ... we talked ...," Martin said.

"What about?" Happy demanded.

"About ... about when the grand wizards first appeared," Martin said.

"That explains it," Happy snarled. "Crusto told me he had an appointment, and he asked me to catch you."

"Crusto sent you ...?" Martin asked.

"Apparently," Happy snorted like a horse and flicked his tail. "Lizardmen; never trust anything that can breathe water ...!"

"Why?" Martin asked.

"Lizardmen are deep ... and secretive," Happy said. "Don't get me wrong; Crusto's a great teammate, but conversations with lizardmen are always one-sided; they take more information than they give ..."

"But ... I don't have any information ...," Martin argued.

"Listening isn't the only way to get information," Happy said. "Just from watching you, I can see part of what he told you."

"Really ...?" Martin asked.

"Crusto told you that lizardmen were civilized before the grand wizards arrived," Happy said.

"How did you know?" Martin stared up at him.

"Strategy," Happy said. "I didn't know ... but now I do."

"He also said that the centaurs were civilized before the grand wizards came," Martin said.

"Did he?" Happy asked. "That surprises me. It's true; centaurs were the second civilization on Heterodox."

"The lizardmen were first ...?" Martin asked.

"No, the elves were first, but elves are transitory," Happy said. "Elves lived in the trees, could move in an instant, and fled when savages came hunting them.

Centaurs were the first fixed civilization; we built the first walls, and then the first buildings, that ever existed here. When savages attacked, we fought and drove them back, wave after wave. When we were overwhelmed, we had to flee, but savages had no use for walls, so we'd come back to find our homes abandoned."

"Why am I here ...?" Martin asked Happy, unable to keep the question inside him.

"So ... that's what you and Crusto were talking about," Happy said, and he tapped one hoof nervously. "That's a dangerous question ... and don't think we're the only ones asking it. Many fear what the answer may be; many, but not centaurs. The oldest and strongest emotion is fear, and the oldest and strongest kind of fear is fear of the unknown. Centaurs alone don't fear the unknown, although the unknown offers the greatest danger."

Martin forced himself to stay silent, hoping for answers.

"Look, I'm not telling you my suspicions, but this is serious," Happy said. "When the first grand wizards arrived, it changed our whole world."

"They didn't arrive together?" Martin asked.

"All but one," Happy said. "All of the other grand wizards appeared five hundred years ago. Then, almost three hundred years later, Grand Wizard Veinlet Prize appeared, conquered half of the abandoned lands, and demanded admittance to the Grand Wizard Council."

"Where did he come from?" Martin asked.

"That's the biggest mystery," Happy said. "No one knows where any of the Grand Wizards came from, but they all seemed to know each other ... from the first day they arrived. Wherever they came from, they all seemed to have come from the same place ... at the same time. Grand Wizard Veinlet Prize's arrival surprised them, for they'd never before met or heard of him."

"But how ...?" Martin began.

"I didn't come here to answer your questions," Happy said. "We've got a tough game coming day after tomorrow, and we must win. You need practice, and I need to find Crusto; I don't like being used as a lizardman's tool."

"Please, don't be angry with him," Martin said.

"I'm not angry," Happy said. "Trust me; when you see an angry centaur, you'll know it ... because you'll be running away ...!"

Practice was much harder. Rather than one-on-one, Veils and Murder attacked Martin together. He was forced to defend ... and usually failed. Stabbing taught him how to use the wooden blocks, and Martin found he had a knack for jumping onto the many levels of the solid wooden blocks, dueling from different heights, and dropping off unexpectedly into the midst of opponents. However, Martin was terrible at stealing and managing the zombie head, and his attempts to pass it failed utterly. He learned that picking up the zombie head with your hands, or kicking it with your feet, was a foul, and finally Murder stopped him.

"Martin, I don't mean to be insulting, but you'd help us best by constantly harassing the other Smalls," Murder said. "When possible, leave the zombie head to Stabbing and I."

Martin frowned, yet he was so bad with the zombie head that he nodded. He couldn't do a fraction of the tricks Murder, Stabbing, and even Veils could.

"What concerns me is that Martin can't practice on the real pitch," Stabbing complained.

"I'm concerned, too," Murder said, and she jumped onto a block and climbed to the top of a pile, leaning over a cliff taller than she. "Martin, come here ... below me ... and try to trip Stabbing."

Stabbing obliged, but before either could attempt to trip the other, Murder stabbed the long end of her hook-staff down between them, striking the smooth floor with a sharp rap, and she voiced a loud imitation of thunder.

"That's what you can expect tomorrow," Rude said, limping forward on his cane. "Lightning bolts raining down from every angle, flashes of light, and booms of thunder."

"You will get struck," Stabbing said. "Every player gets struck. That's the nature of this pitch. You need to shake it off as fast as you can. Consider yourself lucky; Smalls are less of a target than Bigs."

"The hard part is the surprises," Murder said. "You never know when lightning will flash right in your path. If you try to predict it, you'll move too slowly."

"The less you worry about it, the better you'll play,"

Veils said. "You won't get hit any less by standing still."

Murder's jabs blocked both Martin and Stabbing's attacks and defenses ... and still both fell a lot. Stabbing stole Martin's staff several times, and had to return it. Veils joined the fight, attacking both, and struggling to defend herself. Whenever Martin concentrated on her, Stabbing hooked and dropped him, and then he returned the favor. Foremost, Martin was worried about the real combatants ... and the lightning bolts, however less powerful everyone said they were.

Chapter 21

Smiteday / Friday

When science is applied ...

"So, it went well?" Vicky asked after their parents left.

"Huh ...? Martin asked, disturbed from considering possibilities for the next game. "What went ...?"

"Yesterday ... being in charge ...?" Vicky reminded him.

"Oh, that ...," Martin answered. "I made sandwiches and we played video games."

"No arguments?" Vicky asked.

"Our only argument was over which flavor of chips we'd open after lunch," Martin said.

"Again, I'm impressed," Vicky said. "I suspected you'd be angry because you couldn't exercise outside ... and take it out on the boys."

"What's the point ...?" Martin said.

"Exactly," Vicky said. "Months ago, that's what you'd have done, but now ... you're different."

Martin paused and looked at her.

"What do you mean?" Martin asked.

"Something's made you grow up unusually fast," Vicky said. "Care to tell me what that *'something'* is ...?"

"You're dreaming," Martin pretended to scoff at her.

"As you wish," Vicky said. "I will learn your secret. However, today I'm doing laundry ... and I want your purple jersey."

"P-p-purple jersey ...?" Martin stammered, alarmed.

"The one with the white '13' on it," Vicky said. "It needs to be washed."

"Why ...?" Martin asked.

"Because it stinks," Vicky replied.

Wearing a clean, freshly-washed jersey, Martin fell into the hands of Brain. Yet Brain didn't set him down at once; he lifted Martin to his face and sniffed him.

"You smell tasty," Brain said.

"I ... washed," Martin explained.

"Good thing Snitch not here," Brain said, and he set Martin down.

Martin glanced around to make sure they were alone.

"Brain, where do ogres come from?" Martin asked.

Brain seemed puzzled, and then pointed behind him.

"I was on the pitch ...," Brain said.

"No, I mean ... before the grand wizards came, where

did ogres live?" Martin asked.

His confused expression grew more evident.

"Shantdareya," Brain answered.

"Where in Shantdareya?" Martin asked. "In the mountains, the forests, ...?"

Brain shrugged, still looking confused. This was getting nowhere ...

"That's okay," Martin said. "Let's go join the others."

His expression never changed, so Martin reached up, took his huge ogre hand, and led Brain out of the locker room.

Grunts of Snitch, Happy, and Crusto came from the pitch, and Martin stopped and stared at them. With a grinding rumble, a monstrously heavy ball of rock, six feet in diameter, rolled across the pitch, with Snitch pushing it. The stone ball looked like polished, solid granite, and reminded Martin of the ball that had rolled after Indiana Jones in the tunnel ... and almost crushed him. Happy and Crusto were pushing against it from the other side, yet unable to stop Snitch's progress.

"Now!" Crusto shouted.

Crusto and Happy changed the angle of their bodies, and thus the angle of their pushing, and the ball's trajectory turned slightly, making Snitch stumble. With cheers, Happy and Crusto quickly rolled the ball away from Snitch, and started pushing it around some block-barriers, back toward the far end of the pitch. Snitch jumped up and ran after them.

"Ha!" Brain laughed, his eyes on their practice,

apparently having completely forgotten his conversation with Martin.

"I'll be all right," Martin said. "You can go play."

Brain smiled, and then charged after the Bigs and the rolling stone ball.

Seeing none of the others, Martin followed, and climbed up onto some blocks, which appeared to be safe; sets of blocks didn't move when the heavy ball slammed into them and bounced off. However, they stopped playing, and rolled the ball into a divot, into which it 'thumped' very solidly. Then Brain, Happy, and Crusto tried to explain to Snitch that they were changing the sides, that Happy and Brain would be on one side, and Crusto would be on Snitch's side. This took about ten minutes, and then Snitch seemed to understand.

As they were starting to play again, Grand Wizard Bastile Wraithbone, Rude, Stabbing, Murder, and Veils came walking out of the darkness. Veils was holding a small bag, and she and Stabbing were still finishing off their last bites of some BBQ Wyvern Wings.

"Martin ...!" Grand Wizard Bastile called, and he ran over to them. "Sorry we weren't here when you arrived. Our meeting took longer than we expected."

"Meeting ...?" Martin asked.

"Strategy," Rude said. "The Skull-crackers are the only team left with no losses. With the Barkrover Bullies out, there are only four teams left, so no one gets a bye in the semi-finals."

"We had a bye, and the Neverlive Nasties got their bye in Round 2," Murder said. "Neither the Wild Wraiths nor the Grave Gutters have had a bye, so we won't get another."

"Either the Grave Gutters or the Neverlive Nasties will be out after tomorrow's game," Rude said. "If we win, the semi-finals will be over, and we'll be in the finals. If we lose, there will be another semi-finals, and again we won't get the bye. If we lose that game, we don't get into the finals."

"That means we're not guaranteed to get into the finals unless we win this round," Murder said. "If we don't, then we'll have to play another round. If we do, then our next game will be the finals."

"It doesn't matter; we play to win," Grand Wizard Bastile said.

Everyone groaned.

"What is it?" Martin asked.

"If we got to pick one game before the finals, it wouldn't be Trip-Hook Roller," Rude said. "It's too dangerous. Players get hurt ... often. If ... any Small gets hurt, we'll lose automatically."

"Don't the other teams face the same risk?" Martin asked.

"The other teams have backups," Grand Wizard Bastile said. "Trip-Hook Roller is notorious for damaging Smalls."

"I'm playing," Martin said.

"We were considering backing out of this round,"

Rude said. "We'd gain one loss, but have another chance to get into the finals."

"We can't take the chance," Grand Wizard Bastile said. "We must get into the finals!"

"We only need one victory, this week or next, to get into the finals," Stabbing said. "Our odds would be better with most other games."

"Some games are worse," Murder said.

"Only a few," Stabbing said.

"You see why it took longer than we expected?" Bastile said. "Crusto already told me he wants to play. Murder and I want to play. Rude, Stabbing, and Veils want to take a loss and skip this round. What do you say, Martin?"

Martin shrugged.

"You all know the games, I don't," Martin said. "My best strategy would be to let you advise me."

"You're our tie-breaker," Rude said. "What do you say?"

Martin stared at them, biting his lip.

"What ...?" Rude asked. "Have you thought of something?"

"No ... well, yes, but we can't do it," Martin said.

"Why not?" Murder asked.

"Be - because it's cheating," Martin said.

"Cheating ...?" Stabbing asked. "How ...?"

"Because it isn't sports," Martin said. "It's science."

Practice was delayed while Martin explained. They had to go back into the locker room, where Martin used a hunk of chalk to draw on a bare stone wall. Only Bastile seemed to easily grasp what Martin meant, and the others simply didn't believe it.

To prove himself, Martin took Murder and Stabbing and stood under a cloud Grand Wizard Bastile conjured. To their amazement, Martin only got shocked a few times, while Stabbing and Murder, with all their metal jewelry and bare feet, suffered.

"Is it possible ...?" Rude asked.

"Not for the Bigs," Martin said. "But for us Smalls ... maybe ..."

"We've got to try it," Grand Wizard Bastile said. "Martin, can you do it?"

"Probably," Martin said. "I'll need to take their measurements."

"Well, it's up to you," Grand Wizard Bastile said, and he looked at Murder and Stabbing. "Are you willing to try?"

Both looked nervously at each other.

"What have we got to lose?" Murder asked.

Veils came up and kissed his cheek again.

Chapter 22

Rompday / Saturday

The Trip-Hook Roller ...

Martin slept in late; he'd need it. When he did wake up, he dug through his closet and found half of what he needed. The other half he didn't have; he'd have to ask Vicky.

Saturday breakfast was grapefruit, grits, bacon, and toast. Martin ate, but withheld his question, as he didn't want the others to hear. His father announced that he was taking him and his brothers to get haircuts around noon, and Martin sighed; at least he'd look good for the semi-finals.

After breakfast, Martin followed Vicky to her bedroom door.

"Vicky ... can we talk?" Martin asked.

Vicky gave him a strange look.

"Privately ...?" Martin added.

Vicky nodded, then let him into her cluttered room and closed the door. Martin explained what he wanted ... and Vicky smiled.

"I could give you a pair of old ones," Vicky said. "But there's a price ..."

"I don't have much ...," Martin began, but she waved his worry aside.

"I want to know why you're exercising," Vicky said. "The real reason; not the lie."

Martin sighed and bowed his head, then looked at all of the fiction and fantasy books on her shelves. Nothing there could be as crazy as Heterodox.

"You wouldn't believe me," Martin said.

"Try me," Vicky said.

"I ... can't," Martin said. "Not yet. I need ... a week, maybe two."

"What for ...?" Vicky asked.

"I ... can't ...," Martin began.

"I see ...," Vicky said.

"You do ...?" Martin asked.

Vicky reached out and scraped her thumb hard across Martin's cheek. Then she sniffed it.

"Is that BBQ sauce ... or lipstick ...?" Vicky asked.

"What ...?" Martin asked.

"You're lucky mom didn't notice," Vicky said. "Whatever made that mark on you ... it looks like lips ... a kiss ...!"

Martin blushed and looked down.

"In nine days ... maybe thirteen ... I'll be able to tell you," Martin promised, and she smiled.

"Wait here," Vicky said. "I'll get them."

Brain caught Martin, whose arms were full as he landed in the ogre's wide hands. Every member of the Skull-crackers stood there, waiting expectantly.

"Got them!" Martin announced.

"Are you sure this will work?" Murder asked.

"It might," Martin said. "It's called conduction ... and resistance. Electricity always follows the path of least resistance, and sneakers are more insulation than bare feet. We'll need to towel ourselves dry often, as sweat is water, which conducts electricity. We leave all necklaces, rings, and metal off the pitch, including buttons and buckles. It won't fully protect us, but every bolt we avoid is an advantage."

"The Wild Wraiths are mostly women ... and they wear lots of jewelry," Stabbing said.

"If moisture conducts electricity, then you should dry off your hook-staffs, too," Rude said. "Players' hands get sweaty ..."

"Every little bit helps," Martin said. "Also, lightning strikes the tallest objects first, so when you can ... stoop ... and hold your hook-staffs low."

Necklaces, earrings, bracelets, and every other type of jewelry was removed, even from the Bigs, and placed in a cloth bag Rude carried. After tightening the laces and tying his old sneakers onto Murder's feet, and doing the same for Stabbing's long-clawed feet with his sister's old sneakers, Martin led the way out of the locker room and toward the crowd. Murder and Stabbing walked awkwardly; their first attempts at wearing sneakers.

This crowd was bigger, packing the stands and reaching out to the far ends of the stadium. Monsters appeared in amazing variety, combinations of humans, beasts, and things Martin could only describe as alien squeezed to get a closer look. A line of referees stood holding open a narrow passage for them, and they had to walk single-file through it, deafened by cheers and patted by hands and limbs of every description. As he walked, using his arms to ward off the many talons, pincers, claws, and suckers, Martin assumed that the semi-finals attracted more attention, and he could only imagine what chaos the finals would be like.

"Here come the undefeated Shantdareya Skull-crackers!" Evilla screamed over the rising roar of the crowd. "Long-shots-turned-favorites, led by Grand Wizard Bastile Wraithbone, with Allfed Snitchlock, the strongest troll in the league, Brain Stroker, ogre-veteran of six seasons, Crusto Fernwalker, the fastest swimmer in the league, wise Happy Lostcraft, the 'Centaur Mentor', pretty Murder Shelling, the 'Deadly Dryad', Stabbing Kingz, one of the swiftest Smalls ever to play, and that strangest of all players, the only human to ever join our games, let alone thrive in them, Martin Mulberry, better known as ... Martin the Magnificent!"

More cheers rose, and Martin would've blushed, but he saw what was awaiting him as they reached the pitch and stood outside it. Over fifty tiny dark clouds, no larger than basketballs, floated over the brightly-lit pitch like hovering menaces, and frequently a flash of lightning crackled and leaped from a small, dark cloud to the pitch below. Martin noticed that the bright, thin, threatening bolts tended to strike the tallest-stacked blocks, which made him hopeful; monsters may be tougher than humans, but Martin was better educated.

On the other side of the pitch came a team wearing scarlet.

"And here come the Wild Wraiths!" Evilla screamed. "Led by the ever-beautiful Grand Witch Maim La Nuormal, Queen of Wanderlost, whose team failed before the Neverlive Nasties in the quarter-finals! I see that vicious, velvety vampire, Fey Wraith, followed closely by the mysterious Jailnet Lazy, the darkest shadow ever, sexy Lynn DaBlair-Witch, who'll have you howling 'there-wolf', Death Wall-ache, that sewn-together corpse that leaves everyone in stitches, and the infamous Mad Eyelean Con, the only Dragling left in the league, Mykill Gouge, that twice-banned bloodiest ogre ever, Don Alt-Pleasant, the minotaur whose horns once impaled the foul Liverea Squiggly, and lastly, that 'Scourge from the Sewers, the most-feared Ravenous Ratking, Fright Fried!"

Martin's eyes widened as he saw his opponents. Grand Witch Maim La Nuormal was tall and elegant, shapely, with a thick black-feather boa wrapped around her scarlet-robed shoulders, a pearl complexion, and deep, mysterious eyes. Beside her stood tiny Fey Wraith, a pale, long-fanged girl no bigger than Veils, wearing a flimsy black dress with trailing sleeves and a skirt of many slits. Jailnet Lazy looked partially transparent, a chubby girl, taller than most Smalls, and resembled any ghost from a bad horror movie. Lynn DaBlair-Witch was undoubtedly a werewolf, her violet jersey and tight pants the only parts of her not covered in fur, and her face was indeed wolfish, with pointed ears and a snarl on her muzzle. Death Wall-ache was no bigger than he, but covered in stitches like the zombie head; a Small Frankenstein's monster. For the Bigs, Mad Eyelean Con was the first Dragling he'd ever seen, and she looked like a small dragon shaped like an ogre, just as big, with thick, crusty red-scales, huge wings, and a long, lashing tail ... and when she opened her mouth, a flickering red glow, like fire, emanated from the back of her throat. Mykill Gouge was a huge ogre, almost as big as a troll. Don Alt-Pleasant looked like every other minotaur, except that he wore spiked armor like Jackknife the cyclops. Fright Fried was a Ratking, like Stabbing, but of a higher order, as big as Crusto, giant rat-beast, bulging with muscles, but covered in the same ratling greasy-brown hair. Martin had never seen a team that looked so formidable, but he chided himself for being surprised; *the weaker teams got weeded out as you neared the finals.*

Worst of all was that the Wild Wraiths numbered eight, while the Skull-crackers had only seven; they had an extra Small. If one of their Smalls got a serious injury, then a replacement was available. If the Skull-crackers lost a Small, then they'd play the rest of the game outnumbered and not be allowed to finish the playoffs.

"Line up along the outside!" Grand Wizard Bastile said as loudly as his aged voice could speak over the crowd. "Don't step onto the pitch until you have to ... and good luck!"

Martin lined up with the others, and noticed that four referees were sanding on platforms overlooking the pitch; *fouls in this game would cost dearly.*

"Get ready to run!" Murder whispered to Martin, and she handed him his hook-staff. "The zombie head rests atop the ball in the center, and the first team to reach it gains the advantage."

"The semi-finals of the three hundred and fourteenth Grotesquerie Games are about to start!" Evilla cried, posing in a leopard-skin dress that couldn't have been tighter on its original owner. "I am Evilla, your favorite glamour gal, that marvelous maiden of monsters, and I'll be bringing you your most exciting moments of the next few hours ... and commentary on the game! So place your bets, grab a big box of Tangy Tarantulas, and get ready to watch the most amazing thing you've ever seen ... me ... and the Shantdareya Skull-crackers versus the pride of Wanderlost, the Wild Wraiths!"

The crowd's cheers rose and a wave began in the stands.

"I'm told we're about to get started!" Evilla said. "Our chief referee, Conra deVerdict, is signaling ... don't get your antenna twisted! The horn's about to blow! Get ready ...! Let the mayhem begin!"

The horn blew. Martin charged onto the pitch, heedless of the flashes of lightning bursting all around. Only Crusto remained; Happy charged ahead, faster than any of the others. He galloped to the huge stone ball and slammed into it with his hindquarters; the zombie head fell off, and the ball slowly rolled in the opposite direction.

Martin ran around some blocks which Murder and Stabbing jumped atop and bounced off, bounding far ahead. Yet before he got another step, a lightning bolt arced down and caught him. Martin screamed, but it was more tingly than painful, stunning, yet nothing like he'd suffered in his first game, when he'd fouled Aunt Honey Peekings. Yet his nerves felt dazzled, and he stumbled his next few steps, and long moments passed before he regained full control of his limbs.

Martin knew his plan wouldn't fully protect him, but he shrugged it off and kept running. Lightning bolts rained down all over. Snitch and Brain reached the ball, helping Happy push, and only Mad Eyelean Con and Mykill Gouge pushed against them; a bolt of lightning caught one of Don Alt-Pleasant's long, brass-decorated horns, and he fell to his hairy knees.

Murder and Stabbing hook-staff dueled Lynn DaBlair-Witch, who was blocking them from getting behind her, a wolfish snarl on her muzzle. Fey Wraith had the zombie head trapped in her hook-staff, so Martin headed toward her. Then Jailnet Lazy appeared, practically floating at him, waving her hook-staff. Martin parried her weapon easily and tried to run around her, but she moved to block his path. She swiped at his ankles, but he jumped over her hook-staff. Then she flipped her hook-staff over, swiped back, and dropped him onto his butt. Martin jumped up and slashed just above the pitch floor; his hook-staff passed right through her ghostly ankles. Yet he felt some resistance, and she tilted horizontal in midair, floating, although she didn't fall. Martin charged to get past her, but her legs blocked his path. He drove right into her, partly pushing her aside, and then he was startled to have penetrated her skin. Her legs stuck right through his stomach, and he felt as if he were wading through sticky syrup, but he took a firm step to push through her and forced himself free. Then he ducked as a bolt of lightning struck a stack of blocks beside him, and he ran toward the Bigs.

Lynn DaBlair-Witch was still dueling Stabbing, but Murder had slipped past and was fighting with Fey Wraith over control of the zombie head. Martin charged forward, caught her hook-staff with his, and Murder stole the zombie head. Taking the head, Murder ran around the Bigs, and Fey Wraith turned to chase after her, but Martin yanked hard, pulled her hook-staff from her hands, and flung it skittering across the pitch, where it landed in a divot.

Fey Wraith hissed at Martin, her angry face contorted and vampire fangs bared, and then she ran after her hook-staff ... and got struck by lightning only a few feet away. Another bolt flashed nearby, and Martin realized Murder had carried the zombie head more than eight feet away, leaving him susceptible to zaps from the floating clouds. Martin tried to follow Murder, but the wrestling Bigs rolled the heavy ball in his path. Forced to run around a set of blocks, Martin dodged Jailnet Lazy as she floated toward him, and then he ran within the safe-range of the zombie head.

With Fey Wraith chasing her hook-staff, Lynn DaBlair-Witch staff-fighting with Stabbing, and Jailnet Lazy haunting him, Murder safely whirled her staff, keeping the edge of the lightning range directly over their Bigs. Happy, Snitch, and Brain were pushing the huge ball from one side, but their strength was matched by Mad Eyelean Con, Mykill Gouge, and Don Alt-Pleasant. Yet the lightning was raining outside the range-circle, and two bolts struck Mad Eyelean Con, making her fall twitching. Three against two, the Skull-crackers rolled the ball toward their end, but the Wild Wraiths' Bigs kept trying to force the ball into a divot. Then lightning struck Mykill Gouge, and one minotaur couldn't stop a troll, an ogre, and a centaur. Recovered, Mad Eyelean Con came running up, smoke and whispers of flame slipping from her mouth, but the ball was rolling as fast as Snitch could run. Don Alt-Pleasant threw himself down in its path but they rolled the ball right over him ... and into the big hole on their side of the pitch.

A bell rang and the crowd cheered.

"First score to the Skull-crackers!" Evilla shouted over the roars. "Don Alt-Pleasant looks like minotaur-mush, no, wait! He's getting up. Mad Eyelean Con has his arm, and all are departing the pitch while still in the safety zone of the zombie head. The granite marble will soon pop-out in the center, and the game begins again! But who will win? Sidle up by me, you lucky horrors, and we'll see!"

Chapter 23

Rompday / Saturday

Blasting rock and roll ...

The referees waved their wands and the heavy stone ball rolled back to the center, lightning hitting it several times. After it was in place, the zombie head rose and floated to rest atop it. Of course, the lightning from the clouds avoided the zombie head.

The lightning wasn't as bad as Martin feared; the Smalls stayed within the ten-foot protection circle as much as possible, even when fighting each other. Despite being close at hand, the Bigs ignored them, focused on the ball. The Bigs suffered the most from the lightning strikes, when not in the safe-zone, and scoring depended upon them; Martin doubted if all the Smalls of both teams could push that heavy granite ball out of a divot.

"Here we go again!" Evilla shouted. "The refs are signaling! Let chaos rein!"

The horn blew and they charged in. Martin leapt over divots and boxes, hoping to get to the zombie head before getting zapped. However, Murder and Stabbing both got struck, and Martin found himself alone.

Happy again reached the stone ball first, and started pushing, but Snitch and Brain arrived at the same time as Mad Eyelean Con and Mykill Gouge. The minotaur had remained off-pitch, and Fright Fried, the Big, muscular ratking, ran in his place; this was one of the few games where players could switch off in the middle of a half.

Fey Wraith reached the zombie head first, and Martin found himself assailed by Jailnet Lazy and Lynn DaBlair-Witch. He was no match against a shadow and a werewolf. Half of his attacks against Jailnet Lazy phased right through her, and the growls of Lynn DaBlair-Witch were so threateningly wolfish they raised his hackles. His greaves took a beating, and no sooner did Martin regain his feet than he was falling again. He felt bad; Brain got zapped and the ball rolled the wrong way.

Stabbing suddenly pounced into their midst, defending Martin so he could rise.

"Defend me!" Stabbing shouted, and Martin slashed his hook-staff low.

Snitch took two zaps, but he only looked up and

snarled at the dark, floating clouds. Suddenly the zombie head flew over the Bigs, and Stabbing caught it in his crook. The safe area shifted, and Mykill Gouge got zapped. Then Murder came running around the Bigs, chased by Fey Wraith, her hook-staff raised; Murder had stolen the zombie head! Seeing Stabbing with the zombie head, Fey Wraith jumped on top of the ball, walking backwards as it rolled.

"Dumb troll, dumb troll, gotta suck your thumb, troll!" Fey shouted.

Snitch snarled and punched at her. Happy grabbed his arm and tried to stop him, but few could restrain a troll's fist; Fey Wraith blocked with her hook-staff, which broke in two, and still she was knocked backwards. But the referees saw; four lightning bolts zapped forward and struck Snitch, and by extension, Happy. Both sizzled and fell, and the Wild Wraiths rolled the ball around them. Fey smiled and jumped down; Brain alone couldn't control the ball. Yet Fey's hook-staff was broken; she took Jailnet Lazy's staff and joined Lynn DaBlair-Witch. To Martin's surprise, Jailnet Lazy jumped at him, and splashed right into him. Her body enveloped his head, deafened him to the crowd's cheers, and made the world look like a black-and-white silent movie seen through a fish tank. Martin tried to shake her off, stumbled, and they fell in a pile.

A lightning bolt dropped onto them, and both writhed, shaking from the sudden voltage. As they jerked, Jailnet slipped mostly off his head with a squishy, dull sound. Martin pulled himself free of her, jumped up, and ran to help the others. The ball was closing in on the wrong hole, and Happy and Snitch were still on the ground. Jumping up, snatching his hook-staff, and running for the safe-zone, Martin found Murder and Stabbing fighting hard, Fey Wraith on the ground, and Lynn DaBlair-Witch protecting the zombie head trapped in her spinning hook-staff. She was dancing with practiced ease as the long tails of Mad Eyelean Con and Fright Fried lashed, causing the Skull-cracker Smalls to jump to avoid them.

Brain alone couldn't hold them back; as Martin joined the fray, the ball rolled into the hole, and the bell rang.

"Wild Wraiths score!" Evilla shouted. "Tied game!"

The Wraiths jumped off the pitch, and Martin started to follow, but Murder and Stabbing grabbed the zombie head and ran back toward the center, with Brain on their heels. Martin chased after them.

Snitch lay stunned, collapsed on top of Happy, who was struggling to extricate himself, and lightning bolts kept zapping them. Working together, they freed Happy, and under the protection of the zombie head, they struggled to wake Stitch and drag him off the pitch. Snitch was groggy, unaware of where he was.

Crusto, Rude, Grand Wizard Bastile, and Veils ran up next to the pitch.

"He's out," Happy said. "He won't recover today."

"But we'll lose ...!" Veils argued.

"Can you heal him?" Martin asked Grand Wizard Bastile.

"No," Grand Wizard Bastile said. "If we lose, we're still in the playoffs. If you get hurt, then we're out."

"I'll be careful ...!"Martin promised.

"It's not worth it," Grand Wizard Bastile said.

"If we lose, we have to win two games, a second semi-final and the finals," Murder said. "If we win, we only have one game left."

"Crusto must replace him," Stabbing said.

"We need to win," Crusto said. "I can't match a dragling ..."

"Either way is risky," Rude said. "But we have to decide now ... or we'll be late."

"Martin ...?" Grand Wizard Bastile asked.

"I'm here to win," Martin said.

"Very well," Grand Wizard Bastile said, and he raised his staff and began to wiggle his fingers over Snitch.

Crusto rose up and made a strange gesture to the referees.

"Skull-crackers have signaled a medical delay!" Evilla announced, and the crowd groaned. "That's five minutes, folks! Place new bets, buy your team's pennants, and enjoy a fresh, ice-cold Salamander Swill! The game is paused, but you still got me ... Evilla ... in the flesh, and I've got a lot of that!"

Grand Wizard Bastile's magic glow covered Snitch, and lasted several moments, during which Martin hardly dared breathe. Then Snitch's eyes opened.

"It worked!" Veils shouted.

They helped Snitch to his feet while Rude lectured him.

"Never listen to an enemy!" Rude stressed. "Listen to no one wearing scarlet!"

"We've only got ten minutes before halftime," Crusto said. "We're tied, and it's unlikely anyone will score. Play safe; save taking risks for the second half. Better get ready; our delay is almost up."

They lined along the pitch, and the referee signaled. The horn blew, and Evilla started prattling, but Martin was too busy running to listen. Happy reached the ball first, and luckily, as he slammed into it, the zombie head somehow fell onto his back. Happy bucked, and the zombie head flew into the air, arcing toward them. Stabbing caught it; they hadn't reached the ball ... and already they had the zombie head!

The Wild Wraiths arrived as the rest of the Skull-crackers charged up. Snitch and Mad Eyelean Con hit the ball together, and soon all six Bigs were pressing against it. Fey Wraith and Murder dueled viciously, and Stabbing dodged and jumped over Lynn DaBlair-Witch's assaults, trying to keep the zombie head from her. Jailnet Lazy went after Martin again, clashing hook-staffs, and trying to envelop him. Martin had to leap and dodge, avoiding her, when Murder and Fey suddenly broke apart. Fey stepped away, and Murder jumped to help Stabbing, and Lynn DaBlair-Witch savagely attacked them both.

"A scroll ...!" Veils' scream reached Martin's ears. *"The vampira has a scroll ...!"*

Martin glanced to see Fey Wraith holding a paper scroll, and reading it aloud, although the roars of the crowd drowned out whatever she was saying. Murder jumped straight toward her, but Lynn tripped her, and then she blocked Stabbing by running into him.

"Stop her ...!" Stabbing shouted, pointing at Fey.

Sparkling white vapors erupted, flashing with blinding silver sparks, as Fey Wraith's magic scroll burst aflame. As it burned, the sparking white vapors flew from the burning scroll toward each of the Skull-crackers, and enveloped them, completely encasing everyone wearing purple. Trapped in the silver-sparking white vapor, Martin felt tingly, but encumbered, as if he'd fallen into a pool of wet cement.

"It's a Slow-Stopper spell!" Evilla shouted. "The Wild Wraiths used their one spell for the playoffs, and it looks like it worked! Amazing timing; only four minutes before halftime, and the Skull-crackers are Slow-Stopped! The Wild Wraith Bigs have pulled the ball free, and Lynn DaBlair-Witch steals the zombie head! They're rolling it to score ... the Skull-crackers are helpless!"

Martin watched, unable to move, as the sparkling white vapors held him pinned. Laughing, the Wild Wraiths ran off with the zombie head and the ball, leaving them trapped.

"What's going on?" Evilla asked. "They're waiting!

One minute before halftime; they're not going to give the Skull-crackers any chance to even the score! Ha! The Wild Wraiths always were sadistically cruel! Twenty seconds ... ten ... five ... they're pushing the ball ... the Wild Wraiths score!"

The bell rang a moment before the horn blew; halftime ... and the Skull-crackers were losing.

Slowly the white, silver-sparkling vapors dissipated, but the damage was done. The halftime score was two to one. The Wild Wraith's plan had succeeded.

"I'm sorry," Martin said after they'd run off the pitch and huddled together. "My strategy didn't work."

"I think it worked ... once," Stabbing said.

"So do I," Murder said. "But Smalls try to stay inside the safe-zone, so it doesn't get used much."

"You didn't see it because you kept getting attacked by Jailnet Lazy," Veils said. "Shadows don't wear jewelry ..."

"That must be their strategy," Rude said. "She's been assigned to keep you occupied."

"What can I do?" Martin asked. "She's slow, but she's like ... thick air!"

Suddenly Martin had an idea. He first looked at Snitch, but then he turned to Brain.

"Brain, can you blow on me ... really hard?" Martin asked, and to demonstrate, he blew his breath at Brain.

Brain shrugged, took in a deep breath, and blew at Martin so hard he stumbled backwards.

"Perfect!" Martin said. "Brain I need you to blow ...

just like that ... at Jailnet Lazy!"

"Brilliant!" Rude exclaimed. "That should blow her right out of the safe-zone ... maybe out of the game!"

"Do they have any more scrolls?" Martin asked.

"Each team only gets one scroll per season, and one per playoff," Rude said. "Most use theirs in the first game, like we did, only ours didn't work, and I ended up breaking my leg in your bedroom."

"We need to take out the little vampire," Martin said. "I've got an idea there, but we need something to take out their Bigs!"

"We need to make sure they can't take out Snitch again!" Grand Wizard Bastile said. "I can't do another spell."

"How about earplugs ...?" Martin asked. "If he can't hear their taunts ...!"

"Where can we get earplugs?" Stabbing asked.

"I've got it!" Veils said, and she tore two strips off her jersey, made Snitch kneel down ... and she stuffed the rags into his ears.

"If we can control the zombie head, we can let the zaps take care of their Bigs," Murder said. "But we can't guarantee ..."

"In Wet-Feather War, Brain threw me, and then Crusto carried us ...," Martin said.

"That should work!" Crusto said. "There's no rule against it!"

"What ...?" Stabbing asked.

"Happy!" Crusto said. "You're the fastest; Martin,

Murder, and Stabbing could ride you to the ball!"

"They'll have to hold on real tight," Happy warned.

"We will," Murder promised.

"The game's about to start again," Bastile said. "Any other ideas?"

"Yes," Martin said. "Our knowledge of electricity gives us an advantage, but it only works outside the safe-zone. Even if we have to risk ourselves, we need to get the Wraiths away from the zombie head."

"Hurry ...!" Rude shouted.

One in each hand, Brain lifted Stabbing and Martin onto Happy's back, while Murder clasped hands with Happy. He tossed her up and she landed on his flank.

"Back again, you maniacal mongrels, it's ... me!" Evilla shouted into her microphone. "Evilla, the damsel of your dreams, and of course, the second half ... about to begin! Score is two to one, the Wild Wraiths winning thanks to a successful spell, but the Skull-crackers have been down-but-not-out before. Teams are lined up ... ready to start ... here's the horn ...! Let havoc reign...!"

Happy galloped forward, Stabbing clinging to his shoulders, Martin clinging to Stabbing, and Murder clinging to Martin. They reached the ball in only five seconds, long before the Wild Wraiths arrived. Murder seized the zombie head in her crook as Martin and Stabbing tried to help Happy push the ball, but their muscles were too weak for the task.

"Get back!" Happy shouted at them.

Both teams converged on the ball, and as before,

Jailnet Lazy dove at Martin.

"Brain ...!" Martin shouted, pointing at her with the curl of his hook-staff. *"Now ...!"*

Brain paused from shoving the ball with both hands just long enough to inhale deeply, and then he leaned over and blew with all his ogre might. Screaming a ghostly wail, Jailnet Lazy was blasted out of the zone, at least twenty feet backwards, where a bolt of lightning zapped her.

"Great!" Martin cried, and he ran to help Murder.

Martin found Murder trying to defend with the butt of her hook-staff as Fey Wraith attacked. Martin hadn't realized how tough handling the zombie head was ... and why they insisted he let Murder and Stabbing do it. Beside keeping your hook-staff spinning, to keep from dropping the zombie head, you had to move as the stone ball moved, keeping the edge of safe-zone over the center of the stone ball, covering only your Bigs, while being unable to defend against attacking Smalls. Yet his newly-learned hook-staff skills were no match for Fey Wraith's mastery.

"Stabbing ... I need a hand!" Martin shouted.

Confused, Stabbing tore free of Lynn DaBlair-Witch and jumped toward him. Before the werewolf could circle them, Martin grabbed Stabbing's right hand, squeezed hard on one finger, and stabbed the palm of his hand against the sharp point of Stabbing's index claw. Instantly blood welled, and Martin shoved his bleeding hand into Fey Wraith's vision.

"Blood ...!" Martin shouted at her. "Fresh, warm, tasty blood ...!"

Fey froze, fixated on Martin's palm. The dripping red blood seemed to mesmerize her, and Martin slowly drew her away. She followed as if hypnotized, and Martin led her out of the safe-zone.

Fey stared hungrily at him, and Martin glanced up at the dark clouds; *this could backfire!* But he was ducking his head and holding his staff low, while Fey was holding her staff high, dripping sweat, and wearing a thick silver necklace, bracelets, and many rings, and she was barefoot, like most Smalls ...

Zap!

The bolt could've struck either of them, but it clearly arced toward Fey, and she screamed and fell. Martin ran back into the safe-zone, seeing Jailnet Lazy also return, but at Stabbing's request, Brain blew hard on her, and she tumbled away again. Another bolt struck her, as she flew backwards, and then she fled from the pitch.

Stabbing easily kept Lynn DaBlair-Witch busy, freeing Murder to keep her position precise. He tried to drive the werewolf out of the safe-zone but she was too clever for that ... until Martin arrived to help. Together they dropped Lynn DaBlair-Witch onto her backside twice before Fey Wraith managed to rejoin the fray, her once-sleek black hair now frizzled.

Control of the zombie head let Snitch, Brain, and Happy push the ball closer to their edge, and eventually Mad Eyelean Con got zapped again, and without her strength, Mykill Gouge and Fright Fried were overpowered.

"Shantdareya scores!" Evilla cried. "Tied game!"

They jumped off the pitch and circled back, and soon they were lined up, ready to restart. Again, Martin, Stabbing, and Murder began mounted atop Happy's back. When the horn blew, they rode him into play, but Murder, riding in back, got zapped by a random bolt and fell off.

"Murder ...!" Martin shouted, but Stabbing held him still.

"She jumped off ... so Happy wouldn't get zapped ...!" Stabbing said, one hand on Happy and the other on Martin. "Hold on!"

However, as they neared the ball, they saw that they weren't the only strategists; Mad Eyelean Con had thrown Fey Wraith across the pitch, and she got to the zombie head first. Fey jumped onto the stone ball, snatched up the zombie head in her crook, and ran back toward her team.

"Dismount!" Happy shouted at them.

"No!" Stabbing shouted. "We need to protect you ... until we can get the head back!"

Snitch and Brain arrived at the same time as the Wraiths, and the battle began in earnest. Fey Wraith had the head, but Jailnet Lazy hadn't returned; following behind the others, Death Wall-ache, the small girl who was pale green and stitched together like a Frankenstein's monster, had taken her place. For a

Small, she looked strong, but she moved slowly, and Martin led her out of the safe-zone with ease. She had thick metal bolts sticking out of her neck; when the lightning struck, it seemed to target those.

Murder had returned, but Lynn DaBlair-Witch was fending her off, and Stabbing had so far failed to steal the zombie head. Martin thought of helping, but another idea struck him; Martin ran for Happy, jumped for his back, and bounced up onto the top of the rolling stone ball, walking carefully as it rolled.

"Dragon-steaks are delicious!" Martin shouted at Mad Eyelean Con. "When can I cook you?"

She scowled at him.

"Draglings aren't stupid!" she snarled, tiny tongues of flame slipping from between her thick fangs and sharp teeth.

Martin frowned; *his plan had failed!* Then he remembered something Stabbing had said. He reached over and pulled out one of the earplugs from Snitch's ear.

"We blew away your shadow!" Martin taunted the dragling. "I'll bet you can't blow me off this ball!"

Mad Eyelean Con frowned, then opened her wide mouth and sucked in a deep breath. As she did, Martin tossed the cloth earplug at her, and she sucked it in. Suddenly she choked, coughed, and Martin jumped off the ball, away from her.

Flames spewed from her choking maw, right over the top of the ball. Brain ducked, but Happy got burned.

Martin screamed; he hadn't expected that her fire-breath would travel so far, but what happened next occurred exactly as he'd planned.

"Flame-breath is illegal," Stabbing had said. "Draglings who use fire once get stunned, and if twice, then they get banished from the game."

Four referees pointed their wands, and four powerful bolts arced across the pitch. Mad Eyelean Con took all four blasts, and blazed yellow, screaming as only dragons can, before she fell.

Without Mad Eyelean Con, the Wraith Bigs were helpless, as Snitch and Brain pushed the ball steadily forward, yet Martin fell to his knees beside Happy, who had fallen into a divot, badly burned and still burning. Happy was gritting his teeth.

"Go ... help ... them ...!" Happy snarled.

Martin didn't; he pulled off his own jersey and used it to pat out the flames. The dragon-breath seemed to have been a liquid spew that ignited and kept burning, but the fires quickly smothered under his jersey; Martin was glad it wasn't as bad as it had first looked. Mostly, Happy had a two-foot circle of horse hair singed away, but little damage to the skin under it.

A dark cloud floated over them, and Martin got zapped, but he didn't care; he never stopped caring for Happy.

"Skull-crackers score!" Evilla cried. "Three to two, Shantdareya takes the lead!"

Moments later, Stabbing came running up, still

holding the zombie head, Snitch and Brain right behind him. Murder arrived a second later, and all of them helped Happy to his hooves, and Snitch and Brain supported him as he limped off the pitch in the protection of the zombie head.

Stabbing dropped the zombie head face-down onto the edge of the pitch as they left it. As he was little help supporting the huge centaur, Martin stopped to roll the zombie head upright.

"Is he all right?" the zombie head asked.

"I don't know," Martin answered, "but thanks for asking."

The referees were rolling the stone ball back to the center, and one of them pointed their wand at the zombie head, which rose up and floated back toward it.

"You're a real credit to these games!" the zombie head called.

Martin didn't feel like a credit; he'd gotten Mad Eyelean Con zapped, but Happy had suffered her flames.

The game turned into a rout. Don Alt-Pleasant, the minotaur, returned to take the place of Mad Eyelean Con, but he wasn't her equal. Crusto replaced Happy, but Snitch was still the strongest, and without the dragling, Mykill Gouge, Don Alt-Pleasant, and Fright Fried were no match. Martin was more than an equal for Death Wall-ache, and Murder and Stabbing matched Fey Wraith and Lynn DaBlair-Witch. While the Smalls equalized, in this game, the Bigs scored the points, and the Skull-crackers scored twice more.

Yet the Wild Wraiths weren't finished; Fright Fried confronted Martin as the teams met again.

"Stupid human ...!" the monstrous ratking shouted. *"You've taken us out of the playoffs, but we can take you out of the finals ...!"*

Abandoning the ball, Fright Fried jumped high, at Martin, to smash his massive bulk down on top of him ... and crush him. Instinctively Martin swung his hook-staff, but it only broke against the bulging chest muscles of the huge, hurtling ratking.

Suddenly Murder pushed Martin out of the way ...

Fright Fried crashed flat on top of Murder!

"Noooo....!" Martin screamed.

Four bolts from the referees zapped Fright Fried, but three voices screamed. Fright Fried screamed first and loudest, but from underneath him came Murder's muffled scream, and Martin screamed to hear it.

The game-time was almost over, but for the Shantdareya Skull-crackers, the playoffs were ended. When they rolled the singed and smoking Fright Fried over, they found Murder crushed beneath him, in a tangle of broken limbs, and still twitching from being zapped. She'd be out for months, if she recovered at all, and they didn't have a spare Small.

The Shantdareya Skull-crackers were out of the playoffs ...!

Chapter 24

Smashday / Sunday

Side-stepping the rules ...

Martin couldn't sleep all night. Murder was seriously hurt ... *because of him.* Happy had gotten badly burned ... *because of him.*

Happy would be fine before next week, but Murder was out; afterwards, Grand Wizard Bastile had healed her, like he'd healed Rude, but Murder would be bound to a wheelchair for weeks ... and on crutches after that. Even with healing magic, it might be months before she was strong enough to play again.

They didn't have months. They had to field three Bigs and three Smalls on Rompday ... or they'd have to forfeit the finals. Then either the Grave Gutters or the Neverlive Nasties would win by default, and all of

Shantdareya would lose.

Martin's opinion of the fans had taken a deep dive. The crowd had cheered when Fright Fried had tried to avenge the Wild Wraiths by crushing him ... and squashed Murder instead.

Why had she pushed him out of the way ... and taken his place ...?

Sunday dawned cheerlessly. In church, Martin prayed, but he didn't know if prayers extended to monsters. By the time he got back home, he headed to his room and closed his door. An hour later, a knock came.

"Martin ...?" Vicky asked.

"Go away!" Martin replied.

Vicky opened the door, and found him sitting on his bed.

"What's wrong ...?" Vicky asked.

"Who said anything was wrong?" Martin snapped.

Vicky stepped inside and closed the door.

"I'm not prying," Vicky said. "You're obviously upset, and I may have some advice."

"What ...?" Martin growled.

"First, never dismiss advice you haven't heard," Vicky said. "Maybe you'll find it useful, maybe not; you won't know until you hear it ... and take the time to consider it."

Martin clenched his teeth and frowned.

"Second, bad times happen, and being angry solves nothing," Vicky said. "You have to get over the anger or you'll never deal with the problem."

Martin growled softly.

"Third, imagination solves more problems than intelligence," Vicky said. "Not one problem ever had a solution until someone dreamed of it, and all the intelligence and education in the world ... in any world ... can't be properly utilized without imagination."

"Are you through ...?" Martin snarled.

"Imagination isn't just dreaming up weird stuff," Vicky said, and she opened the door and stepped out of his room. "Imaginative people are observant and insightful. They see puzzles in everything, the pieces, the people, and the patterns into which they combine. They identify and analyze everything. Then they find new ways to arrange the pieces and people, sometimes to force them into new patterns, but the best way is to shift the players so they naturally rearrange themselves ... and flow into the pattern you want. Observant re-arrangers, that's what imaginative people are ... and that's how they confront all problems, not to fight the problem, because fighters often lose. Imaginative people rearrange the players, the pieces and the people, into patterns that work for them."

Vicky closed his door behind her.

Martin fell into Crusto's arms, and he set Martin on the floor, looking around at all his teammates.

"The Wizard's Council says we have until Rompday to replace Murder," Grand Wizard Bastile said.

"Can we ...?" Martin asked.

"Monsters don't play on credit," Crusto said.

"We're broke," Grand Wizard Bastile said. "Whatever we offer, Veinlet Prize will offer twice that to keep others from joining us."

"His coffers are unlimited," Happy said.

"Where's Murder?" Martin asked.

Brain stepped aside. Murder sat in a wheelchair, mostly covered in bandages. One arm and both legs were splinted, and a tight band was holding her head erect to a pole running up her back. Martin ran to her, knelt down before her, and took her hand gently.

"Murder *... why ...?"* Martin pleaded.

Her eyes lowered to him, although her head didn't tilt.

"A ... teammate ... was in trouble ...," Murder spoke weakly, her voice trembling. "Would ... you ... have done ... any less ...?"

"No, but I wish you hadn't," Martin said. "I don't know what to say ...!"

"I ... understand," Murder said. "One of us ... but it's done. You ... must continue ..."

Veils came up and placed her hand on Martin's shoulder.

"We'll do all we can," Veils promised Murder.

"Martin, we need to talk," Grand Wizard Bastile said. "We only have two Smalls ... and we tried all night to hire another. After the Neverlive Nasties lost, I even tried to rent Craze Kinki from them, but Grand Wizard

Clod Pains refused."

"Many grand wizards don't want a team with a human on it to win," Crusto said. "They think if the Skull-crackers have to bow out without playing, then humans might be banned from the games."

"It's just prejudice," Stabbing said. "The same prejudice we ratlings get from ratkings."

"How can we get a new Small?" Martin asked.

"We can't," Grand Wizard Bastile said.

"What about magic?" Martin asked. "Could we bring another human ...?"

"I doubt it," Bastile said. "The argument that let you remain was that you'd already played in Round 1, even if only for the last few moments. I doubt I could get them to accept another."

"Could we make one?" Martin asked. "A zombie ... or a small golem ...?"

"Those spells take months ... assuming I could," Grand Wizard Bastile said. "My specialty is healing. Animation spells are difficult ... require years of study ..."

"We've thought of all these options," Rude said. "We hoped ... you'd have better ideas ..."

"What about Crusto ...?" Martin said. "We don't need a spare Big. If you could shrink him ...!"

"Crusto has to play," Stabbing said. "Happy ..."

"My burns ... are worse than we thought," Happy said, and he turned so Martin could see the huge bandage covering his flank. "I could play ... but one bump would render me invalid, and we'd lose."

"We can't lose," Brain said. "Shantdareya sinks ...!"

"He knows, Brain," Grand Wizard Bastile said. "I'm too old, Rude, Murder, and Happy are injured, and there's no one else ..."

"Veils ...?" Martin suggested.

"She's too young," Grand Wizard Bastile said. "They would never ...!"

"Could we disguise her?" Martin asked.

"It wouldn't work," Rude said. "They know Veils. They know she's too young."

Martin turned ... and looked at Veils. Her eyes met his ... separated only by a few months of birth ...

"Could ... magic ... age ... Veils?" Martin asked. "At least, make her old enough to play ...?"

"I ... I've never done a spell like that," Bastile said.

"But it's possible ...?" Martin asked. "It ... could work ...?"

"Let's do it!" Veils agreed.

"It would be dangerous ... and it would only last a few hours, maybe half a day," Bastile said. "If I started now, and did nothing but study all week ... I might be prepared by Rompday."

Martin glanced around ... at each of his teammates. Snitch looked confused ... and sad, as if he sensed the emotions around him even if he didn't understand them. Brain looked worried, as if he barely grasped their problem's complexity; he certainly couldn't think of a solution. Happy looked angry ... or maybe pained; Martin couldn't tell which. Crusto looked the same; it was hard to divine the expressions of a lizardman. In her wheelchair, Murder looked exhausted, as if she were straining to stay conscious. Stabbing looked hopeful and glanced at Veils expectantly. Rude instantly noticed Martin's stare and nodded to him. Only Grand Wizard Bastile looked hesitant.

"Veils, my precious granddaughter," Grand Wizard Bastile said. "There's a dozen ways this spell could go wrong. The spell could fail; I could age you too much ... or too little, or the spell could change you permanently ... or even kill you."

"I want to ...!" Veils said.

"I know you'll risk anything to play," Grand Wizard Bastile said. "The reservation is mine; I'm not willing to risk losing you. I love you, my sweet, and I can't ..."

"It's not just me," Veils said. "Shantdareya is mostly sunk ...!"

"Never has anyone asked me to do something I feared so much," Grand Wizard Bastile said. "You're asking me to risk half of everything I love ... you ... for the rest of everything I love."

"Bastile ...," Murder whispered.

Everyone fell silent, and Grand Wizard Bastile leaned toward Murder.

"Trust ... Veils ...," Murder whispered. "Do it ... for me ..."

Grand Wizard Bastile bowed and shook his head.

"I will begin my studies," Grand Wizard Bastile sighed. "My last spell broke Rude's leg ... and I spent a month preparing that one. If this one isn't better ...!"

"It will be," Martin said.

"How do you know ...?" Rude asked.

"Because everything depends on it," Martin said.

Veils stepped forward and placed her hand on Grand Wizard Bastile's robe.

"Grandfather, I have faith in you," Veils said.

Grand Wizard Bastile looked down and sighed heavily, then he turned and slowly walked toward the door.

"I'll be in the Wizard's Archive," Grand Wizard Bastile said. "I may be there a while ..."

They watched him leave in silence ... no one moving. However, after the door closed behind him, Veils smiled brightly.

"Thank you, Martin," Veils said, and many repeated her thanks.

"We don't have time for thanks," Martin said. "What's the next game?"

"Pole-Jump Smash," Happy said. "It's not good; it's a risky game at best."

"It's a fast game," Crusto said. "A high-scoring game that many get hurt playing ..."

"Rules later," Rude said. "First, Martin needs to learn to jump ..."

They walked together out to the pitch. The stands were empty, but tall again, as they'd been when Martin had sat in them and watched the Net-Door Maze game. The Trip-Hook Roller pitch was gone, the divots, blocks, and floating dark clouds replaced. Now he saw a series of four tall, curved walls. As they neared them, Martin saw that each end boasted a tower, a raised platform ten feet high, and two ten foot high curved walls radiated out from each platform. The middle section, where the curved walls almost met in the center, had wide open spaces to each side.

"Pole-Jump Smash," Rude said. "Veils, Stabbing, show him."

Crusto pushed Murder closer, and Veils and Stabbing walked forward. To Martin's surprise, they picked up long poles that were laying on the ground, raised them horizontally, and ran at a wall. At the last moment, they dipped the front end of the pole into a small hole, sprung up on the poles as they bent, and vaulted over a wall.

"Pole vaulting!" Martin cried.

"What ...?" many voices asked.

"You know this game ...?" Rude asked.

"I know pole vaulting, but humans jump over a raised pole, and the one that goes highest wins," Martin said.

"Our fiberglass jump-poles do come from the human world," Happy said.

"Jumping highest doesn't help," Rude said. "Smalls just have to get over the walls ... and up onto the platform."

"With the zombie head," Crusto added. "Whenever you get all of one team's Smalls, and the zombie head, up onto a platform, then you score one point."

"What's the difficulty?" Martin asked.

"The Bigs can temporarily lift a wall ... make it higher," Crusto said. "Two Bigs are chained together by one hand, and they range out through the narrow doors. Their other hand carries a flexible rubber club. They can hit Bigs of the other team with their clubs, but Smalls can't be hit by clubs. The third Big stays in the back circle and defends the platform, and he can't attack Smalls, either, unless they attack him."

"Does he get a club?" Martin asked.

"No, but Bigs can grab your jump-pole ... and yank it out from underneath you as you try to top the tower," Rude said. "Smalls have to be quick ... and balanced ... or they fall hard."

"There are thick pads on the ground lining the foot of each wall," Happy said. "Bigs can't step on them ... that's a foul, but a Small that tops any wall can fall straight down on the other side, and land safely on its pad."

"There are no pads in the center," Rude said. "Smalls that get dropped onto dirt get hurt."

"No Big can hold onto a pole once the Small is no longer touching it; they have to drop it right away," Crusto said. "Bigs can't carry or throw a Small of their own team, but they can throw Smalls of the opponent's team, using their poles, but only over one wall ... usually in the worst direction. Bigs can't climb over a wall; they have to use a door."

"There are steel plates in front of each wall-section," Happy said. "When Bigs stomp on a plate, that section of wall raises eight feet. Our poles are too short to get over a raised wall."

"The walls-tops are flat ... and a handspan wide," Rude said. "Smalls can climb on them, walk on them, or stand on them, but you don't want to be on a wall-section when it rises; few could hold on, and that's a long way to fall."

"Can Smalls use the doors?" Martin asked.

"Of course not," Rude grinned. "That would make it too easy. Not to mention that it's a foul for a Small to pass through a door ... and enemy Bigs love to throw Smalls through doors ...!"

"How do you get your pole over a wall after you jump?" Martin asked.

"There are spare poles littering the ground in every section," Rude said. "You just pick them up. Of course, that makes running more difficult; you have to jump over them as you run. Also, poles can be used as weapons against other poles, which really works when an enemy is trying to jump away with the zombie head: a Small can swing his pole and swat another Small's pole right out from underneath him."

"Each tower has a ladder for climbing down," Stabbing added. "We can climb up the ladder, but it's risky; Smalls of the other team can vault at us and knock us off before we get to the top."

"That sounds dangerous," Martin said.

"It is, but it's also the finals, the last game of the season," Happy said.

"Unless Bastile botches the aging spell, in which case our last game ... was our last game," Crusto said. "If we don't have three Smalls on Rompday, Grand Wizard Veinlet Prize automatically wins the finals, and gains the staff of Borgias Killoff, and Shantdareya sinks into the sea. However, just in case, let's let Martin practice, shall we ...?"

Chapter 25

Stompday / Monday

To gift a solution ...

Martin kept quiet until after his parents left.

"Vicky, when someone gets hurt ... helping you ... how do you thank them?"

"Who got hurt?" Vicky asked.

"Hypothetical," Martin said.

Vicky frowned.

"How badly hurt?" Vicky asked.

"Wheelchair ... broken legs ... and burns," Martin said.

Vicky looked deeply troubled ... and then she grew serious.

"Gifts can be what others need, want, tokens, or what

you want," Vicky said. "The best gifts are what people need; if they're hurt, they need treatment, medicines, and care ... and sometimes just company, someone to be with them, to do what they can't. You can't heal broken legs, but those are painful, and may need painkillers. Burns need antiseptic ointments; there's a small tube of burn cream in mom's medicine cabinet. When someone can't do without something, you provide it; not only does that give them what they need, but shows you cared enough to be thoughtful about their needs.

"What people want is equally thoughtful. You have to put their desires before yours, even if you wouldn't want that for yourself. Everyone dreams of something; find out what they dream about, and make their dream come true.

"Tokens are unthoughtful, gifts people bring when they don't know what the other wants, like flowers and chocolates; they're good gifts, and people like them, but they're usually not targeted to specific needs or wants.

"The worst gifts are what you want, rather than what they want. You may think a new baseball glove is a great gift, but that doesn't mean everyone thinks that. Giving people gifts that you want, rather than what they want, shows thoughtlessness and vanity, and those are the worst gifts."

Martin thought hard, and in his head added up all the money that he owned.

"Vicky, I'm going outside to exercise," Martin said. "After dinner, I need to go shopping. Could you drive me ... please ...?"

Martin fell into Brain's hands carrying a big plastic bag in one hand and a bouquet of flowers in the other. His teammates looked shocked, but once Brain set him down, he went straight to Murder and presented her with the flowers.

"These are for you," Martin smiled, and he dug inside his bag and pulled out a plastic bottle. "These are aspirin, which helps lessen pain. You swallow them with lots of water, without chewing them, and they'll help. I wish I could give you something stronger, but it's all I could get. And this ..." Martin pulled two large tubes out of his bag and handed both to Happy. "... these are burn creams. You gently cover burns with them, and they cool the pain and make them heal faster. And here's a bottle of aspirin for you, too. I'm sorry you both got hurt. Where's Bastile?"

"He ... he's in the Wizard Archives," Rude said.

From his bag, Martin pulled out a thin stack of papers.

"I printed these from a medical website," Martin said. "They're instructions for caring for burns and broken limbs ... I thought they might help ..."

"I'll take them ... and see he gets them," Rude took the papers as if they were priceless treasures. "What's a website?"

"I'll tell you later," Martin said, and he pulled more papers out of his bag. "These are for all of us Smalls. I searched for ... well, these are human documents written by our best pole vaulters ... on the techniques they use ... their methods for jumping higher than anyone else. They might have some clues to improve our game."

"How did you get these?" Veils asked excitedly, and she leaned over his shoulder to look at the words and diagrams. "Can you read them?"

"Of course," Martin said. "We'll read them on the pitch ... so we can practice them."

"That's invaluable!" Crusto exclaimed.

"I can get these on any sport," Martin said. "Boxing, wrestling ... even swimming."

"Crusto was born in the ocean!" Stabbing laughed.

"Wisdom should never be discounted," Rude said. "The secrets of experts; these must've cost a fortune!"

"They're free ... if you take the time to do the research," Martin said.

Every eye bulged.

"Well, the next time I visit the human world, I must stay longer!" Rude said.

"Anytime ... except now," Martin said. "Murder, Happy, ... I'm sorry you got hurt, and I'd do anything to undo your injuries, but since I can't, I'll do all I can to make sure we win the Grotesquerie Games."

His teammates cheered, and many hands patted his back. Veils hugged him tightly, and Murder made him lean close to her face so she could kiss his cheek.

"Thank you, Martin," Murder said, holding her flowers lovingly with her uninjured hand. "You ... really are magnificent!"

The whole team walked out to the pitch, Brain carrying Murder, which was gentler on her than rolling her wheelchair across the dirt and grass. Martin, Stabbing, and Veils entered the pitch, and began sorting through the papers while the others watched and listened.

"Look at this picture," Martin said to Stabbing and Veils. "Look at how she holds the pole. Every human pole vaulter holds their pole like this. They've figured out what's the best way to get the maximum height out of every jump, and they all agree these are the right hand positions."

Stabbing picked up a pole and tried it.

"Looks strange," Stabbing said. "Feels strange."

"That's because you're not used to it," Martin said. "Try it ... and see if it helps. But not yet; there's more. It says you don't just carry the pole, you hold it up, like this, and run like you're pushing it. Keep your back and head straight; you need to go up, so you want to start out as tall as you can. Keep your hands apart, and when your pole starts to bend, push your forward arm to its fullest extension, straight and rigid, and pull down hard with your back hand; this will extend the bow of your pole to its maximum, which helps lift you higher. Now, humans run a set distance they choose for each attempt; we need to count our steps and see what works best for us."

Except we'll have Bigs chasing us, or have to jump

over chains and fallen poles ...!" Stabbing argued.

"Let him finish!" Veils scolded.

"We'll have to alter these techniques," Martin said. "We're playing a different game, so we have different goals. We'll study these rules, take from them every advantage we can, and not worry about the rest. Now, these ruts we stab our poles into ... they call them boxes, and here's how to best aim at them ..."

Martin read for another ten minutes, describing the run, the bend of the pole, the best positions of the body, how to lift and extend, and even how to properly land on the pad below for maximum safety. Stabbing looked doubtful, but afterwards, he tried doing what Martin had described ... and jumped so high he cried out in fright, and had to drop down to land atop the wall. He stared down disbelieving, and then dropped off onto the padded mat on their side.

"It worked!" Stabbing exclaimed.

"Knowledge is strategy," Martin said loudly, and he glanced back at Rude. "The man ... I mean, the monster who knows the most techniques can choose the ones that work best for them."

"Don't worry," Veils said to him, and she gently squeezed his arm. "You may come from the human world, but as far as we're concerned, you're a monster."

"Thank you," Martin said, trying not to laugh at how that would sound in a conversation on Earth. "Now, Veils, you give it a try."

Veils matched the described hand positions. She

held her pole horizontally, ran straight, and pushed it hard into a box, one of the many small holes which were positioned before every section of wall. Her pole bent almost double, and she flew completely over the wall and dropped onto the other side. As she fell, they could hear her cheer.

"That was amazing!" Veils shouted as she ran through the door.

"Let's read some more, and then I need to try it," Martin said. "I need practice, too."

Reading instructions from the papers proved much easier than performing their teachings. Martin kept missing the rut in the dirt, the box, and several times his pole pulled from his grip at the limit of its bend, and Martin tripped over the thick pad and slammed into the rock wall. When he did make it to the top of the wall, twice he got his feet hooked on the top of the wall while he still clung to his pole, which never came close enough to the wall for him to mount, and he had no choice but to fall safely to the pad. Several times he didn't make it, but caught the top edge of the wall with one hand, and had to let go of the pole to clamber up.

Stabbing and Veils liked the new techniques, but they'd done this many times, and their advice and tutelage helped Martin make it over the wall for the first time. He made a mental note: when a person with personal experience tells you how to do something, consider the possibility that they may know what they're talking about.

As he thanked everyone for their help and encouragement, Rude laid a hand on his shoulder.

"Martin, we're teaching you our games, but you're changing our games," Rude said. "You think circles around most monsters, and your ideas are revolutionary. Teams across Heterodox will be studying your strategies for years. If you really want to help us, tell us: how do you always know what to do?"

"I don't," Martin said. "I'm ... just winging it."

"Winging ... without wings ...?" Rude asked.

"What he's trying to ask, I think," Happy interrupted, "... is, how do you do it? Are you just a natural strategist? Are you just smart ... or do you know things we don't ...?"

"Actually, no," Martin said. "It's not brains or knowledge. I'm ... imaginative."

Martin paused; *was he really repeating his sister Vicky's advice?*

"Imagination ...?" Rude asked. "That's the key to a door I'd like to unlock. But how ...?"

"I ... watch ... and think," Martin explained. "Every problem is a puzzle. It has people, things, and actions, and if you look deeply enough, you see their patterns. You can fight against a problem ... or you can ... rearrange the people and things, and alter their actions, and let their new relationships change the patterns ... and let the problem solve itself. Anyone can do it ... you just have to look at the whole problem, from everyone's perspective, not just look at the part that affects you."

Chapter 26

Smiteday / Tuesday

Jump into a secret meeting ...

"What are you doing?!?" Vicky screamed.

Martin froze, looking down at his sister, who was looking up at him with wide-eyed terror. He was walking across the highest beam of his swing set, balancing upon its thin, top-most steel bar.

"Get down from there ... slowly ... and carefully!!!"

Martin chuckled, jumped off, and caught himself at the last moment, his hands gripping the top pole, before he dropped to the ground. Suddenly Vicky was shaking him violently.

"Don't you ever do that again! That was dangerous!"

Martin waited until she was done, although her frantic, wide-eyed expression didn't lessen.

"I'm not taking risks," Martin said. "I'm training."

"Training to break your neck ...?" Vicky demanded.

"Training to do things most people can't," Martin said. "That's what sports are all about."

"Are you kidding me?" Vicky asked. *"You could've gotten killed!"*

Martin stepped back, out of her reach, and suddenly he did a back-flip. While Vicky watched, disbelieving, Martin leapt onto the climbing rope and pulled himself up, using only his arms, and then swung to the pole and scissored his legs around it, then slid slowly down without using his arms, and just before he reached bottom, he dropped his upper body, hands to the ground, and cartwheeled back to his feet.

Vicky stared, her mouth agape, but finally she swallowed and spoke.

"Martin, you're never to do that again ...!"

"But ...!" Martin argued.

"Never!" Vicky shouted. "I'm responsible for you, and I'm not going to explain to mom and dad how I let you crack your skull doing stupid tricks without proper safety tools! Athletes who try stuff like that wear harnesses and practice over pads and nets."

"I don't have those!" Martin argued.

"Until you do, you stay on the ground!" Vicky ordered. "I see you up there again ... and you'll never exercise again ... not once ... not while I'm in charge!"

Martin arrived ready to practice. He was angry at Vicky, and determined to do whatever it took to prepare himself to win the finals, no matter what. Brain caught him as he arrived. Rude, Snitch, and Crusto were there, and all welcomed him. They walked out to the pitch together.

"We've been thinking," Rude said as they walked. "We still have to worry about next year. After the finals, maybe you could come to Shantdareya, and teach us more about how you do strategy ...?"

"I'd be glad to, but for right now, I need to stay focused," Martin said.

"Of course," Rude said. "Plenty of time for that later."

Happy was standing beside Murder, who was still holding the flowers Martin had given her. She was watching Veils and Stabbing practice jumping over the nearest wall. In the distance, he saw the Grave Gutters leaving the pitch; Slug Gormet-Wreather, the huge sphinx that had nearly crushed Jackknife Illson, the minotaur Jerk Goldboom, and the yeti and bigfoot, Bruise Clambell and Pansthorny Chopkins. Those Bigs had knocked the Barkrover Bullies out of the playoffs, and they wouldn't be going any easier against the Skull-crackers in the finals. He knew Jangelly Kurtails, Barbaric Steal, and the banshee Damhell Hairy were somewhere close, even though he couldn't see them, and he'd soon have to face the Smalls that had beaten

Aunt Honey Peekings.

Murder called him over and gave him another kiss on the cheek, thanking him again for the aspirin and flowers. Martin blushed, but then he walked straight onto the pitch and picked up a pole. He tried stepping on a metal plate, just to see what it did, but he didn't weigh enough to trigger it. Martin jumped and stomped on the plate three times, kicking with all his might, before it triggered. The top of the wall-section shot up eight feet higher ... so fast it startled Martin. Only a second passed between the stomp and the rising of the wall; Martin could never hope to jump an eighteen foot wall with a twelve or fourteen foot pole, which seemed to be all that they had.

Martin practiced as he'd never done before, focusing on each step of every jump, the run, the stabbing of the box, the bending of the pole, the holding on tightly as it snapped straight, and the clearing of the wall. He exercised until sweat soaked his jersey, which was still burned from extinguishing the flames on Happy. Trolls, ogres, and certainly Slug Gormet-Wreather could reach up and pluck a Small off the top of a ten-foot wall, so he focused on making it completely over the wall each time. He also practiced mounting the platforms at each end, by vaulting or climbing its ladder, but he wondered how he'd jump and score at the same time.

"The zombie head will be inside a loose rope net," Stabbing explained. "You can snag it easily, and loop any strand over your arm."

"That rope net is a danger, too," Veils said. "It's easy to grab, and enemy Smalls will try to snatch it from you, if they get close enough. Remember, we can toss the zombie head to each other, even over walls."

"Yes, but to score, all the active Smalls of one team must be together on the platform with the zombie head," Stabbing said. "In Pole-Jump Smash, once two Smalls have the zombie head on their pitch, then every member of the other team will try to block their last Small from reaching them. You can't attack a Small or steal the zombie head once they're on the platform, and you can only keep the zombie head on your platform for five minutes, or it's a foul. If it looks like five minutes will pass before Veils and I get to you, you have to jump off ... with the zombie head, or just kick it off, or you'll get zapped."

"Can we get the zombie head ... in the net, so we can practice with it?" Martin asked.

"Sure," Stabbing said. "I'll get it; you two need the practice, especially Veils."

"Me ...?" Veils asked.

"You," Stabbing replied to Veils' surprised expression. "You're a great Small ... right now ... but the only way we'll get to play tomorrow is if Bastile's spell works right ... and his last one failed utterly. If it does work, you'll need to be aged enough that no one recognizes you, which means that you'll have a different body than you have today, and you won't have a chance to find out how it moves until you're on the pitch."

Stabbing turned to go, but then he looked back at Martin and Veils.

"While I'm gone, you two keep practicing, but do so safely," Stabbing said. "We all need practice, but don't take any risks. We can't afford an injury tonight."

Martin and Veils practiced, racing each other from one platform, jumping over all four walls, to the other platform. Veils got ahead of him, but he soon caught up, and then he passed her, and jumped over a wall while she was still running to get a pole.

Suddenly a gray mist enshrouded Martin. He looked up and saw a tall, dignified, handsome man standing before him, wearing a black wizard's robe trimmed in deep orange.

"Good evening, Martin Mulberry," he said. "I am Grand Wizard Veinlet Prize."

Martin froze; after his fall to the padding, he had no weapons, not even a pole. He jumped to his feet, wondering what he should do.

"Please, don't be alarmed," Grand Wizard Veinlet Prize said. "I'm not here to hurt you. I just wish to speak, and have a friendly conversation, with you."

"Veils ...!" Martin shouted. *"Stabbing ...!"*

"Oh, they can't hear you," Grand Wizard Veinlet Prize said. "I wished our conversation to be private, and it wouldn't be fair of me to expect you to waste your precious practice time talking to me. No, this fog gives us a few special moments, outside of normal time. We won't be interrupted in here."

Martin stepped to the side and peered through one of the open doors; Veils was motionless, reaching for a pole on the ground while Murder, Rude, and their Bigs watched her.

"What do you want ...?" Martin asked defensively.

"My friend, that attitude is undeserved," Grand Wizard Veinlet Prize said. "You're not my prisoner. You can walk through that door, or out of my cloud in any direction, and you'll return to normal time. Of course, our chance to speak will be gone forever. Is that really what you want?"

"I don't know," Martin said. "What do we have to talk about ...?"

"First, I wish to congratulate you," Grand Wizard Veinlet Prize said. "It's been a long time since I visited the human world, and I must say, your human race is as impressive as ever. I'm glad you're here. You've had a wondrous effect on our population ... on every monster in Heterodox."

"Is that why you let me stay ...?" Martin asked.

Grand Wizard Veinlet Prize smiled.

"There you go again, showing superior intellect," Grand Wizard Veinlet Prize said. "Except for the grand wizards, the monsters of Heterodox have never seen intelligence as great as yours ... and never guessed that intelligent strategy could defeat strength and savagery. It's a lesson that's doing them good."

"You let me stay ... to help civilize the monsters?" Martin asked.

"Why ... yes," Grand Wizard Veinlet Prize said. "The grand wizards stopped them from killing each other when we started providing their food, and we've taught them to grow and raise food of their own, so they won't be dependent upon us forever."

"What happens to the monsters when you stop providing their food?" Martin asked.

"The same thing that happened when Adam and Eve were kicked out of the Garden of Eden," Grand Wizard Veinlet Prize said. "Monsters will become the masters of their own lives ... and find their own destiny. We grand wizards want to give them every chance to do that. That's why we needed you."

"Why ...?" Martin asked.

"You tell me," Grand Wizard Veinlet Prize said.

Martin paused and thought about it. If everything that Grand Wizard Veinlet Prize had said was true ...

"You need the monsters to learn to think for themselves ...," Martin said, "... to value thinking."

"Exactly," Grand Wizard Veinlet Prize said. "We want them to expand their interests; a monster who limits his interests limits his life. We can teach them everything they need to know, but they expect a grand wizard to be smarter than a monster. We needed someone they wouldn't expect would be smarter than they are ..."

"But I'm not," Martin said. "My advantage is books, television, and movies. I've seen more things, and watched a thousand more stories, so I'm able to draw upon more experiences than any one person could have in a single lifetime. I've read enough books and seen enough shows that I've collected a wider base of experiences ... from which I can draw better conclusions."

"That's very observant!" Grand Wizard Veinlet Prize said. "Perhaps we should expand their practices of theater and story-telling."

"Yes, because plots repeat each other, again and again, and after a while, you can see how things really are ... see their patterns ... even if someone's trying to hide the truth from you," Martin said. *"Wouldn't you agree that's true ... Master Grand Wizard Borgias Killoff ...?"*

The grand wizard stared at him.

"How did you know ...?" he asked.

Martin smiled knowingly.

"Master Grand Wizard Borgias Killoff surrendered his staff, the most powerful staff ever, and vanished," Martin said. "Shortly afterwards, Grand Wizard Veinlet Prize appeared out of nowhere, with all the powers of a great wizard, and none of the other grand wizards knew who he was or where he came from. That's an easy connection ... and a plot I've seen a hundred times."

"You are an amazing young man," Master Grand Wizard Borgias Killoff said. "Tell me, what do you intend to do with this knowledge ...?"

"In a story, I'd blackmail you and force you to lose the finals on purpose," Martin said.

"I trust you have more honor than that," Master

Grand Wizard Borgias Killoff said. "Besides, I could change the laws for the next season .... to block humans from playing in our games ..."

"Why ...?" Martin demanded. "Why did you abandon your staff and walk away?"

"Grand Witch Maim La Nuormal," Master Grand Wizard Borgias Killoff said. "She's so beautiful ...! I was short, and old, and I loved her as only a grand wizard could, but she refused me."

"So you abandoned your previous life, changed your appearance ... and now ...?" Martin asked.

"Grand Witch Maim La Nuormal and I have been dating for two hundred years," Master Grand Wizard Borgias Killoff said.

"You've kept your secret for two centuries?" Martin gasped. "Why ...? Why not tell her ...?"

"Grand Witch Maim La Nuormal is an excessively proud woman," Master Grand Wizard Borgias Killoff said. "By the time I realized how angry she'd be to learn that she'd been tricked, it was too late; my funeral ship had sailed ... and my mistakes were embalmed. It's been no easy task to deceive her ... that stupid flying castle of hers has many powers, and threatened to reveal everything ...!"

"So you sent her to duel Grand Wizard Bastile Wraithbone ...?" Martin exclaimed.

"I couldn't drop her castle into the sea myself; she'd have never forgiven me," Master Grand Wizard Borgias Killoff said. "So I tricked others into goading her, rather than do it myself. I never meant for her to sink the whole island of Shantdareya ...!"

"You're to blame for everything ...!" Martin shouted.

"Grand Wizard Bastile Wraithbone was too gentle with her," Master Grand Wizard Borgias Killoff said. "I suspect he also craves the affections of Grand Witch Maim La Nuormal; most of the grand wizards do ... and they all hate me for dating her."

"You have to tell her ...!" Martin said.

"No, I ...," Master Grand Wizard Borgias Killoff began.

"You have no choice!" Martin said. "You spoke of honor; there's no honor in deceiving the one you love."

"If I could ...," Master Grand Wizard Borgias Killoff said.

"You could, but you won't," Martin said. "Otherwise you'd have done it by now."

Master Grand Wizard Borgias Killoff stared at him.

"You didn't come here to discuss your love-life," Martin said.

"No, I came to offer you gold ... a mountain of gold ... to quit the Skull-crackers tonight," Master Grand Wizard Borgias Killoff said. "I could make you the richest man in the human world. However, hearing you talk, I doubt if any amount of gold would suffice ..."

"You said I had honor," Martin replied. "No honorable man would accept such an offer ... or make such an offer. Maybe that's why the Grand Wizards have failed to civilize Heterodox ... because they haven't civilized themselves."

"How are we wizards not civilized?" Master Grand Wizard Borgias Killoff asked.

"Besides lying to your girlfriend, you could lend Grand Wizard Bastile your staff, the Staff of Master Grand Wizard Borgias Killoff," Martin said. "He just needs it to raise his island ..."

"No promise could insure its return ... and no power could take it from him," Master Grand Wizard Borgias Killoff said. "I need my staff back ..."

"Trust is abundant among the civilized," Martin said.

"Have the Skull-crackers found a third Small?" Master Grand Wizard Borgias Killoff asked.

"It's possible," Martin said, carefully not revealing any secrets.

"You will lose tomorrow," Master Grand Wizard Borgias Killoff said. "If you're lucky, you'll only lose the game ...!"

"Whether I win or lose tomorrow, you've lost ... today," Martin said.

Without another word, Master Grand Wizard Borgias Killoff raised his staff, the gray mist vanished, and with it, the master grand wizard disappeared.

A moment later Veils came jumping over the wall.

"Aha! I caught up with you!" she said, and then she stopped smiling. "Martin, what's wrong ...?"

Martin couldn't answer her. All he knew was ... no matter what happened ... *he had to win tomorrow ...!*

Chapter 27

Rompday / Wednesday

Heed advice to win ...

"Vicky, I'm sorry," Martin said. "I shouldn't have been taking risks ..."

"Vicky, I'm sorry," Martin said. "I shouldn't have been taking risks ..."

"Do you know how much trouble I'd have gotten into if you'd gotten hurt?" Vicky asked. "Can you imagine how terrible I'd feel if you died while I was supposed to be watching you?"

"I know," Martin said. *"I'm sorry."*

Happy caught Martin as he fell into Heterodox thirty

minutes early. He first noticed Snitch, Brain, and Crusto, who were wearing thick plates of spiked armor, like Jackknife Illson, only more, with matching steel helmets. Martin understood; Bigs needed them for this game. The whole rest of the team was there ... except ...

"Where's Bastile?" Martin asked.

"He's finishing the text of his new scroll," Happy said.

"He said he wants to devote every minute to make sure it's correct ...," Crusto said, "... because ... if it isn't ...!"

Every eye turned to look at Veils. She looked nervous, wearing a plain white robe that reached to her ankles. Snitch looked confused, but everyone else looked worried.

The door opened, and from the crowd around the pitch, distant cheers echoed inside. Grand Wizard Bastile Wraithbone entered, and closed the door behind him. He was wearing a fancier purple robe than Martin had ever seen before, but he looked weary, pale, as if he hadn't slept in days. In his hand, he carried a large scroll.

He approached them in silent solemnity. The Skull-crackers parted, leaving Veils standing alone in the center. Grand Wizard Bastile stepped toward her.

"It's ready, and I've done my best," Grand Wizard Bastile said to Veils. "I'm still willing to call it off, even if it costs us the game; nothing is as important to me as you."

"No," Veils said. "Whatever the risk ... I'm willing to

take it."

"I know that, and I know better than to argue with you," Grand Wizard Bastile said. "You know the risks. I love you, and I'm as ready as I can get. Are you prepared …?"

"Do it," Veils said.

Bastile opened and lifted up the scroll, and Martin glanced at it. Beside the words, every inch of it was covered in complex magical symbols and signs.

Bastile cleared his throat and began to read.

"Time flows deep,
slow and pleasant,
Unto us,
does the future endow,
Override, I command,
flow of the present,
Bring to us
the future now."

Everything that could move did. Every monster, and Martin, began to shift, as if they were moving in every direction simultaneously, becoming a thousand ghosts of themselves. Time displayed every possibility, and their ghosts grew younger, or older, all at once. A loud wail filled their ears, and a deep rumble vibrated the stones beneath their feet. All of the magical symbols on the scroll leapt off the page, into the air, swirling and moving, cycling like the hands of countless clocks, turning like gears, and flipping like the pages of countless calendars. The paper of the scroll burst aflame into a brilliant light, and flashed to Veils, enveloped her, and shined so brightly everyone closed and shielded their eyes.

Slowly the wail died, and the floor stopped shaking. Martin looked, and saw everyone uncovering their eyes.

Veils stood, a child no longer. She was taller, firmer, expanded into the shape of a strong, mature young woman. She looked both ... slender and curvaceous, her dark hair much longer. Her face was ... perfect; Veils was beautiful beyond description. She looked to be about nineteen years old, and the robe that had reached to her ankles now reached only to her knees, revealing a pair of shapely calves. Even the points on her ears seemed longer.

Veils looked around at all of the wide eyes staring at her.

"Did ... did it work ...?" she asked, and then her hand touched her throat; her voice was that of a woman, not a little girl.

"Veils, you look ... fantastic!" Rude said. "No one will know who you are!"

"She's astounding!" Happy exclaimed.

"Bastile, you did it!" Crusto hissed.

Veils looked at Martin, whose jaw was hanging open.

"Martin ...?" she asked.

Martin swallowed hard, unable to speak. His eyes dropped to her bare feet, then rose up her shapely figure all the way to the face of the most beautiful woman he'd ever seen.

"Ummmm ... y-y-you ... g-great ...," Martin stuttered, unsure what to say.

"You'd best take a new name," Crusto said. "We can't call you Veils and keep your secret."

"What name?" Veils asked.

"I was thinking you might use your grandmother's name," Grand Wizard Bastile said.

"May I?" Veils asked.

"She would be honored," Grand Wizard Bastile said.

"What was her name?" Stabbing asked.

"Yuck Wand DeSnarlo," Grand Wizard Bastile and Veils said together.

"Just call me Yuck Wand," Veils added.

"Yuck Wand, I have some clothes that might fit you," Murder said softly. "Could you ... wheel me back to our dressing room?"

As soon as both women vanished, congratulations rained on Grand Wizard Bastile. Even Snitch insisted on shaking his hand, although Martin suspected he really didn't understand what had just happened. Martin also shook his hand, and Grand Wizard Bastile actually blushed, cheeks reddening, and large, smiling teeth shined between his heavy gray mustache and beard.

When the women returned, Martin gasped, surprised; Veils was wearing a thin, hooded purple cloak that fell to the floor and covered all but her face, of which only a thin slit could be seen. He had to look up to her; she was over a foot taller.

"It's time," Grand Wizard Bastile said, his voice

tremulous. "The final game of the playoffs is about to begin, and everything depends on us. You each know what you need to do. Let's go win ... for Shantdareya!"

They headed up the stairs and outside.

Cheers erupted as they stepped from the stadium's doors. The crowd was twice as big, and twice as loud, as Martin had ever seen it. Monsters were going crazy, leaping and cheering and waving signs and banners so fast Martin could barely tell which color they were. Most looked purple, but a lot of orange showed. This was their Superbowl event ... their ultimate celebration of sports.

A referee, in a yellow-striped robe, waited for them, and escorted them down a narrow path lined by floating red cords, holding back the crowd on both sides. The referee held his wand before him, which was sparking threateningly, and the one werewolf that jumped over the floating red cords was instantly zapped, and hurled back into the crowd, his every hair singed black. Limbs of every type reached over and patted Skull-cracker shoulders, all except Veils, who rode cloaked on Happy's back, while Brain carried Murder in her wheelchair. No one knew who Veils was, and the mystery of her kept all hands away.

"Here they come!" Evilla's voice blasted from the speakers. "Never before has any team entered the finals of the Grotesquerie Games undefeated! This is the team to watch! No one knows what to expect from them, and their unique tactics have turned Heterodox upside down!"

Martin frowned; *she meant that they'd allowed him, a human, onto the team ... but from Master Grand Wizard Borgias Killoff he'd learned the truth ... a truth he'd told no one ...!*

"Grand Wizard Bastile Wraithbone is leading them," Evilla continued. "There's Brain Stroker, the only ogre still in the playoffs, carrying Murder Shelling, that stately dryad who sacrificed herself to save a teammate from the revenge of Fright Fried, who was truly fried for his blatant foul, and may suffer a permanent banishment from the league. And here comes Allfed Snitchlock, that 'Troll who Pays every Toll', and Crusto Fernwalker, the most likable lizardman in the league. Behind him is Happy Lostcraft, who won't be playing today; the unlucky centaur bore the agony of Mad Eyelean Con's illegal fire-burst. Who's that ... the cloaked figure riding Happy ... is that their new Small ...? As you know, only Stabbing Kingz, the 'Ruinous Ratling', and Martin Mulberry, 'Martin the Magnificent', were left uninjured after their defeat of the Wild Wraiths. If they can't mount the pitch with three Smalls, this is going to be a very short game. And there they are: Stabbing Kingz and Martin the Magnificent!"

The cheers of the crowd swelled up and overwhelmed the speakers. Evilla's speech was cut off until they reached the edge of the pitch. There, Brain and Snitch picked up some stout shackles linked by a long chain, locked them on to opposite wrists, and picked up matching, flexible clubs.

"Here come the favorites!" Evilla shouted, and from the edge of the pitch Martin could see her, on her raised announcer's platform, wearing a sparkling black dress with hair to match. "From Lilliesput, here to challenge the last hope of Shantdareya, the legendary Grave Gutters of Grand Wizard Veinlet Prize! Leading them is the 'Egyptian Terror', Slug Gormet-Wreather, the most powerful sphinx ever, with that 'Stomping Bigfoot', Pansthorny Chopkins, and the 'Abomination of the Alps', yeti Bruise Clambell! Behind them comes possibly the best rookie this season, the 'Mighty Minotaur' Jerk Goldboom! And there she is, the favorite of the crowd, and mine, that 'Fairest Fouler', the 'Banshee of Beauty', Damhell Hairy!" Evilla waved both of her hands and jumped up and down, bouncing prettily. "Hi, Damhell! And here come her fellow Smalls! Jangelly Kurtails, the best brownie in the league, looking fully recovered, and that 'Darling from the Deep', naiad Barbaric Steal, who holds the highest-ever record for zombie-head snatches for the third season in a row! And look who's back: out from retirement, the 'Sweet Satyr', Caroling Jokers! Her return gives them a spare Big and a spare Small, neither of which their opponents have! Yes, here they come ... to play their guts out, Grand Wizard Veinlet Prize's greatest team ever, the Grave Gutters!"

Cheers exploded, the crowd bursting with excitement.

"And here are the august team leaders and members

of the Grand Wizard Council, to oversee the handing over of the staff of Master Grand Wizard Borgias Killoff," Evilla said, and Martin noticed the front row right behind Evilla was seated by dignified wizards in long, dark robes. "With great respect and gratitude, we welcome and honor Grand Wizards Beluga La Grossie, Lion Changeling, Clod Pains, Crass Gopherly, Pester Crushings, Peevish Lore, and, of course, Grand Witch Maim La Nuormal. They will judge any disagreements and witness the victory. Beside the pitch, Grand Wizards Bastile Wraithbone and Veinlet Prize stand with their teams, and tonight, one of them will triumph, and be rewarded with the greatest prize on Heterodox, the powerful magic staff of Master Grand Wizard Borgias Killoff!"

The crowd cheered again, but not as loudly; they came for drama and violence, not to honor wizards.

"Both teams stand beside the pitch, but will we have a game tonight?" Evilla asked. "Concern has mounted, and now is the time! Did the Shantdareya Skull-crackers find a third Small? Now we'll know! Players, mount the pitch, and prepare for the ultimate competition to begin, the finals of the three hundred and fourteenth Grotesquerie Games!"

"Good luck to all ... and good game!" Grand Wizard Bastile said.

Crusto led the way, followed by Snitch and Brain. Stabbing followed them, Martin right behind him, with Veils trailing.

"Twelve players are entering the pitch!" Evilla announced. "Looks like we will have a game tonight! But who is the mystery player inside the cloak?"

Their Bigs stepped in front of the platform, onto the hard dirt, and Stabbing, Martin, and Veils climbed the ladder leading up to their platform. Then Crusto signaled to Evilla, and waved for the crowd to be silent.

"Hold on, everyone!" Evilla said. "I think we're about to learn something ...!"

When the noise of the crowd dropped, Crusto raised his hissing voice so he could be heard.

"Beautiful Evilla, and honored Grand Wizards," Crusto spoke loudly to the whole stadium, "I give you the newest Small on the Shantdareya Skull-crackers: Yuck Wand DeSnarlo!"

With a dramatic gesture, Veils spun and threw off her thin purple cloak. Her long, dark hair flipped around her, landing over one shoulder, and the crowd gasped. Veils was taller than most Smalls, and attractive, a young woman with all the right curves. She was wearing a purple leather vest, purple leather gloves, and dark black skirt over matching shorts. She wore no shoes, but had a necklace of amethysts around her neck, with matching bracelets and anklets. Her long, pale legs, and bare shoulders and arms, looked muscular, trim but strong, and she stared out at the entire packed stadium as if challenging every player, wizard, and monster. The crowd stared in stunned disbelief ... and then exploded in applause and cheers.

Evilla also paused, staring in disbelief at the beautiful, majestic figure of Veils, eight years older than her true age. Then she seemed to realize she was saying nothing, and struggled to speak.

"Why ... ummmm ... Welcome, Yuck Wand DeSnarlo!" Evilla shouted, a false-looking smile plastered on her face. "Welcome to the newest Small of the Shantdareya Skull-crackers!"

The crowd kept cheering wildly, and Evilla struggled to draw their attention.

"The final playoff of the three hundred and fourteenth Grotesquerie Games is about to begin!" Evilla shouted. "Hold tight onto something ... preferably me ... and we'll get started. Just waiting on the signal from the referees ... and there it is! Prepare yourself, Heterodox! Here comes the horn ...! Let the mayhem begin!"

The trumpet blew, and Stabbing, Veils, and Martin jumped to the ladder and slid down to the dirt. All three Smalls ran for the nearest poles scattered around the pitch, and Martin was shocked when Brain and Snitch, still shackled together by a long chain, ran toward a solid wall section, and as they approached it, a door opened in the center of it, and then closed after they both ran through it.

"Hey, how did that happen?" Martin shouted, preparing for his first jump.

"Doors open when Bigs approach certain walls," Veils shouted.

"I wish somebody had told me!" Martin shouted

back.

Running at the wall, Martin targeted his box, which was really just a deep rut in the hard-packed dirt, and he shoved his pole inside it. Keeping his forward arm stiff, he bent the back end down as he kept running, and let his pole spring him over the wall. He, Veils, and Stabbing crashed onto the pad in the free zone, between the middle section and the platform sections. Other than them, it was empty; Snitch and Brain were gone.

They grabbed more poles and ran at the next wall. Springing over it, they dropped into the middle section into utter chaos. Snitch and Brain were there, fighting Pansthorny Chopkins, the hairy bigfoot armored, helmeted, and carrying a club exactly like Snitch and Brain, and Slug Gormet-Wreather, who wore armor and a helmet, but fought with her sphinx-strength, striking with her massive lion's paws. They fought savagely, smashing into each other, yet each pair of Bigs were still chained together.

As the Smalls dropped into the middle section, where the Bigs fought, Damhell Hairy, Jangelly Kurtails, and Barbaric Steal came flying to the top of the wall on the far side of the middle section. Martin recognized them all from their Net-Door Maze game against the Barkrover Bullies. He tried not to pause and watch the Bigs battle; Stabbing and Veils both ran to scrounge a pole, and Martin followed their example.

"Damhell has the head!" Stabbing shouted.

"Martin, get over that wall!" Veils shouted.

They snatched up poles, and to Martin's surprise, divided. Stabbing ran toward the Gutter's Smalls, and Veils ran along the walls they'd just leapt over. Martin obeyed, grabbed a pole, and ran toward the next wall. The Gutter's Smalls ignored him, but as soon as they got to their feet, they grabbed poles and ran for the wall behind Martin. Stabbing swung his pole at Jangelly Kurtails, who blocked his pole with her own, and Barbaric Steal ran in front of Damhell Hairy, and both charged straight at Veils. Barbaric Steal swung her pole, as Stabbing had, but Veils caught it and tried to dodge past her, toward Damhell Hairy.

Alone and unhindered, Martin jumped, carefully caught the top of the wall, and stood up upon it, bending his knees to keep his hold on his pole, which helped him balance. The free-zone beyond this wall was empty, so Martin watched the battle behind him from the top of the wall.

Damhell Hairy had a clear path to the other wall, but Stabbing and Jangelly Kurtails ran right behind her. Dangling from one arm, Damhell Hairy carried the zombie head in its large, loose, fully-enclosed net. She jumped to the wall, barely made it to the top, and scrambled up and fell over. Jangelly Kurtails and Stabbing both jumped right behind her. Jangelly Kurtails struggled, as Damhell had, but Stabbing cleared the wall with ease and vanished over it.

Veils and Barbaric Steal both ran away as the fighting Bigs neared them, and then they ran side-by-side toward the far wall. Either could have fouled the other, yet neither tried. Both made it over the wall and dropped out of sight, and Martin stood there, wondering why they'd left him behind.

He watched the Bigs fight; their flexible clubs smacked loudly, bending like rubber, clanging against their armored bodies, but the tough Bigs endured the blows and kept fighting. Slug Gormet-Wreather fought like a lion, her large, armored human head taking blows without flinching. Snitch struggled to shove her off him, and swung his hard rubber club whenever he could. Brain and Pansthorny Chopkins traded blows, clangs ringing across the pitch, mixing with the loud cheers of the crowd.

"Damhell is running, Crusto chasing her!" Evilla shouted into her microphone. "Jangelly Kurtails swings her pole at him; unlikely that a Small can hurt a Big! Stabbing converges! Yuck Wand DeSnarlo cuts off Barbaric Steal ... Barbaric throws her pole at Crusto Fernwalker ... she tripped him! Damhell Hairy runs, she jumps ... she has the zombie head atop the platform! Jangelly Kurtails is jumping, she's there, too! Barbaric Steal is running around; Crusto is chasing her, Stabbing and Yuck Wand DeSnarlo are trying to cut her off ... too late! She jumps ....! Barbaric Steal makes it to the platform ... Grave Gutters score!"

Martin groaned. *Why had they left him stranded atop a distant wall ...? He could've helped ...!*

In the distance, Martin saw Stabbing jump over the

wall.

"Stabbing Kingz drops into the free-zone!" Evilla shouted. "The Gutter Smalls can't leave the platform until the zombie head is picked up by ... Yuck Wand DeSnarlo has grabbed the zombie head! She's running to jump, but the Gutters are sliding down the ladder, hot on her trail!"

Martin saw the net-enclosed zombie head fly over the wall from the platform section into the free-zone. Suddenly he knew what was coming, and he dropped into the enemy free-zone and grabbed a fallen pole. Then he ran to the center and waited. Moments later, the zombie head came flying over the wall and crashed onto the dirt. Martin snatched it up, looped it on his arm, lifted his pole correctly, and ran toward the last wall.

Martin almost dropped over into the enemy platform section, but then he saw Bruise Clambell charging at him. Carrying the zombie head, Martin ran along the top of the wall, getting off the section he'd landed on just as the yeti reached the metal plate and stomped on it. Right behind Martin, that section of wall shot up eight feet, almost taking him with it. Then Stabbing leaped over, onto the far side. He dropped down onto the pad, rolled to his feet, and ran out into the open.

"Martin!" Stabbing shouted. "Throw me the head!"

Bruise Clambell was about to stomp on the next steel plate, yet Martin hurled the zombie head over the yeti's head, flinging it right to Stabbing. Caught with ease,

Stabbing took off running with the head, and he jumped over abandoned poles ... and didn't pick one up. The yeti ran after Stabbing, but Stabbing ran around to the back of the platform, and Bruise couldn't get at him. Every time he moved in one direction, Stabbing moved in the other.

"Get atop the platform!" Stabbing shouted.

Martin dropped down, picked up a pole, and ran toward the platform. It had boxes all around it, and Stabbing got Bruise to circle around to the far side, and then Martin jumped and topped the platform with ease.

"Here ...!" Stabbing shouted, and he threw the zombie head up to Martin. "Stay there!"

Martin caught the zombie head. Stabbing ran backwards and grabbed a pole, but at just that moment, Veils jumped over the last wall, into the platform area.

"Here they come!" Veils shouted.

Moments later, Damhell Hairy and Barbaric Steal topped the wall together and dropped down. Veils had grabbed two poles and kicked a third aside; she threw one pole at Bruise Clambell, and used the other to jump onto the platform. Bruise turned and scowled when the pole struck him, but too late.

"Yuck Wand DeSnarlo speared Bruise!" Evilla shouted. "He turns, and Stabbing uses the distraction! He's running, Damhell Hairy right behind him. She's got a pole! She's trying to block him! Stabbing jumps, Damhell swats the pole right out from underneath him ... he almost made it! He's clinging to its top edge by his fingers, about to fall ... No! Martin the Magnificent and Yuck Wand DeSnarlo have dropped to their knees on the edge of the platform! They've grabbed Stabbing's arms ... they're pulling him up ... the Skull-crackers score! The game is tied!"

Chapter 28

Rompday / Wednesday

The Pole-Jump Smash ...

Pole-Jump Smash was insanely vigorous. Martin was gasping for breath, and started for the ladder, but Veils grabbed his arm.

"You'll get zapped!" she warned. "We can't leave the platform top until the Grave Gutters control the zombie head!"

Stabbing threw the zombie head down, but their Smalls ignored it, and Damhell jumped over into the adjacent free-zone. In the distance, Martin could see Barbaric Steal resting on the wall between the middle and the other free-zone, watching the game, exactly as he'd done. From the top of the platform, the two walls on the Gutter's side looked like concentric half-circles flowing from the platform, and the far side of the pitch looked exactly the same. The middle-zone, where the Bigs were fighting, divided the two mirror-image halves. Where the middle walls were closest was the most dangerous place.

"Get ready!" Stabbing said. "I go, then Vei..."

"Yuck Wand ...!" Veils corrected him.

"Yes, and then Mart ...," Stabbing began, but Jangelly Kurtails suddenly snatched up the zombie head and threw it over the wall. Stabbing wasted no time or breath; he jumped to the ladder and slid down it. While waiting for Veils, Martin saw Barbaric Steal drop down to the far side of her wall, and as he reached for the ladder, Jangelly was vaulting to the top of the wall to the free-zone, and in the distance, Damhell, with the zombie head, was leaping over the wall to the middle.

By the time Martin had slid down the ladder to the dirt, Veils was running toward the wall, her pole horizontal. Her older body served her well; she drove her pole into the box and flew over the wall. Martin glanced at the Gutter's yeti, Bruise Clambell, who was their goalie, defending the scoring zone, as he lifted a pole, set his hands properly, and began to run. Despite the fighting, the long poles made terrible weapons, and the Bigs couldn't directly attack the Smalls, only grab at their poles, so scoring points was far easier than defending.

As Martin reached the top of the wall, looking down into the free-zone, he saw Jangelly jump from the middle toward the other free-zone, but the wall before her suddenly shot up eight feet; Snitch or Brain must have stomped on its metal plate. Jangelly smacked hard into the blank wall, and slid down her pole ... and suddenly she flew upwards, backwards, over the wall into the free-zone. *A Big must've caught her on her pole and tossed her!* She tried to grab the wall as she passed over it, but she missed, and flailed wildly before she landed away from a pad, onto the hard dirt, but with an expert roll, kicking up a cloud of dust.

Martin dropped to the cushion and regained his feet before Jangelly staggered back up. He snatched up a pole, preparing to run, when he saw how dazed she looked.

"Are you okay ...?" Martin asked.

Jangelly was clutching her knee, grimacing, but she looked up at him surprised. Then she nodded to him, and tried to put her weight upon her leg, and almost fell. She grabbed and lifted a pole, using it as a crutch, and hobbled back to where she could run. Martin watched her dumbfounded; *was she crazy? No one could pole vault while limping!*

"Bet you can't catch me!" Jangelly taunted.

Then she smiled at him, and ran, with no limp at all, and easily vaulted the wall. *She'd been faking!* Martin heaved his pole up and chased after her, using the box next to the one she'd chosen, and leaped to the middle.

There Martin saw Jangelly shout to Slug Gormet-Wreather. The giant sphinx turned and saw him, and she shouted to Pansthorny Chopkins. Both turned and ran away from Snitch and Brain, but not straight toward Martin. Then Martin saw it, ten feet of heavy chain dangled between them, each end shackled to one wrist of each Big, flying toward him. It caught him in his midsection ... and slammed him back against the wall. Martin doubled over, stunned, his stomach feeling like Snitch had punched him, the back of his head sore from slamming into the wall.

"Again ...!" Slug Gormet-Wreather shouted, wicked laughter in her voice.

Slug Gormet-Wreather and Pansthorny Chopkins drew back their shackled limbs, then slashed them forward. At the last second, Martin dropped flat onto the cushion, and the heavy chain hammered the wall just above him, showering chips of stone onto him.

"Martin ...!" Brain shouted, and he leapt atop Slug Gormet-Wreather, hammering his club down upon her helmet. Snitch plowed into Pansthorny Chopkins and slammed him against the wall, and suddenly a door opened, and Snitch's next push knocked Pansthorny Chopkins through the door into the free-zone, and then the door closed. With abominable savagery, Snitch then jumped at Slug Gormet-Wreather as she struggled to buck Brain off her back, and both began beating her.

Pained, Martin ran to get away from the combatting Bigs, afraid of getting hammered again ... or stepped on.

"Martin the Magnificent escapes certain death!" Evilla shouted. "He looks dazed, barely alive, but ... Jangelly

Kurtails is in the scoring area! Barbaric is on the platform with the head, Stabbing is dueling Damhell. Damhell and Jangelly start their runs ..., they jump ...! Crusto has grabbed Jangelly's pole! No! Jangelly jumped onto Crusto's head, and then bounced to the top ... Grave Gutters score!"

Martin grabbed a pole and leapt to the top of the wall between the middle and free-zone, and then realized his mistake. He dropped back, grabbed the same pole, and ran across the middle to the other wall, back toward their tower. The zombie head would be coming back, and he had to be ready to catch it.

Martin made it to the top of their middle wall and looked back just in time to see Veils fly over the wall into the free-zone behind him, and Stabbing dropped from the wall into the middle and grabbed a pole, looking back to see when the zombie head would come flying toward him. Pansthorny Chopkins had managed to get the door opened, and returned to the middle to rescue Slug Gormet-Wreather, but Bruise Clambell was still ahead, waiting for Martin to enter the scoring zone. Into the free-zone, Martin dropped down carefully, and snatched a fallen pole which had fallen across the cushions, and waited breathless seconds. Then the net containing the zombie head came flying over the wall, and he ran and caught it.

"You okay?" Martin shouted at the zombie head as he slung it over his arm.

"Better than rotting in a hole ...!" the zombie head

chuckled.

Stabbing bounced over, and they reached the top of the next wall together. Dropping down, they tossed the zombie head back and forth twice, playing 'keep-away' from the yeti, but then Stabbing reached the ladder and climbed to the top with the head. Furious, the yeti charged at Martin, fangs snarling and claws extended.

"You can't attack me!" Martin shouted at him. "You'll get zapped!"

Bruise Clambell stopped and frowned; he'd been trying to intimidate Martin, but couldn't directly attack him. However, Martin ran and jumped toward his opponent, as he had in Wet-Feather War. He jumped at the yeti, grabbed his long-haired arm, and swung behind him. By the time Bruise realized what had happened, Martin had snatched up a pole and was running for the platform.

Veils jumped to the top of the wall, then pulled up her pole and turned it horizontal, parallel to the wall. Damhell and Jangelly came leaping up a moment later, but Veils shoved her pole at them, and blocked both of them from reaching the top, although their combined impact knocked her backwards. Veils lightly dropped down onto the scoring side, while they both fell back into the free-zone. Then Veils lifted her pole, as Bruise charged her, and she ran straight at him, and didn't turn her angle of direction until her pole passed between his legs. Bruise tripped, and Veils ran for the ladder.

"Yuck Wand DeSnarlo is climbing! Where did she

come from? She's certainly a talented Small! From this distance, she's also rather attractive ... she's at the top! The Skull-crackers score!"

Now that he'd figured out the game, Martin breathed easier, although his chest still hurt. Yet the Grave Gutters soon scored again, just before the horn trumpeted the signal for halftime. The score was five to four, and Martin dropped his pole and hurried to get water, which he gulped deeply.

"Don't drink too fast," Happy said to him. "You're doing well out there."

"Yes, but they're winning!" Rude said.

"Only by one," Happy said. "We start the second half with the zombie head."

"So ... we can tie the score, but we need to get ahead!" Rude said. "If the game ends with us tied or losing ...!"

"Neither team has managed to steal the zombie head," Grand Wizard Bastile said. "So far, it's been a clean game. No one has gotten zapped."

"Any ideas, Martin?" Rude asked. "This is our last chance ...!"

Martin took a deep breath and let it out before answering.

"The only way to upset a clean game ... is to dirty it up," Martin said.

Hearing this, every Skull-cracker smiled.

"Huddle up!" Martin said. "Every villain in every story I've ever seen has used dirty tricks ... and I know all of them!"

As this was the finals, the halftime had a show. A monster marching band came out and performed, but they marched as badly as they played, and kept walking into each other. Then some dancing hobgoblins with batons came out to perform, dressed like cheerleaders, but between dropping their batons and accidentally hitting each other, they began fighting in earnest, and six referees waving wands and zapping combatants had to run out, separate them, and drive them off the pitch. Lastly, a handsome, tall elf came out and sang a tribute to all Heterodox in a deep baritone, a sort of anthem, and all of the monsters applauded when he finished.

When halftime was almost over the speakers began blasting again.

"Well, back to the game!" Evilla cried. "Once again, it's me, your scintillating sweetheart, Evilla, your gal glamorous, about to bring to you the exciting second half of the finals, to decide between the Grave Gutters and the Skull-crackers who shall reign supreme over the Grand Wizard's Council ... and who shall slink home in disgrace. So grab a Larva Lemonade and a fistful of Schezwan Scorpions, because the game is about to recommence!"

Martin and his teammates walked back onto the pitch and entered their scoring area. Martin watched Veils climb up the ladder, admiring the shape of her new, tall, fully-developed body, but he shook his head; he had a game to win, and no distractions, no matter how pretty, would help.

The zombie head was waiting for them at the top of their platform. Martin picked it up.

"Any suggestions?" Martin asked him.

"Just ... please ... cut me out of this net after the game," the zombie head pleaded. "I don't want to be trapped in here until the start of next season."

"It's a promise," Martin said. "Right after the game."

"The referees are signaling!" Evilla cried. "Now, for the championship, let insanity prevail!"

The trumpet blew, and the second half began exactly as the first half had, only the Skull-crackers scored first, tying the score at five. However, when the first Grave Gutter Smalls vaulted into the free-zone with the zombie head, Barbaric and the female satyr, Caroling Jokers, Martin met them with a fistful of dirt in each hand, which he flung into their eyes. Damhell, the only Grave Gutter Small without dirt in her eyes, chased Martin away, but Stabbing and Veils came flying over the wall, and together they pulled the zombie head from the blinded veteran. Less than two minutes later, the Skull-crackers scored again.

"A nasty trick ... but it worked!" Evilla shouted as the crowd cheered wildly. "Skull-crackers winning, six to five! Damhell looks angry; she knows the cry of the banshee is illegal, but who knows? Every claw is out, and the Grave Gutters want revenge!"

The Grave Gutters tied the score on the next

turnover, and then Stabbing got the zombie head to the platform ... and they scored again. Next, Damhell Hairy came flying over the wall, carrying the zombie head, and Martin lifted a pole and charged straight at her.

"Martin, you can't lance a Small!" Veils screamed.

Martin ignored her and charged Damhell, who stood, smiling huge banshee teeth; she'd gladly let Martin spear her, if he'd get zapped for it. However, at the last second, Martin dipped the end of his pole and stabbed it into the box between her feet, bent it as deeply as he could, and then let it go. The released pole snapped back to its straight position ... and whacked Damhell right between the eyes. Rather than foul her, Martin had pulled the hackneyed 'bend-the-tree-branch' plot device, which always hits the person chasing them. As Damhell staggered, stunned, Martin tore the zombie head from her hands and passed it to Veils.

"Unbelievable ...!" Evilla screamed. "Damhell Hairy is down! Yuck Wand DeSnarlo has the zombie head, but Jangelly Kurtails, returned to the game, and Barbaric Steal, are converging on her from opposite sides! Yuck Wand throws to Stabbing ... and drops to the dirt! Caroling Jokers and Barbaric Steal smash into each other! Both are down!"

All three Shantdareya Smalls vaulted into the scoring zone.

"The Skull-crackers head for the platform!" Evilla screamed. "Bruise Clambell can't defend against all of them! Will we have a two-point lead ...? Yes! Skull-crackers score! Eight to six! What a game!"

Atop the platform, with the zombie head, Martin, Veils, and Stabbing smiled at each other.

"Skull-crackers control the middle, too!" Evilla cried. "Brain Stroker tangled their chains, wrapped them around Slug Gormet-Wreather's lion-legs, and Allfed Snitchlock pulled her off her feet! They're tying them up in their own chains ... like a Death-Night present! Slug Gormet-Wreather and Pansthorny Chopkins are trapped, and Allfed Snitchlock and Brain Stroker are beating both with clubs!"

On the next turnover, Caroling Jokers returned to the pitch, and she tried to jump out of the middle zone, but one of Slug Gormet-Wreather's flailing paws accidentally hit the steel plate, and the wall before her shot upwards and blocked her passage.

"Slug Gormet-Wreather walls Caroling Jokers!" Evilla shouted. "Her own teammate! She's down ... and Martin the Magnificent has stolen the zombie head again! He passes to Stabbing ... but what's this? Caroling Jokers has lowered her horns! She's charging Martin from behind ... he sees her ... Caroling Jokers rams Martin the Magnificent ...! He's down, but here come the zaps! Caroling Jokers, for her obvious foul, takes four lightning bolts ... and serves her right!"

Knocked to the ground, Martin gasped and writhed, his chest hurting even worse. He'd turned too late to get out of her way, and taken the brunt of her attack on his upper ribs ... while still hurting from getting chained against the wall. Slowly he arose, aching all over, and feeling like he had several broken ribs.

"Martin looks shaky," Evilla said. "Hello ...? Caroling Jokers is rising, still smoking from getting zapped. She looks groggy, too, but she's not out of the game! That's what comes from being a veteran of seven seasons ... Caroling Jokers can take punishment ... and keep playing!"

Martin jumped for the free-zone ... and cried out from the agony he felt. He knew he was badly hurt, and that he should give up, but the voice of Murder kept echoing in his ears. Martin fell, unable to top the wall, but then he looked across the pitch to see Murder watching him, in her wheelchair beside Grand Wizard Bastile, Rude, and Happy ... *he couldn't give up!* He tried again ... topped the wall, and jumped down as lightly as he could. Pain stabbed as he landed, but he grabbed another pole and ran across the free-zone.

Martin topped the last wall to see Stabbing and Veils, with the zombie head atop the platform, waiting for him, and he paused atop the wall. Bruise Clambell, Damhell Hairy, and Barbaric Steal stood between him and scoring. As he watched, Caroling Jokers dropped over the wall behind him; she'd be coming soon!

Martin turned back and faced the free-zone.

"Come on, goat-head!" Martin taunted Caroling Jokers, standing tall atop the narrow wall, despite the pain it caused. "You can't stop me, you stupid satyr!"

Furious, Caroling Jokers picked up a pole and

charged straight at him. She bounded up, her pole bent deep, and she rose fast, both hooves kicking hard ...!

Martin ducked low, and she passed right over him. He even reached up and helped push her to fly farther from the wall ... too far to reach the pad ... and she fell right on top of Bruise Clambell!

"Martin the Magnificent takes out a Grave Gutters Big with a Grave Gutters Small!" Evilla shrieked, and the crowd howled with laughter. "He jumps down in the confusion ... he looks hurt! He's grabbed a pole, but he can't jump! He's running around the platform with Damhell Hairy and Barbaric Steal on his heels! He can't make room to run for a jump, or have time to climb the ladder. What ...? Martin has lifted his pole up to Stabbing Kingz and Yuck Wand DeSnarlo ... they're pulling him up! Damhell and Barbaric are jumping, trying to grab his ankles ... no chance! Skull-crackers score! Nine to six! A three-point spread!"

Martin gasped painfully as he moved.

"How long ...?" Martin asked.

"About thirty minutes left ...," the zombie head said.

"No ...," Martin gasped. "How long can we ... keep the head up here?" Martin asked. "We're winning ... need to slow ... the game ...!"

"Not long," Stabbing said. "If we wait, it'll be a foul ... and we'll all get zapped."

"Don't risk zaps," Martin said.

"Can you make it?" Veils asked. "We're winning, and you could stay up here ..."

"No," Martin said. "I'll keep playing ... for Murder and Happy ... we have no choice ...!"

"Do you have any more tricks ...?" Stabbing asked.

Martin shook his head.

"Not unless you have a rolling boulder in your pocket, or a falling anvil ... or ... we could paint a realistic tunnel opening on a wall ...," Martin said.

"He's delirious," Veils said.

"If he says he can play, we let him," Stabbing said.

"Time's almost up," the zombie head said.

"Drop him off ... behind the platform," Martin said. "I'll be in the free-zone."

In the last few seconds, Stabbing dropped the zombie head behind the platform, forcing Caroling to jog behind it to pick it up. By the time she had it back around the platform, Stabbing had descended, grabbed a pole, and cut her off. His pole swished through the air as she dodged, and then threw the net holding the zombie head into the free-zone. Stabbing scowled, and Veils jumped over the wall only a second later. Stabbing hefted his pole, ran, and vaulted after her.

Martin climbed down slowly. He felt horrible, and by the time he reached the bottom, Caroling Jokers was just starting her run. Their eyes met for a brief second; they both looked near death. She vaulted weakly up, caught the wall, and barely climbed atop it, then dropped down to the other side. Martin grimaced against the pain in his sides, lifted a pole, and began his run. He also barely made it to the top, and grabbed it with one arm while still holding his pole, and swung a leg up and over the edge. Slowly he climbed up, looking out across the pitch. Snitch and Brain were standing in the middle, only occasionally raising a club and swinging it down. The Skull-cracker Bigs had taken the pitch, but they were tightly chained to Slug Gormet-Wreather and Pansthorny Chopkins, and couldn't reach most of the steel plates.

"No!" Evilla screamed. "Crusto Fernwalker was reaching for Damhell's pole, and she slid down it! His claws have snagged the zombie head! Bigs can't hold the zombie head, but the ropes are caught in his webbed hands ...!"

ZZZzzzaaaaappppp!!!!!

All four lightning bolts flew, and Martin saw sparks rise in front of the far platform.

"Crusto Fernwalker is hurt!" Evilla shouted. "He's staggering ... he falls! The Shantdareya Skull-crackers have lost their goal-tender! Barbaric Steal recovers the zombie head, and here comes Caroling Jokers! The Grave Gutters score! Woah! They threw the zombie head right at Yuck Wand DeSnarlo! She caught it! The head is in play! Stabbing jumping as the Grave Gutters slide down the ladder, and Yuck Wand tosses the head blindly into the free-zone before Stabbing even gets there! She's grabbing a pole, but so are the others! She's trying to block them, but there goes Barbaric and Caroling! They separated, and Yuck Wand DeSnarlo can't block them all!"

Martin looked down at the free-zone; Stabbing had a clear run to him, and he wasn't sure he'd make it back up, if he jumped down. Gritting his teeth against the pain in his chest and side, Martin pulled his pole, which he was still holding, closer, and gently slid down it, back to the platform side.

Snarling his yeti teeth, Bruise Clambell watched as Martin limped past him and started climbing the ladder. The Big couldn't attack him directly, and Martin hurt too much to be intimidated.

Martin reached the top of the platform and looked back to see Stabbing racing toward him ... with all of the Gutter Smalls chasing him. Only Bruise stood in his way. With amazing dexterity, Stabbing jumped to the top of the last wall, pulled his pole over, and jumped down, landing running. Bruise stepped back against the platform's base, blocking the stairs with his body. Stabbing charged right at him, and stabbed his pole into the box.

As Stabbing lifted off the ground, Bruise charged forward. The yeti caught Stabbing's pole with both hairy hands and plowed his shoulder into it. Stabbing let go, but Bruise swung the pole like a hockey stick, caught Stabbing's chest squarely, and kept running forward. As he neared the wall, the door opened right in front of him ... and he threw Stabbing through the door ...!

ZZZzzzaaaaapppppp!!!!!

Martin saw the four bolts strike Stabbing. Screaming, Stabbing arced his back and keeled over, ablaze with light... and he dropped the zombie head. He fell twitching, and the last thing Martin saw, as the closing door cut off his sight, was Stabbing lying unconscious on the pitch, and Damhell grabbing the fallen zombie head.

"Grave Gutters recover the head!" Evilla screamed. "Damhell passes to Barbaric, Barbaric passes it over Yuck Wand DeSnarlo's head! Caroling Jokers has the zombie head ... and she's headed back! No Skull-crackers block her way!"

Martin sighed; he glanced at the ladder, wondering if he could climb down it without passing out.

He had to try ... Stabbing was out ... and Veils couldn't play alone.

Martin started down the ladder. Each movement shot bolts of agony worse than any lightning through him, yet he kept going, precariously clinging to consciousness ...

Bruise Clambell suddenly kicked the whole platform, and it shook violently. Martin lost his grip on the rungs ... and fell off ...!

Martin heard the *crack!* as he felt the stabbing sting *... never in his life had he hurt so badly!* He tried to move, but his left arm was twisted beneath him ... *broken ...!*

"The Grave Gutters score!" Evilla cried. "Yuck Wand DeSnarlo can't defend, alone against three! Martin looks hurt ... will he be able to finish? The zombie head lands at her feet! Yuck Wand will have only seconds before the Gutters are after her ... she picks up a pole ... and she's grabbed the head! Here come the

Gutters!"

Broken and battered, Martin looked up at Bruise, who was smiling with delight. Martin was helpless ... and had only one chance to help clear Veil's path ...

"Are all yetis as ugly and stupid as you?" Martin asked.

Bruise Clambell looked shocked, and then he snarled menacingly.

"I heard yetis are the dumbest monsters on Heterodox," Martin said. "I certainly can't see anything to disprove that!"

Bruise Clambell roared, and stomped a huge, hairy foot right next to Martin's head.

"What was that squeak?" Martin asked. "Was that you ... or did somebody step on a mouse ...?"

The towering yeti leaned low over Martin, their faces only inches apart. Martin's face was blasted by the yeti's foul breath.

"Is that your stink ...?" Martin asked. "You smell ... like a human ...!"

Yeti eyes bulged, red and angry, but Bruise spoke in a whispering growl.

"I'll deal with you after the match," Bruise Clambell snarled softly. "But first, I'm gonna throw your rookie girl off the pitch!"

Painfully, Martin slowly climbed to his feet, his right hand holding his aching, broken left arm. He stared right back into the yeti's eyes; *they could break his body, but not his spirit ...!*

As Veils came flying over the wall, Bruise Clambell ran to meet her. She dodged, but he cut her off, staying between her and the platform. Then Damhell Hairy, Barbaric Steal, and Caroling Jokers came chasing after her, and Veils was surrounded.

"Martin ...!" Veils cried, and she threw the zombie head at him.

Despite the pain, Martin reached up with his one usable hand and caught the zombie head, but he was too weak ... it knocked him backwards, against the ladder, and he collapsed onto the dirt at the foot of the platform.

"Martin ...!" Veils screamed.

Barbaric Steal reached Martin first, and laughed at him as she grabbed the zombie head and a fallen pole at the same time. In what seemed an instant, she, Caroling Jokers, and Damhell Hairy had all jumped over the wall and vanished.

Veils ran to Martin and fell to her knees beside him.

"Martin ...?" she asked, and he could only groan in reply. "Here ... I'll carry you up ..."

"No ...," Martin whispered, straining to voice each word. "Do as I say: forget about me. Get the zombie head ... and get yourself up onto the platform with it. Let me ... worry about me."

"But ...!" Veils argued.

"We don't have time to argue!" Martin hissed, and then he coughed painfully. "Regulation is about to end ... *you're our only hope!"*

Veils slid her fingers across his dirty cheek.

"I can't lose you ...!" Veils said.

"Go ...!" Martin ordered as forcefully as he could.

Veils didn't hesitate again. She grabbed a pole and ran at the wall, and in an instant she was gone.

"The Grave Gutters score!" Evilla cried. "What a finals! Only minutes left, and the game is tied ...! Next score will win ...! Three Grave Gutters Smalls remain ... and Yuck Wand DeSnarlo is practically alone!"

With great effort, Martin staggered to his feet, clutching his broken arm, and gritting his teeth with the strain of just standing. He looked at Bruise Clambell, but he could do nothing to the grinning yeti. With great effort, he limped away from the platform, all the way to the edge of the pitch.

"That's it; run away!" Bruise laughed at him. "Nothing can save you now! You're a human ... and you'll always be a loser!"

"I ... know ... something ... you ... don't ...," Martin whispered, his words spaced by gasps of pain.

"What ...?" Bruise demanded haughtily. "What do you know ...?"

Martin mumbled something, but his voice was too weak for speaking over the roars and laughter of the crowd. Bruise hesitated, then finally walked over and lowered one hairy white ear to Martin.

"I ... know ... that ... you're ... a ... fool!" Martin whispered to him.

As Bruise looked at him in surprise, Veils came flying over the center of the wall and dropped to the pad, holding the zombie head. Martin smiled; Bruise was too far away from the platform. Nothing stood in Veils' path.

Veils glanced at Martin, her face full of doubt, but Martin shook his head and pointed up, and Veils ran for the ladder. Bruise pounded after her, as Barbaric Steal, Caroling Jokers, and Damhell Hairy came hurtling over the last wall. Veils jumped to the ladder and nimbly climbed to the top, and then she topped the platform, holding the zombie head ... but she stood alone.

Martin looked up; he was badly hurt, his left arm broken, and he could barely walk. All he wanted to do was lay down and die ... but he couldn't. To score, every Small in play had to be atop that platform, with the zombie head, and Martin couldn't climb, let alone jump, and ranged before him was Barbaric Steal, Caroling Jokers, and Damhell Hairy, and even if he could get past them, there was still Bruise Clambell. Martin could barely move ... he could never get past four angry Grave Gutters. The crowd quieted, eager to watch Martin's final defeat.

The horn blew suddenly, the only sound Martin cared to hear.

"Martin is about to lose ...!" Evilla said. "That's the end of regulation ... and the score is tied! Yuck Wand DeSnarlo will get zapped soon unless she drops the head! The next team to score wins ...!"

Martin sucked in as deep a breath and turned to face the referees.

"My arm is broken ...!" Martin shouted at the nearest referee. "I can't continue! I have to step out! I quit! I quit this game!"

With difficulty, Martin turned and limped off the pitch.

A dead silence fell over the stadium. Two stands full of monsters, and a thick crowd of monsters encircling the pitch, gaped, speechless and astounded, as Martin left the field of play, limped off the pitch, and then he crumbled ... to slowly collapse onto the ground.

"What happened ...?" Evilla gasped. "What happens now? Martin the Magnificent has quit, and left the pitch, badly injured! Only Yuck Wand DeSnarlo remains, the last Skull-cracker Small, and she's atop the platform ... with the zombie head ...! Does that mean ...?"

The referees all glanced at each other, visibly shrugging. The crowd held its breath.

"The referees are signaling!" Evilla shouted into the silent stadium. "Conra deVerdict himself is signaling ... it's a score! Yuck Wand DeSnarlo scores the final point! It's over! The Shantdareya Skull-crackers win ...!"

Cheers exploded. Every monster in the stands jumped to their feet. Not even loudspeakers could drown out the howls, roars, hoots, and screeches that deafened even those making the noise.

Martin barely clung to consciousness, wincing against the pain of even breathing. *But ... he'd done it! He'd taught them that humans weren't losers! He'd shown every monster on Heterodox that ...!*

Martin passed out ... and never finished that thought.

Epilogue

With home restored.

"... and that's what happened ... and how I got injured," Martin said to his parents. "We won ... because I quit. Grand Wizard Bastile Wraithbone healed me as best he could, but ..."

Martin tried to shrug but it hurt to move his arm.

"You ... expect us ... to believe that?" Martin's father asked.

"Honey, that was just a dream," Martin's mother said. "Monsters aren't real."

"No, I was there ...!" Martin argued.

"We don't have time for this nonsense," Martin's dad said. "We're both late. You're grounded until you tell us what really happened."

"But ...!" Martin objected.

"Martin, we check on you ... every night ... sometimes very late ... before we go to bed," his mother said. "We look in on all of you, after midnight, and you've always been asleep, never out of your bed. Wherever you thought you were, it was only a dream."

Martin's jaw fell, and he felt flabbergasted. *Never out of his bed ...?*

"He was dreaming ... and fell out of bed," his father concluded.

"It could be broken," his mother said. "He should go to the hospital ..."

"I've got three meetings ...!" his father said.

"I've got a presentation ...!" his mother said.

Both sighed heavily.

"Go to work," his father said. "I can attend my meetings over my phone ..."

"Thanks, dear," his mother said, and she stood up and grabbed her purse. His mother paused to pat Martin's good hand, and then she hurried into the living room to pick up her things and leave.

"I've got two phone calls I have to make," Martin's father said. "I'll go in my room, and I want it quiet in here. We leave for the hospital in fifteen minutes."

His father got up, pulled out his phone, and walked into his bedroom, his phone already dialing. He closed the door behind him.

Martin sat there, stunned, not knowing what to think.

Had it all been a dream ...?

"So ... Heterodox," Vicky said, standing in the doorway. "Sounds like a fun place."

She stepped into the kitchen, holding her latest book, and she stood looking at Martin with a strange smile.

"They check on us ... every night ...?" Martin asked slowly. *"I was never out of bed ...?"*

"Don't let that bother you," Vicky said. "I never leave my bed."

"You ... *you've been to Heterodox?"* Martin exclaimed.

"Oh, no," Vicky smiled. "In my world, Zantheriak, elves fly starships and battle evil Slurks with proto-plasma cannons ... a weapon I designed. I can take you there, if you'd like, but not everyone can enter our worlds. Mom and dad never dream deeply. They have no fantasies, no deep, heart-wrenching reveries. Even when they watch TV or a movie, they're quietly thinking about their jobs ... or paying bills ... that's their only world. Besides, TV and movies are someone else's dreams. Books ... books are where readers like you and I find our dreams."

"Books ...?" Martin asked. "Are there books about the Grotesquerie Games ...?"

"Not yet," Vicky said. "But I suspect that there will be ... soon. I suggest you start writing them."

"But ... Bastile, Rude, Murder, ... all my friends ...! Are they real ... or just a dream?" Martin asked.

"There's no such thing as *'just a dream',"* Vicky said.

"You handed me your 'Wet-Feather War' bola, didn't you? The cord with dripping bags on each end? You walked around all day squishing in shoes that still smell like a lake. You've gotten nasty bruises ... and been wearing that silly purple jersey all summer ... and you got kissed ...!"

"It's real ...!" Martin exclaimed.

"And you've become quite an athlete, exercising in the backyard every day," Vicky said. "Mother might be able to stop you from going out for sports now, but what happens when dad gets a call from your gym teacher ... asking him to let you play? That phone call will come; you've earned it. Before you get into high school ... and then college ... you'll have changed mom and dad's opinions of sports ... from the skills you acquired playing in the Grotesquerie Games."

"But ... the finals are over," Martin said. "Will ... will I ever get back to Heterodox?"

"I'm sure you will," Vicky smiled. "What was her name ... Veils? She'll make sure you come back ..."

"How do you know ...?" Martin asked.

"Because that's where she'll be," Vicky smiled, "... waiting for you."

Topsail Tower was a tall volcano, smoking, but fortunately, not erupting. It rose thirty feet out of the sea, and on its rugged, steep sides, monsters of every kind crowded together, makeshift camps squeezed side-by-side, covering every inch of its rocky hillside. Martin stood beside his sister, Vicky, who was smiling brightly, delighted, and not at all surprised, as she stood close beside Brain, who was holding Murder in her wheelchair, being careful not to shake her. All of his teammates surrounded him, dressed in purple, and every face he could see was looking at them. Foremost stood Grand Wizard Bastile Wraithbone, wearing another thick, flowing purple robe. Grand Wizard Bastile smiled, and held aloft the legendary staff of Master Grand Wizard Borgias Killoff, whose secret identity only Martin knew.

Grand Wizard Bastile waved his staff and shouted.

"Powers of the Night and Day!
Spell of Evil, we thou slay!
Let these sunken days end!
Shantdareya, now ascend!"

Brilliant violet lights erupted from the legendary staff, and the roaring waves of the sea rose in fury. Crashing water thundered, and the ocean beneath them boiled. Topsail Tower trembled and shook, so hard that many monsters fell, clutching to the trembling rocks to keep from being thrown off.

Shantdareya arose. As the ocean frothed, the mountain shot upwards, tall and mighty, and the roaring sea fell away. Foam thick enough to wash away cities slid far from them, revealing tall hills and green forests, and then wide farms, and finally, villages and towns, the largest of which was summited by a shining purple castle.

The monsters cheered uproariously. Their island had risen back up, out of the sea, and now they could go home.

After the long cheer died, Martin turned to Vicky. Vicky's smile couldn't have been brighter, and then he glanced at Veils, young again, who was holding his hand, and staring at her familiar home, returned to her and her fellow monsters, with tears of joy in her eyes.

"So, sis ..., what do you think?" Martin asked Vicky.

"Seems like a wild place," Vicky said, grinning widely. "I'll bet we'll have a lot of wild adventures here!"

Martin smiled; he couldn't agree more.

THE END

All Books by Jay Palmer

The VIKINGS! Trilogy:
- DeathQuest
- The Mourning Trail
- Quest for Valhalla

The EGYPTIANS! Trilogy:
- SoulQuest
- Song of the Sphinx
- Quest for Osiris

The Magic of Play

The Heart of Play

The Grotesquerie Games

The Grotesquerie Gambit

Souls of Steam

The Seneschal

Jeremy Wrecker - Pirate of Land and Sea

Viking Son

Viking Daughter

Dracula - Deathless Desire

ABOUT THE AUTHOR

Born in Tripler Army Medical Center, Honolulu, Hawaii,
Jay Palmer works as a technical writer in the software industry in Seattle, Washington. Jay enjoys parties, reading everything in sight, woodworking, obscure board games, and riding his Kawasaki Vulcan. Jay is a knight in the SCA, frequently attends writer conferences, SciFi Conventions, and he and Karen are both avid ballroom dancers. But most of all, Jay enjoys writing.

JayPalmerBooks.com

Made in the USA
Monee, IL
06 February 2024

52566219R00184